Memory Bank

A Novel By

Sandi Marchetti

Published By
Barclay Books, LLC

St. Petersburg Florida
www.barclaybooks.com

PUBLISHED BY BARCLAY BOOKS, LLC
6161 51ST STREET SOUTH
ST. PETERSBURG, FLORIDA 33715
www.barclaybooks.com

Copyright © 2001 by Sandi Marchetti

All rights reserved. No part of this book may be reproduced or transmitted in any form by any means, electronic or mechanical, including photocopying, recording, or by any information and storage retrieval system, without the express written consent of the publisher.

This novel is a work of fiction. The characters, names, incidents, places, dialogue, and plot are the products of the author's imagination or are used fictitiously. Any resemblance to actual persons, living or dead, or events is purely coincidental.

Printed and bound in the United States of America
Cover design by Barclay Books, LLC

ISBN: 1-931402-12-4

Dedication

This book is for my mom and dad, Edward and Esta Marchetti, whom I would do anything in this world for. No questions asked; they are always there.

For my children whom I love each the best.

Jane, my closest friend. You're always there. You always were.

Gerri, my only sibling. But I refuse to live with you in a white house in Maine.

For Jeff S., Rick and Sistie. . . . If writing is in your soul, go for it!

And to Bob, a friend so dear to my heart. "And justice for all."

A short note to Barclay Books

Becki and Brantley, you may very well be the best publishers in this here United States. From the first word that ever came across the e-mail between us, Becki, you have been there for me. You have both been patient and understanding with my concerns. You have been encouraging and optimistic about Memory Bank and future books and I love you both for it. And more than that, you are a friend to all us writers who are under your delicate and sometimes emotional care. I'm sure I speak for us all . . .

Prologue

"That's the way choking is. You squeeze until the windpipe snaps and the eyeballs pop." Al Capone's words floated through his mind, as he put the barrel of the gun deep inside his mouth.

Instantly, he could taste the cold metal of the nozzle against his tongue. He could feel the bile rise, as he struggled to keep from gagging.

He once read that being stabbed felt like ice penetrating the body. He read where it didn't hurt until the knife was pulled from the tautness of the skin. You didn't die until your body fluid ebbed from the veins, leaving you weak and giddy.

He had investigated almost all forms of death. He'd even considered pills and drifting off peacefully. But there was always the chance of someone finding him and saving him. So, in the end, blowing his brains out was the answer. Blowing his brains out was quick, painless, and merciful.

He realized that any form of death was a blessing in lieu of living through this hell of an existence. Who wanted to live to watch loved ones and human counterparts waste away to their own death? Who wanted to be the last human, or one of the last humans to start this world over again?

A cynical giggle forced his way into his throat. As a kid, he had remembered being so afraid of the potential "atomic bomb."

He had been just sixteen and in high school. Another war had begun and another threat of nuclear war had hit the nation, sending all the people on this earth into a frantic tizzy.

"One of these days," his father had warned him one night just before he'd gone to bed, "after numerous threats, a nuclear warhead will hit and annihilate us all! Fry us all to a crisp, I tell ya!"

And he had been wrong. He would never have admitted it if he were alive, but he had been *dead* wrong. *Look how it's really going to end. Could we have ever known?*

A virus. A Goddamn virus will put us all away.

His giggle turned into a loud tearful laugh.

He pulled the trigger . . .

One

It was very silent. So silent, it was ethereal. There wasn't a sound except for the rustle of a piece of paper or a leaf skipping along the ground. Something sullen and sad was in the air, and nothing was, as it appeared to be.

The Skyrail Station had never seen such abandonment. Had it been able to talk, it would question when the next incoming train announcement would be made. It would wonder when all the hustle and bustle would begin as it watched for the clamoring of people pushing each other through the doors to catch their train to work.

But this wasn't the case at all. For, at a glance, one would think that amid all the activity that had once permeated this station, something had come and swooped everyone up, leaving behind half-full cups of coffee, magazines opened to pages of love advice and fashion, half-full vending machines, and torn tickets floating aimlessly about.

Where had all those people gone? Where were all the chattering tongues and the cries of babies? Where were the punks threatening the elderly, the addicts stealing pennies for a fix, and the man on the corner prompting those who passed by to "find what shell it's under?" How about the two men selling imitation Rolex watches from briefcases; where had they gone?

Where was all the laughter? Where were the children that should be running through the station happily screaming among themselves, the old ladies exchanging recipes while they waited for their train, the young men bragging about the piece of ass they'd scored for themselves the night before?
They were all gone. They had all vanished.

***

On the outside of the terminal, there were but a handful of people walking the streets, their heads bent in silence with no care as to where they were going.
Even if they could bring it all back—all that wonderful laughter, scrambling, and even crime for that matter—there would be just too much to re-do. No one had the energy anymore. Besides, no one would even live long enough to see it. Not even close.
Yet, amongst all this bleakness, the sun still shone bright and the sky was as blue as the sea. The trees and flowers still bloomed and the birds and animals flourished, leaving a feeling that all was right with the world.
But, it was just a feeling; not to be confused with reality.
So, what was the answer? The answer was silence. The silence was anger.

***

There was a woman sitting on one of the benches at terminal nine. She looked the way a woman looked when she'd stopped giving a damn; her hair was disheveled, her face furrowed, her mascara mottled, and her clothes looked as though they'd been retrieved from the bottom of a damp dirty laundry basket. Her shoes, worn and wide, scraped whenever she walked.
The woman tried to stand up. There was a thump. She hadn't collapsed and she hadn't lowered herself intentionally, but somehow she was on the floor. And . . . she began to laugh . . . laughing a soft laugh that said, "I give up . . ." before sliding

over to a bench where she curled up into a ball and fell fitfully asleep.

***

A seventeen-year-old girl stood by the pizza parlor door. Her pale small features were accented by heavy makeup and framed by a halo of long dark curls. She was wearing blue jeans with a black and gold top that looked like something a pimp would demand that she wear.

Who was she waiting for? And, for who was she made up? What kept her stamina going so strong, to the very extent that she had applied makeup and had carefully chose her clothing? What could possibly explain her actions?

Surely she knew that there were no more pimps; there were no more hookers—ladies of the night, call girls, strippers or dancers. There were no more nude bars or whorehouses. There was virtually no more sex.

***

Still, from an overview, this looked like a pretty normal world. Yet, it was silent. It was without the sound of lawnmowers and car engines and void of planes in the sky . . .

The oceans were in need of boat motors and surfers crashing through waves.

The parks were lacking children's laughter.

The schools were missing the desire to learn.

The churches were minus the faithful.

The world was a mess, and its occupants the cause.

***

"We are the world. . . . We are the children"
Fooled ya. . . .

Two

There were people in the room. Men and women seeming like only caricatures in August Webster's eyes. A parody of figures and faces reading magazines, staring perplexingly, or watching the suspended television screen. There were murmurs and whispers coming from the small group and an occasional audible sigh or whisper.

Webster bypassed them on his way into his office, feeling a slight revulsion to the morose scene.

It was just after nine in the morning. Walking directly to his large bay window, he looked out onto the streets below.

The pedestrians that moved about seemed sluggish. It was as if they had no purpose in life. But then, they couldn't see life the way he did. They couldn't possibly feel what he was feeling, nor could they see the Elysian Fields ahead.

From the day he had first set foot into this building, the regal structure with its wide staircase and dark walnut paneling had served as a special retreat to him. Hours often passed like minutes when he absorbed himself in his work. And for what, he thought, inhaling deeply?

He pulled his watch from his vest pocket and pushed the button signaling his secretary to send in his first patient. It would all be worth it. He had been working towards a common goal with all the leaders of the world.

He knew what this earth needed. A visionary. Someone who could realize a Utopia. Someone who could appreciate that the earth could be, and should be, in a state of ideal perfection. A unified world under one leader.

His heart was beating furiously with excitement, as it so often did while these thoughts surged through his mind. *He could be that leader, and he knew beyond all shadows of a doubt, that he would be that leader.*

But, like all great potentates, he would need the time to win over his people.

His first appointment arrived. She was a young woman, named Mary, with whom he had already had numerous sessions. And just like before, as in those other sessions, she sauntered into his office, slowly and easily, instantly annoying him as his deliberations of the future ebbed from his mind. He hated disturbance.

To Webster, she looked like a pathetic moppet, easily pliable and emotionally compliant. Had she lived before, she in all probability would have made an excellent candidate for this Regression Act. She was easily hypnotized and related well her opinions, fears, and dislikes.

But, that's not what made the world go around these days. A past life did. And she hadn't lived before, therefore she was not as perfect as she seemed. In his line of work, perfection and accommodation were clear-cut dividends. At least, that's what he insisted upon.

Perhaps it was good to be so sure about what he wanted. Perhaps it made him a stronger individual because everyday he could feel his strength increasing dramatically. Everyday he grew closer and closer to his goals, working ten to fifteen hours a day to achieve them, sometimes even sleeping at his desk.

The human body wasn't meant to take such abuse. But, if one had the drive, nothing was unattainable. And if a goal was so blatantly attainable, then the human body remained in good form out of sheer desire.

Webster turned around slightly from his fixation on the city.

He was scanning the tops of the dirty buildings that housed disease-carrying pigeons, way past the city limits of his desires. The skyscrapers silhouetted each other in the horizon and to all intents and purposes, the city looked relatively normal.

But Webster knew better. Anyone who had lived in the city for any amount of time knew better. Things were just not as they seemed.

He thought about the residents of the city, the country, and the world. He hadn't taken full possession as of yet, but he could feel it like hot coals in his belly. He had been so close. Someday, he would have reign over all of it. The people would come to love and trust him. And then, he would realize his Utopia. Then, he would rule his Utopia.

Webster finally decided to take notice of the young woman sitting on the opposite side of his desk. *Pathetic.*

Mary hung her head and shook it. Then, she began to speak, almost as if she were in a trance. Almost as if she had started from a conversation of another session and had never left here, just continuing on from there.

"I don't like it. Not this kind of thing," she said sighing. "It frightens me."

"There, there," he said slowly sitting down. "You're making it sound as if it were something appalling, dear."

The soft spoken, cunning Webster crooned. "It's just a modern component of life now. You should be happy that you have a brand new start. And when you do begin again, you'll be special, Mary. Not like you are now. Now you are a nothing, dear. You just exist. You have no depth. You have no substance and your unfortunate life is simply worth zero."

He patted her hand, which silently repulsed him. "And, as you know, dear, you are not the only person in this situation. There are many, many more just like you who are striving for a new beginning." He patted her hand again. Small tapping pats, repeatedly. "Many, many more. And I am doing the same for them. I'm giving them a totally new and meaningful existence."

August Webster never got tired of this. At least once a day he had to tell someone that they were going to have to die in order for him to give them a new life once more.

He explained to them that they had to achieve a past life, as he liked to phrase it, in order to put forth future endeavors. Never again could the earth be put into the position it suffers now.

And telling these poor souls about their impending demise didn't bother him in the least. After all, wasn't his performance at his agency somewhat along the lines of the program that the government had designed? He was just doing his job.

The tall, slender, gray haired man adjusted his glasses as he picked up the file before him. "You have to understand, Mary. This is the year 2034. It isn't like it used to be where there was all the time in the world to see a life through."

"But, I want to live *now.*" Her eyes were imploring pools of blue apprehension. "I *want* to see this life through."

"Of course you do. But you are too sensitive, my dear, extremely sensitive, in a supersensible way. And, therefore, you are unfortunately limited. There is nowhere else for you to go except the route that I have laid out for you. And those like you."

He cleared his throat now that he could see he had regained her attention. "First off, you need a job that will enable you to learn while you work and acquire adequate merits, by my standards, in order for you to be useful in a future life."

"Why can't I just stay at that job? Won't I naturally acquire more knowledge the longer I work?" She looked at him pathetically. "I'll learn as much as I can. I promise!"

Webster shook his head, losing patience by the minute. "Very rarely does one stay at a job for a lifetime. You'll only tire of it and try to move on. Eventually, it will be as if this never happened and you will be a lost soul. You will forget what you are here for. You will forget my mission and all will be lost."

He stood up, totally annoyed at this miserable moppet. "In doing it my way, you will be grasping a trade and learning it completely so that you will be educated into enhancing the productivity of the future of the earth. Then, I shall have you withdraw your privilege of sustaining life at this stage and soon, you will be born again into your second lifetime." He clapped his hands excitedly. "Something you've never had before. You will have procured a true resume'."

Webster could see the pulse in her neck beating wildly, and he pictured her heart bouncing around in the cavity of her chest like a scared rabbit. That excited him more.

Mary shook her head wildly. "No. I can't allow you to end my life. How would you do it? How would it happen?" She looked at him closely, trying to analyze his psyche. He had a wonderfully human face, she thought. Why then was his soul so black? How could he be so inhuman and still have such a caring countenance?

She had been almost positive, from what she had read, that this was not how the Regression Act was set up. Yet, when she tried discussing it with other agencies, they refused to speak with her or even listen to her complaints against the Webster Center. They wouldn't listen as she bellowed out her frustration, screaming about his trying to end this life of hers and others, in order to procure a past life. It was some sort of a consideration towards him and his center, some kind of professional courtesy.

Webster placed her file back on the desk. "You ask, 'how will it happen?'" He repeated her question. "Very gently. You won't be afraid, because you won't recollect any of this session, or any session in the past. You will see. It will happen very suddenly, very peacefully, and quite unexpectedly."

"The other agencies don't work this way," she said in a near whisper.

Webster's eyes grew dark as he glared at her. "You've already been there, Mary. I've been informed. You should know how they work." The sarcasm couldn't escape his words. But his smile returned just as quickly as it had left. "In any event, they all work in similar ways, my dear."

"I can't believe that," she said bravely.

Webster inhaled deeply, controlling his desire to grab the little mite by her throat. "We are all governed by the same Federal Government, my dear. We all have to follow rules. We are watched very carefully and you'd be wasting your time, of course, seeking out one agency after another." He suddenly scowled at her. "Besides, no other unit would take you out of your territory."

Webster cleared his throat and continued. "After this existence, you will proceed to other lives, which will become more and more consummate."

He stood up and faced the window again. "Now, I really hate redundancy, Mary, so I shan't repeat any of this again! The simple fact is this. You will not remember any part of this conversation when this session is at an end. For this reason only, do I forgive your outlandish behavior." He lowered his voice to a monotonous balanced drone. "Take five minutes to meditate on the righteousness of it all."

Webster fell silent and sat back down. He rested his head against his chair, lingering for a latent response, marveling at the powers of hypnosis, although he did know that hypnosis didn't always expunge memory.

Fleetingly, he remembered the year that the government had issued and enacted the new law. This had been in June of 2033.

It had stated that each newborn child would have a timed microcomputer chip inserted into the base of their skull. Prior to their eighteenth birthday, a prearranged appointment would be set in preparation for the chip's activation. This timed activation would trigger the chip into the memories of all of the past lives that this young person may have lived through.

As for the others, the chip would be implanted into the inner ear. As with the inoculations of the early twentieth century, these implants would be recorded so that no one would be without. This was now Federal law.

On the birthday of these already growing and grown humans, following the implantation, an appointment for follow-up at the nearest center would be made, and there the subject would be hypnotized into regression. The chip would be activated and hopefully, past journeys would begin.

"Dr. Webster," Mary lifted her head and spoke again. "I don't understand."

Webster marveled at the tenacity of this young woman. They looked at each other. His hard, sharp features were inadequately expressing the gentler emotion, like affection and sympathy that he tried so desperately to convey. She needed to be more relaxed, he decided. She needed to be ultimately under his power.

In the glances that they exchanged, was a familiarity that neither one of them dare admit.

"Again, Dr. Webster. I don't understand about this law. I just don't see why new souls cannot go onward and live out their first lives. I don't mean to sound repetitive, but there can't really be any harm in this." Her voice was broken and ineffective. Her bowels churned with the realization that her very existence—past, present, and future—was now in the hands of this one man.

Webster leaned forward and picked up his black and gold pen. "We don't have the time, Mary. That's all there is to it." Leaning back, deep into his chair, he brought the tips of his fingers together. "You see, this planet is suffering such an urgency, that we must all assist in putting it back on its feet once more. And that means each and every one of us, including you, Mary.

"If it means giving up our life for this great planet, so be it. Therefore, there is really no time, no time at all, to tarry around waiting for a new soul to live out its very first life. We need history to build. We need the 'greats' of the past. So, if there is ever another planetary crisis, the search for former souls that have advanced us once before, can be readily called upon to assist us again."

Webster continued speaking as if in his own trance. Words that he had said and thought numerous times before filled his mouth and rolled off his tongue once more. But, in such instances as this one, they had ultimately fallen on deafened ears.

"It is sadly a well known fact that the earth and its humans are advancing far too slowly, according to the guidelines that were set up for it.

"Due to the life expectancy reaching the incredible age of one hundred and ten, which is much too long for a soul with no past to live, the intelligence level is way too low, as well as the environmental level.

"By now, the pollution should be at a minimal degree and the space age should have already opened up totally new horizons for us. Instead, it too appears to stand stagnant.

"The government's objective is to pick some of the brains of our scholars from decades gone by. Maybe touch upon Newton, Socrates, Lincoln, Napoleon, and even those hundreds of thousands of men and women who made the vast difference felt on this earth today. We need a little of everyone, past and present, to help rebuild this planet. Hence, the computer chip, as you know it, Mary."

***

After Mary left, Webster picked up his notes. He was concerned that she hadn't slipped completely under his control.

Most certainly, he wasn't going by the exact rules and regulations that the government had laid out for him. He knew, of course, that all the other agencies were playing true to form. That's why they'd never get anywhere.

That's why he couldn't be like them. He was different from all the other agency leaders. He had to do it his way, which meant that all new souls had to die. There was no other way. Once they were exterminated by a simple undetectable injection all records were destroyed, except for his own, which were securely locked in a safe in his office.

The subjects were usually found in their own homes and pronounced dead of natural causes. In some instances, they somehow were able to make it to a hospital, experiencing symptoms such as heart attack or stroke, and then inevitably die anyway. Absolutely foolproof!

Webster's grin turned into an evil-looking, twisted smirk. He had the world in the palm of his hands. It was all too easy, he thought chuckling, all too easy.

MEMORY BANK

***

Mary was not psychic. She did not see signs and portents in the sky. The lines in her palm revealed nothing to her and told her nothing about her future. But one thing she did know would happen, and that was that August Webster was not going to allow her to live.

It seemed absurd, she thought, that she was not able to find a way out. But it was fact. Even trying the other centers were of no help. They wouldn't even listen to her.

On the evening news she'd sometimes hear something about someone not making it out of a house in a fire, or plunging their car into a canal and not being able to get out.

She could never really figure out why they couldn't make it to safety. Surely there was another window or door in that burning house that they could have tried. And as far as the car plunging down an embankment, if they knew they were heading into a canal, surely they had time to bail out or open a window so that they could swim through.

Mary knew she was being irrational. Sometimes there just wasn't a way out of a situation. All the logical thinking in the world couldn't get you out of it.

What if she disappeared? She had already been regressed. There was nothing there. She had not lived before. This was her first life. How unfair Dr. Webster was by not allowing her to live her one and only life. How then could she be hurt by a past life? Dr. Webster certainly couldn't have the means to locate her if she managed to get far enough away.

Her mind was now working overtime. Who did she have to leave behind, anyway?

Hurrying down the street, she noticed a place that sold luggage. She had no luggage. She never took a vacation.

Mary slid in, hopefully unnoticed, and bought two large suitcases. One for the meager amount of clothes she possessed and the other for personals and memorabilia. She did have a lot of memories about her family, many years ago. They were gone now, but their memories lived on in her.

***

Excitedly, Mary dragged the suitcases up the stairs and into her apartment. There was so much to do. She had to get into her computer and locate a place that Dr. Webster wouldn't even think of looking. It had to be in the United States. She couldn't even begin to think of living in another country, although Canada might be nice.

Once she'd decided on the destination, she would order the tickets, color and cut her hair, and get out of here. She had time. She hadn't even begun her new job yet. Dr. Webster was going to arrange a new job for her so that she could build a resume.

Even if she'd liked her job, there was no way she would allow that man to choose her occupation. She couldn't work the way he wanted her to and know that at the end of her term she would be put to death.

Mary picked up the phone and called her friend at the hospital. "I need to see you," she pleaded. "I need your help."

***

Regression intrigued Webster, simply because he had relatively few comforts and certainties of religious beliefs to sustain him. In such a climate of doubt, he had to look for something more in the way of scientific evidence concerning life after death. He could no longer rely on faith alone, which was also in a serious decline. And so, when the government had instituted this new program, he'd rapidly learned all there was to know about it—more of a selfish act than a patriotic one.

Regression had been proven in 2010, years before the law had been enacted. It had been Sadait Arumait who'd first brought proof of this to the world. He'd traveled extensively around the world to research the subject, and according to Webster, Arumait's findings had been startling. They had even negated some religious beliefs, while actually confirming others. One simple example of this was found within the Hindu and Buddhist religions.

The Hindu and Buddhist belief findings were, unexpectedly, remarkable. They believe that the human, or the soul within the human, is reborn in accordance with the merits one has acquired during the previous lifetime.

Although some sects of Hinduism hold that a being doesn't necessarily assume a human form in the next life, they ascertain this with good cause. Accordingly, one is believed to be governed by one's actions. If a person had been involved with crime or any other lechery, they may just as well come back as a cactus, snake, or other such low-life.

Webster had reflected upon the Hindu belief for some time. It was seemingly more believable than the Buddhist, who, on the other hand, believed that a being's elements of sensation, cognition, emotion, and consciousness fall apart at the moment of death. They cease to exist, and a new individual life begins in accordance to the quality of the previous life. Soon, the person is able to reach the level of innate perfection and eternal bliss.

Webster smiled. He was born, at last, at a most opportune period.

The phone startled him out of his thoughts. At the same time, his eyes focused on the clock. "Yes," he answered abruptly. "Who is it?"

"It's Gerald Foltz, Dr. Webster." Gerald was a young intern practicing at the City of Hope Hospital. "We've a young woman here. Just came in with no identification, and you know that I call you first in these matters, sir."

"Well, enlighten me, Mr. Foltz. Why would you suppose I know her?" Webster at best, was mildly angered, as well as apprehensive at this disturbing phone call and its distressing news.

"She has no identification, like I said, sir. But, I did notice a business card in her jacket pocket with your name, an appointment date, and time on it." The young man cleared his throat and dared to speak the next words. "Her appointment was with you this morning. Sir, I suppose she came in directly from your office."

Wasn't this ridiculous news, Webster thought, twisting a paper clip into a tight coil? "What are you in such a sweat over, Foltz?"

"Well, did you have an appointment with a tall, thin woman in her late twenties, early thirties?"

Webster's lips tightened in a grimace. Had one not felt the turmoil chasing the fear throughout his body, one would think him in tremendous pain. Yet, anyone who knew him well recognized it as an expression of temper control. "I did. May I inquire as to why you ask?"

"Simply because she is dead, Dr. Webster. She's dead, and I believe it is a clear-cut case of suicide."

Thank God. Webster exhaling loudly before proceeding with his convincing tale of her despondency, being careful to show an appropriate sympathy for the loss of his patient. *Dead men can't speak*, he thought, *but someday, a Mary in my life will not perform her suicidal role. Someday, someone will put one and two together and try to take him down,* he thought as he returned the phone to its cradle. *No, I can't let that happen.*

Even though he never had expunged the memory of his clients, he knew that hypnotism was not an exact art. He tried to set their minds into not remembering their last session, but mistakes could and very often did happen. And if that day came—if that mistake was ever made—he would be in need of some credible answers.

August Webster walked back into the regression room, never turning on the light. He shuffled over to the sofa and sat down.

As if in a daze, he lifted his legs into a reclining position, with his head raised slightly on a small pillow. Closing his eyes, he tried to ease the dull throb that was building in the back of his head.

He was baffled at why people sometimes didn't understand what he was trying to do. They didn't understand that he was following his course with the precision and security of a sleepwalker.

Webster's mind began to drift and he saw himself standing at a window with scores of people below, with their arms extended toward him. He was the leader of sixty-seven million people. He could not make a mistake. He could not be mistaken. What he did and what he said was to become historical.

His face suddenly smoothed itself of wrinkles. A slight twisted smile appeared in its place. *No one is as equipped as I am to bring the earth to the position of supremacy, which it believes it so richly deserves, but is so unable to achieve on its own.*

Had one been watching, they would quickly and undeniably realize that wherever it was that he was visiting, was exactly where he should have remained. It was exactly where he belonged.

It hadn't taken much longer than a half hour, and slowly, Webster's consciousness took him to the present. He remained in the same position, hardly moving at all. He wanted to bask in the past. The past was where he got his strength. He needed it just to survive this life.

August Webster would not lose sight of his Utopia.

Three

Something was wrong. The goose-down pillows that were under his head when he'd gone to bed that night were now scattered around him like a barricade. He had to push them aside to see.

The blinds were angled against whatever light the sky may have been giving, but his time sense told him it was still night.

David Wilder had no idea what had awakened him, but whatever it was, it hovered so close he could feel it in his bones.

Sitting up, he rubbed at his eyes, which felt as if tiny granules of sand had been grinding deeply into them. No sleep. Worry. Confusion.

Patting the pillows back into place behind him, he lay down once more and closed his eyes. He could feel the age creeping along his body. He was only thirty-five years old, yet he felt fifty.

David yearned for his youth again. He could almost visualize his small-framed six-year old body running across the fields in the back of his house in Connecticut, with his blonde straight hair blowing in the breeze, and his blue eyes taking in all the mysteries of life. He remembered his mom always at the front door waiting for a hug when he came home and she always had something baking in the oven for him. Where had those days gone? He sighed. Where had his youth gone? When had that child turned into a man and lost the light that burned so brightly in those happy blue eyes? When did the creases in his forehead, from laughing, turn into little rivets of worry?

David's eyes had become burning slits of coal. As he turned onto his side, he could feel small beads of perspiration sliding down his cheek. Sweat gleamed on the steep ridges of his cheekbones.

And, to think that this miserable state that he had been in for the last two months—his obsession, yielding these sleepless nights—was all due to August Webster.

David had reached his activation date two months ago. According to the setup that the government had devised for the agencies, David's initial confirmation for his appointment, right to the hour of his session, had been done to protocol. But, for some reason, he had been left with an inadequate feeling. Something wasn't exactly fitting because David was left with a feeling that he still had remnants of his past life with him when the session had ended. He had recurrent daydreams of whippings and drudgery.

He had flashes of emaciated black men and women in hot fields of corn, fighting off insects and fever. And, although they came to him in a flash of a second's time, it was something that he had not experienced before.

David remembered his regression. It wasn't a painful memory, as much as it was uncomfortable. He was a Negro slave. He didn't quite remember what year it was, only that there were points of fear and despair throughout those memories. He knew it hadn't been expunged, but he wasn't sure why.

There was something strange about the agency. He couldn't ascertain exactly what had been bothering him, but it nagged at him day and night. It was like an annoying question seated at the edge of his mind, and for some ungodly reason, it nagged at him mostly in his sleeping hours.

A buzzing sound disturbed his thoughts. He glanced at the digital clock on the table next to him and pushed the snooze button. He took a small brown leather pillbox out of the drawer, removed two tiny blue capsules and swallowed them dry. He was only able to sleep three to four hours a night, and David felt frustrated. He had dreams he couldn't hold onto, yet they had him sitting up shivering with fear. He was left tired and irritable, since he knew no recourse to his dilemma.

As he drifted off, he thought about the positives in his life. He was a partner in the Wilder, Tuchman Laboratories on 6th Street. Being a scientist, he had a naturally inquisitive, as well as skeptical mind. Added together, he found himself struggling to ascertain whether these dreams were related to the session with August Webster and some sort of parody of some life he may have lived in the past, or whether it was an overworked, strained, and exhausted mind on over time.

It was close to two o'clock; he got up for the last time. He put on a pot of coffee and prepared to get ready for the day . . . Look at this city, he thought, looking out his window. There was a dramatic change since the century turned over. The George Washington Bridge was still standing, but antiquated. It wasn't traveled anymore, and since there has been little to no repair or restoration made to the old artifact, it was blocked off to any and all transportation.

The street lamps that once glowed warmly over the buildings and homes were now implanted beneath the ground, outlining the streets coldly. They had been designed to soften the city by a new electronic device, but they had never gotten to the point of putting that electronic wizard in place.

When he was a child, David dreamed of the New World to come. He dreamed of the real Star Wars coming to life and futuristic gadgets here and there. He dreamed of the world that movies and books promised him; the world that beamed people to where they wanted to go, a world of amazement and wonder.

Instead, he was faced with the stark, cold, steel world he wasn't too keen to be a part of anymore.

You couldn't stop people though, he mused. The city still bustled with limited activity. He wished he could read the minds of the hundreds of people that were scurrying to shelter themselves from the heavy rainstorm that had already erupted. These people were quickly becoming one with August Webster, he thought angrily. Again, he wasn't sure, but he could sense that they were going through the same restlessness that he was experiencing.

It may have been the thick darkness that made David's obsession seem more urgent tonight. It was like a disease, taking him by the throat and squeezing hard. Once he was in its grip, he struggled with an insatiable appetite to quell it. Like a drug rushing through his veins, and then like withdrawal once he was without it.

David even went so far as to investigate the other agencies around the country. It seemed that Webster's practices were extremely conflicting compared to the others. Unlike Webster's center, the other centers didn't have as devastating a history. The people were definitely more relaxed and content, as well. Unlike Webster's, the other centers didn't have as devastating a client history. The suicide rate wasn't as high; and the over-all recovery periods were far more positive and quicker.

The distinction in centers had been the fear that the others had in not following the strict government procedure that was set forth. Webster, it seemed, had no fear. He was more than aware that this Act took hold in an experimental stage. Time was running out and there was no margin for error.

The phone rang like an explosion in the room.

"David?" the voice was deep. "It's Pat. You okay?"

Dr. Patrick Tuchman was the other half of The Wilder, Tuchman Laboratories. He was a straight, studious sort of man with a dry wit about him even while telling a humorous story now and then. He was a gentle man and looked it. He had the appearance of being very fragile and thin, but the strength in his convictions outweighed some of the most powerful men.

The two had known each other since college, but their careers sent them in opposite directions. Then, they coincidentally met at a convention in Bangor, Maine some years later, and after a brief conversation, discovered that they had much more than they expected in common. That exhilarated conversation quickly turned to more vigorous plans of the future laboratory, and eventually a friendship and working team was formed.

The marriage had been a good one, and the results of their work were greater than their wildest expectations.

"Yeah . . . Pat. I'm just beat." He glanced at his watch. It was three o'clock in the morning. "What's up?"

"On my way home I saw your lights on and decided to take a chance that you'd be up." He cleared his throat.

David knew that when Patrick cleared his throat it meant that he was going to try something new on him. Some new invention or thought that whipped through his genius mind.

"Came across a new vaccine tonight. Purely accidental. But, I'd like to check some formulas out against the others." He hesitated for just a second. "I've been working on this day and night, David, ever since I stumbled across it."

David obviously did not respond fast enough.

"What's the matter with you?" Patrick asked. "First of all, you sound like hell, and second of all, you don't seem the least bit interested."

"It's not that I'm not interested, Pat. It seems that all our work may just be wasted. At least here in New York."

"What are you talking about?"

"I've been thinking about August Webster. The way it's going, he may be wiping the city out faster than the disease had."

Patrick sat down with a thud. "I'm not catching your drift here, David."

"I'm absolutely positive that the government isn't aware of his procedures, Pat. I'm going to bring proof to them that what I believe is seriously going on in this center *is* going on. Ever since my own regression, things have changed, which I'll explain at another time. But, I've got to get some cold hard facts on that agency. I need documented proof that what I suspect is actually happening before I go starting a ruckus and getting thrown out on my ass." He exhaled loudly. "Maybe I'm whistling the wrong tune to Dixie, and maybe I'm imagining a lot of this, but . . ."

"Weaseling out, old man?" Pat snickered. "I've never known you to have a suspicion and be wrong. Why now? I'm just as concerned, and I'm just as suspicious."

"You haven't been through your regression yet, have you?"

"Pretty soon. But some family members have and a few friends. They changed afterwards. They changed only to a point that others had to be looking for the change to notice one. Like us, David, that's how I recognized the problem. "

"And you never said anything about this?"

"You never did either."

David laughed. "Touché, my friend. So you do know that we are, in all probability, going to cause some mighty big explosions by digging dirt up on this man, don't you?"

"That's bullshit and you know it. We're not going to stir up anything yet, because no one is going to know what we're up to. So, don't go chicken on me. We both know that the slime ball is up to something as dirty as sewage. Why shouldn't we get to the core of it, so that all our work isn't just flushed right down the toilet?" Patrick inhaled deeply and said, "Damn David. That moron is killing people faster than the virus!"

"Calm down," David said rubbing at his irritated eyes again. "You're dead right. And I'm not going chicken. I guess I'm just drained over trying to deal with this myself. I was wondering when you'd open your big mouth. You in?"

"I'm in."

"Come on over and we can go over some of the equations to your vaccine," David offered.

"It can wait. You rest and we'll come up with something tomorrow regarding Webster. You know, we can map a path out to investigate that agency, and I say we go for it."

David was overwhelmed with weariness, but much too anxious to relax. His mind was on the young man who blew his own head off last night. No one knew why. David did.

Last week, Patrick single-handedly broke into Webster's center and copied some files. The man who killed himself was James Proud. His "resume`," so to speak, was one of those that

David knew to be the pitfall of this agency.

James Proud was born in Atlanta, Georgia in September of 2001. Before that, he had lived in 1592 as a very wealthy man. That was his last and only life. As of yesterday, Mr. Proud was a pauper. As of today, he was dead.

What in the hell, wondered David, did this man do in his last life to deserve such a reduced form in this life? It was only revealed to him, by James Proud's family, that Mr. Proud was having a difficult time handling the radical change. For it seemed, he suddenly remembered very clearly his last life on earth. Poverty is painful, but more so, once you've lived like a king and remembered it all.

Once again David questioned this. Wasn't that memory supposed to be expunged? And yet it wasn't. That's why the rise in suicides. That's why the rush toward counseling. These people just can't handle what they've learned about themselves. They can't live with it.

David threw the folder down and grabbed his jacket. He needed to go to the lab. He felt more productive there. Right now, he was actually dazed and frustrated, because he could find no remedy to this obscurity. He smelled a rat. And when he smelled a rat, there was nothing better to do than get onto the scent and follow it until the right time approached for extermination.

It was cold for May and the wind and rain hadn't helped. This was a year of unusually odd weather changes. Tonight was no exception. It seemed as if the entire eastern seaboard was blanketed in a long, gray belt of clouds that slowly and steadily drenched the lands with inch after inch of rain. "It's days like this . . ." he muttered, fumbling with the zipper of his lightweight jacket.

Despite the chill in the air, David ran the air-conditioning in his car. He adjusted his rearview mirror, catching a glimpse of his tired face. His hair was disheveled, sticking up in the back and some longer strands falling on his forehead. His otherwise brilliant blue eyes were now dull with exhausted bewilderment.

He was just three blocks away from the gray, nineteenth

century brick and stone, four story building that he rented for six and a half years. And now, as of six weeks ago, he owned it.

Real Estate came easier in these days because of the disease. It was a terrible thing to admit, but when his landlord died, and his landlord's son followed, it had been easy going to buy this building.

This building, with its abundant square footage, gave him the adequate privacy and space he required for his research on the Homeosis program.

Homeosis was a mutant of the long-lived immune deficient virus from the middle to latter part of the twentieth century. So far, a vaccine was helping fight the deadly disease, but now, with the new chemical Patrick was working on, the presently afflicted HV carriers, and those that are full blown, would have their chance of reversal. Already, one of five families was losing someone dear to them from the disease; high odds for a morbidly small population on earth.

This disease called HV (Homeosis Virus) was once known as HIV. But, since early 2010, there hadn't been a single HIV case reported. The new strain, HV, rapidly took over, killing even more people than its sister. The rule of life had seemed to be that just when a new medication or vaccine was released, a new strain of disease negated it immediately, as well as the scientists and doctors who worked so diligently at producing and perfecting it. The earth couldn't win.

David was trying to perfect a chemical so that along with a combination of Dextricline and Tripodise, it could be readily used in a pill form. This was near completion, and he had received government grant money to finance the project so there had been very little of his own money vested into the project. But, until his research was complete, there would still be death and panic outside the laboratory world. Even the FDA was not a milestone for David. They were kindly passing through just about everything that would give the population a fighting chance from becoming completely extinct.

On the street before Keller Avenue, he turned right and drove the length of a long building. At the end of the structure, he took another right, then slowed as he drove over an unusually elevated speed bump located just before the security checkpoint. Slipping his card into the meter, the gates opened and he drove on through.

David gazed at the newly renovated sight before him. The stone and brick had been acid washed and he had new windows installed, which replaced the cracked, peeled, wooden framed ones. It was good, this feeling of ownership. It was a success in a different sort of way, with a different sort of meaning to him.

A woman walking her dog watched as David drove through the security gate. She looked at him for a brief second, but not long enough to seem interested in what he was doing. She looked disheveled and very old for her years. Even the dog looked tired and old.

The dog, David mused. Animals were beginning to out number humans. These poor, dumb things had somehow outsmarted the higher species of life on this earth. Beats me, he thought, sadly shaking his head.

David lived a life of little means as a child. When his dad took him to New York City on a few occasions, he often wondered who owned the tall buildings that nearly took away his view of the sky. He remembered straining his head upward to see where the buildings ended. How did these people live? Were they very rich? Where did they live? Did they also have a mom and dad?

David's father worked the subways, keeping the grounds below the city sidewalks clean. He was a man that smoked heavily and drank too much, but somehow, he remained untouched health wise until he reached sixty. Only then did he begin to slide downhill. Mother worried about him in the early days. But, even that ended. With the smell of the subways in his clothing and hair, and the whiskey and tobacco in his mouth, she soon stopped caring. And when he died, she just sat by his coffin, no tears in her eyes and whispered, "You're all right now, Sam. You're all right. We're all right now."

David thought how sad it was that Sam wasn't more like his own father. Grandfather had invested his money in real estate instead of booze and cigarettes. He had worked hard all his life in a clean manner. David was the one like him.

Now, as David looked at the building before him, he realized now that he was a building owner just like the ones he had wondered about as a child. So to him, this was a special kind of success.

Entering through the elaborate Georgian entranceway, David stopped to view the lobby. Unlike all the glass and marble of the modern buildings, his remained old fashion and rich. But, that was only in the lobby. What was once meant to be an elegant building of some type, was not just a warehouse with a wonderful entranceway.

At the top of the stairs, he looked down at the immense amount of square footage sprawled out over the complex with its yards and yards of exposed pipes and valves. Some parts of it reminded him of a school building with its wooden floors and the smell of old plaster that lingered about the area.

He unlocked the office door and switched on the lamp that sat on his desk. He hated overhead florescent lighting. It cast an ethereal glow about the room but it was a fit for a very old room in a very old building.

"That you, Dr. Wilder?" A small raspy voice called from the utility room in the back. It was Victor Moody, the security guard that worked the night shift for David. He was seventy years old, thin, with white hair and a face so black one could only see the pink of his lips and the whites of his eyes in the dark.

Victor came to New York from the back hills of Tennessee. He relocated because his daughter had married a city man and he had moved them here. His wife had passed on with the virus and Vick really needed to be near his only child and new grandchild. To Victor, leaving Tennessee was the only choice he could make.

"It's me, Vick. Just finishing up on some work."

"Oh, that work of yours Dr. Wilder," Vick mumbled through gummed lips, as he sauntered over to David. "Jeez, I swears that work is gonna up and kill you someday, boy, eh?

Ain't you a piece of work." He handed David a cigar. "Now, lookit here, you're suppose to be keepin an eye out for a young lass that'll make you a fine wife and mother of your chilen." He shook his head emphatically. 'You cain't be workin all these late hours, Dr. Wilder. Hot damn if you ain't gonna kill yaself. Never you mind, suh. You go on an find yourself a lady friend."

David laughed. "Don't you go worrying your head about me, Victor Moody. My lady will come in due time. My work comes first at the moment." He raised his hand as if in a salute. "Take care now."

David went to his desk, which sat among boxes, an old credenza that was his fathers, and a long table that he used to develop his chemicals; to mix, to create, to invent.

For a few minutes, he sat down and tried to regain a sense of emotional equilibrium. He wouldn't get any work done. He knew this. He just needed an excuse to mull about his desk and think. He needed to keep his brain from pushing the overload button.

God, he thought. *The world has become such a pathetic place.* He would bring himself to tears if he allowed himself to dwell upon the earth's misfortune.

Funny how he envied his friend Patrick. He has such a dedication to his work that it even took the place of a wife and children. And as far as David knew, Patrick never once displayed a want for family. At least, not in front of him.

In fact, David thought that Pat's dedication went to the point of an actual maternal expression. When David was regressed, the first few weeks were a nightmare with all the flashbacks. Patrick was there trying to formulate some way to rid him of these disturbing memories. Maybe there was a pill of some sort, maybe an injection. But, whatever they may or may not be, Patrick's quarry in developing something didn't last long. Suddenly, he showed up at David's apartment with a small black box.

He had come up with the wonderful idea of decoding the microchips that were imbedded within humankind. As long as the chip was feeding the memory, it stayed activated. But, with this gadget Patrick created, he could deactivate that chip by simple remote control. He called it the DR2.

David had even more help in another friend. Ashleigh Bennett. She came with as much value as Patrick did. Patrick may have had the decoder, but what good was a decoder if they didn't have anyone to decode?

Ashleigh was the counselor at the Webster Center, appointed by the government to help people through the fear of regression. Of course, this was all to be before the sessions took place, not after. There was to be no memory of the regression, and this was so in the other agencies but not so in New York City and its surrounding areas.

Ashleigh also voiced her concerns about the behaviors of the people she was counseling. She had some access to August Webster's files, although many times, his clients came in to see her without his knowledge. That started a day after the first session of one of his clients. She received a phone call that the patient desperately needed to see her again, although she had seen him, as required, just before the regression session. This gentleman was having severe flashbacks. He needed her help. Since then, it had never stopped. The calls kept coming in one right after the other.

Now Ashleigh herself was growing suspicious. She began to realize that there were many more secrets locked in those file cabinets in his office than what she was ever privy to.

Suddenly, everything came together at once for David. He had the answer. The three of them could put this man out of business simply by using the decoder that Patrick had developed and the files that Ashleigh had her hands on.

Implanting them in adult chimps had already proven successful. Patrick realized, at the time, even animals had past lives. For when the chip activated itself, the animal's emotional disposition was definitely and dramatically altered. At the precise moment the decoder was applied to decode the chip, the animal immediately resumed his normal emotional personality.

David already had in mind the first subject for the DR2. It was a young woman that Ashleigh had mentioned to him not too long ago.

It seemed that she had actually lived the life of a Salem witch. She was apparently burned at the stake simply for bantering around with her friends one evening where she foolishly predicted something that coincidentally came to pass within a few days.

As for her first regression session, she was not sure just what it was that she had predicted, but she was nonetheless condemned to burn when the townspeople got word of it.

Kayla Smith was persistently having nightmares about fire and intense agony. Her past memories had been hanging in the back of her mind like a nagging mother's warnings. She didn't want to listen to that sneaky little voice that crept inside her brain and whispered about the flames that were crawling up her body and blistering her fair skin but it all seemed too real.

Even as the screams tickled the back of her throat, she tried to recognize that it was just a memory. Just a horrible bad memory of . . . of what? She didn't know. But she knew that she couldn't stand it anymore.

As Ashleigh relayed what Kayla was going through to David, he knew that if the decoder was successful, Kayla Smith would be the first of Webster's victims to sleep peacefully tonight.

Four

Angela Jillian

Case Number 234

There wasn't a thing in this world that would or could coax Angela Jillian to leave her home. She had been in the house for better than ten years. She was now forty-one years old and when her husband succumbed to the virus that seemed to be knocking on the city's doors, she decided that it was by sheer luck that she hadn't been touched by it. So, she would never roam from the house again.

Anyway, what did she need? She had her groceries delivered on the front steps, she shopped from a catalog and she paid her bills by check and left the mail in the mailbox. There was nothing she needed, except to live. That was all she cared about.

Angela had the deepest fear of death. Sometimes she stayed up all night thinking about it. How did it feel to take that last breath? Where did the soul and mind go as it drifted for the final time from the body?

She felt better not knowing anyone who had died in tears because of fear. Everyone she knew since she was a small child died peacefully or suddenly without even a chance to realize what was happening to them.

And it was during these nights, when she couldn't sleep, that she thought about that dreaded coffin. It looked ominous. From the deepest darkest earliest days, she could remember that box. From the books she'd read and the movies she'd seen, it was the *same* rectangular box with the satin interior that housed the body for the very last time. That same box had been used *for* years and years and years on end. It never changed. No one made a happy box to be buried in. It was always a remorse-looking thing with no room to move and no windows. She couldn't imagine being still, in one place, for so long with nothing to see and nothing to think about. She couldn't accept that in that box, she'd be dead.

She didn't forget the ground either. To be alone in the damp cold earth frightened her beyond imagination. On rainy days and on snowy days she wondered if those people under the ground, beneath those heavy monuments, were cold and lonely. She wondered how many of those coffins had scratches on the inside of the cover from those who had awakened years ago and realized where they were. What kind of panic did they suffer through?

Oh Jesus, sweet Jesus, she thought, panic tugging at her heart, clutching at her throat. It was going to happen to her. There was no way out. No escape. As sure as she was alive and breathing, she would be dead and silent. She couldn't stop it no matter what she did. She could only prolong it and not go outside, keeping herself from being subjected to anyone's cold or flu by not being in the presence of anyone with the virus. And if she ate sensibly and exercised regularly, there'd be no reason she couldn't live a very long and healthy life.

And how did she want to die, since she had no choice? She didn't want to experience it, that's for sure. She wanted to go in her sleep or suffer senility so that she would never know or understand what was happening to her. That's how she wanted to go.

But Angela Jillian forgot about one thing. The regression centers. Her birthday was nearing. She had escaped it the last couple of years and her chip never once activated. Could she make it through another year? No one even came for her as they were instructed to if she proved to be a no-show at the center.

Angela didn't want to have to go to the Webster Regression Center. She didn't want to know if she had other lives because she didn't want to know that she had experienced death before.

But, the proper reasoning led her to believe that if she had, in fact died before, how bad could the experience have been? Funny thing to say, but she survived it, didn't she?

Maybe she should go. Maybe she should dress up with bleached, sterile clothing, take some antibiotics to ward off germs, wear a doctor's mask and quickly get to the center.

Two years ago, she'd thought about this as well, but when push came to shove, she couldn't make herself take a step through that door. She was prepared. She thought she was prepared, discussing it with herself every day and night. It would be good to know she had lived before. At least she would not fear the coffin as much. Yes . . . this year she would go. Her birthday was only one week away. She would convince herself for real this time to make an appearance. She would not back out.

***

There was no sleeping for Angela for the next few days. She was petrified of the session with August Webster. She was petrified to go out the door lest she catch her death of cold. She was petrified to think that she could get hit by a car, a train, a bus, fall in a manhole, or get shot. Any number of things could happen to her while she was out. How could she do this? How could she put herself in such peril? It was a stupid idea. She couldn't bring herself to do it. How stupid of her to think that she was brave enough to weather a regression center? Her decision was made. She would take the chance of escaping the center one more time.

***

Angela woke up the day after her birthday, achy and with a slight clicking noise in her ear. Every time she moved her head, she could feel, as well as hear, a click, click in her ear. It was annoying her to the point that she shoved cotton way down into her ear cavity to drown out the noise. For a while, the cotton was successful. Every now and again she thought she could hear something, but ignored it, as it was so infrequent. It was the achy feeling that bothered her. Where on earth could she have caught a cold? She has always been in the habit of taking the very best care of herself so that this very thing would never happen.

Angela practically tripped as she rushed into the kitchen to make herself a conglomeration of fruits and vegetables in the blender along with fourteen different vitamin supplements. She was determined to head this flu off at the get-go.

By the nightfall, Angela was feeling worse than she had when she woke up. Several things bothered her. Those severe chills she was having, whether from the cool weather or an impending cold, were serious enough to incapacitate her. That damn clicking sound was worse than ever. She didn't know if she was in any true physical danger, but judging from what she had felt that morning, she thought it was more than a little possible. Whether triggered by her imagination or some physical condition, the events were real.

Of course she preferred to believe that there was some underlying physical cause, something easily adjusted with medication or a good night's sleep. That would most certainly be the simplest and most logical cause and solution.

Unfortunately, the only possible explanation she could come up with for her physical condition pointed to the chip. Her chip was activating.

***

It was the cold that woke her. She huddled under her comforter wondering if there was a sudden drop in the temperature outside or if her body temperature was rising, causing her to chill so badly. Even so, the nest of blankets she had made for herself should have contained some heat.

Next, she looked at the clock and raised her eyebrows in surprise. It was almost three in the morning. She laughed softly, giddy with relief and happiness. There was no more clicking sound. It was a cold, not her chip. She was safe. Oh Lord, she was safe for one more year.

But not for long. Angela abruptly stiffened, staring at the clock. Suddenly, she jerked back against the headboard and then again and again. She convulsed for what seemed to be hours, but in reality it was only minutes.

Short cries emitted from clenched lips. She was conscious enough to realize it was indeed her chip. It was indeed.

And then it stopped. Suddenly and without warning, all the chills subsided, the convulsive jerking abruptly ceased and her mind was clear and sharp.

"Son of a bitch!" She cried. "Son of a bitch."

Angela felt great. What it was, she didn't know, but it was definitely gone.

Sitting up, she tested her legs, rotating them, stretching them and rubbing them and then she tested her arms. She raised them straight into the air and then back and forward two or three times. No aches. No pains. No chills.

Angela Jillian felt wonderful. Better than she had in years. And then, she decided that she wanted to go out. She wanted to dress to kill. She hadn't gotten dressed in so long she wasn't sure what she even looked like all prettied up. But now, she wanted to give it a whirl. After all, no one knew her. No one suspected her in all those killings. Why, she was as free as a bird, getting rid of one Goddamn imbecile man after another. Hated them bastards, she did. Just hated them.

They thought she had only killed her husbands. *They thought*! That was the key. They just didn't know.

Her pleasure was not only in husbands that she took to herself, but also in boyfriends, acquaintances and even the little twerps that bought her drinks in the neighborhood bars.

Angela quickly went into her closet and threw one article of clothing after another on the floor. "What is this?" she muttered. "Whose clothes are these?" She wouldn't be caught dead in these clothes. And what about this house, she thought. How unglamorous. Such an unattractive, down-at-heel little place. She didn't remember coming here. These weren't her clothes. These weren't her belongings.

Amazed at her surroundings, she totally lost her sense of direction. She didn't exactly know where she was and she didn't recognize anything in the room.

Angela's heart began to pump at a pace that even she was surprised didn't explode. Where was she?

She picked up a picture from the night table. There was a man and a woman most unfamiliar to her.

Turning around, her eyes caught a glimpse of someone across the room, an older woman with graying hair and hollow cheeks. She looked petrified, as though she had just seen a ghost.

The woman across the room put her hand to her face in horror. So did Angela.

Angela turned and picked the picture up from the end table and realized that it was the stranger on the other side of the room. She turned once more and lifted the picture to get a better idea of the resemblance between the two women. But, the woman picked up the picture as well.

***

The crash could have been heard all the way to the Wickford town line. The screams were heard even further.

Angela Jillian didn't know who she was. Angela Jillian certainly didn't know where she was because Angela Jillian couldn't possibly live in this house.

And one last horrific thought passed through Angela Jillian's mind as she collapsed into a dead heap onto the floor. What was her name? Where had she gone? Where had the Black Widow gone?

Five

Ashleigh Bennett felt the lock on her heart pop open. Her lips curved into a smile, as she pulled her afghan up under her chin, and looked at the small-framed photograph that sat on her end table

She couldn't sleep. Once again the twilight was being swept in ahead of schedule, she thought, sighing.

Glancing at the photograph again, she saw a child in the arms of her father. It was taken in a park among abundant flowers and luxuriant sunshine. It seemed that the sun had not only permeated throughout the picture, but also the little corner of the sofa that she sat on.

The rays of sun created an aura around the child's strawberry blonde hair that curled softly to her shoulders. Her green eyes glistened, as she looked up in devotion at the older man.

This picture was taken once upon a time when there was no such thing as compulsory regressions and hypnosis. It was taken at a time when life was meant for living and flowers were meant for love. It was taken at a time when there was no such thing as a planetary crisis.

Ashleigh had the express feeling that she was taking the whole crisis upon her own shoulders. Being a counselor wasn't an ideal job in this day and age. Especially when many of her clients were dealing with their own mortality a few lifetimes ago. And most of her clients didn't even want to live anymore at all.

At first, it was alleged that ESP, rather than that of regression, explained all the uncannily accurate information a medium might relate to a sitter. This purported to come from a dead relative or friend.

Yet, Ashleigh believed that a human mind could almost literally "pick the brains" of a subject without being conscious of doing so.

Added to this, was the power of mythopeia. This, she believed, was the case with most of the self, as well as hypnotic regression phenomenon.

She knew it was the ability to create myths of detailed stories and places that frequently surfaced as "past lives." And at one time, Ashleigh confessed that she considered this subconscious forgery. But with the microchip now in existence, all that she once thought was negated.

She stood up and stretched. Though she rarely drank alcohol, she hastily mixed herself a Bloody Mary. The session with Kayla Smith this morning disturbed her. No matter how much she prodded and pried, she couldn't get the girl to search deep enough to decipher the mystery of what it was that she had predicted to her friends. Maybe if she could get that to surface, Kayla would see a clear avenue to a solution and serenity.

Taking a sip of her drink, she pictured Kayla's face this morning. It was of a woman who had given up. Her dull stare and low, unsteady voice told Ashleigh that she didn't care anymore.

"Kayla," Ashleigh whispered. "I can't seem to help you. You're lost in a world imprisoned by outrageous walls of the past and I can't find a way to free you."

Kayla was a beautiful girl with soft, almost platinum colored hair that cascaded past her waist. Her skin was milky white and her eyes were crystal clear. She reminded Ashleigh of a fairy princess of the old days she'd read about as a child.

Unfortunately, the nightmares the girl experienced were not happening to a child or fairy princess. On one side of this chalky white continence was what appeared to be a level headed woman. Yet, on the other side, fright and frustration was written all over her face.

Was she trying to deal with a caustic case of déjà vu; actual déjà vu that proved a past life experience?

Ashleigh had a rule. Whenever she experienced such a feeling of déjà vu, she recalled one of her English professor's elaborate explanation of such phenomena to his class, and then through experimentation using one of his own students as a subject, he'd go on and dispute the very idea of déjà vu.

"It's merely an act of association, Ladies and Gentlemen," he argued. "You recognize something familiar, without actually focusing on it and you swear that you've been there before." He'd smile smugly. "Simple as that!" And then he'd perform his experiment for the class.

At that time, he chose a young man whom he obviously thought a perfect subject and made an appointment to visit with him in the confines of his office within the next few weeks. During the period of time between making the appointment and the appointment itself, the professor called the young man's mother and asked that she send something from his room at home that would be familiar to him as an every day object in his younger life.

Within the week, a small package arrived and the professor opened it to find a Donald Duck bank, accompanied by a short note to say that this particular bank had held her son's paper route money throughout his schooling.

The professor then placed the bank in a discernible place among bric-a-brac, trophies and books on his wall unit, but not within feasible conspicuity.

The meeting started with general small talk about the class subject, experiments, even Shakespeare and Poe. And just as the professor surmised, within five minutes into the conversation, the young man suddenly stopped chatting and laughed. "You know," he said. "It's funny. But, I feel as if we've done this before, yet, I know we haven't."

End of experiment. End of discussion.

Immediately after the explanation of the procedure, there wasn't a doubt in anyone's mind that the subject of déjà vu was taboo. It was a simple experiment to disprove it, and when one thought of its premise, it all seemed so logical and reliable. Tried and true, so to speak.

***

But, in Ashleigh's mind, with regression a proven happening, she still couldn't buy the invalidation of déjà vu. She still found it a substantial, conceivable, yet undetermined experience.

One of the first steps in determining her own past life was to distinguish it from her present one. At that time, she realized that déjà vu doesn't discriminate between the past and the present. It just opens up doors and offers both past and present feelings and images.

But the preference was up to her whether the memory was from her present life or from one of her past lives. Now, she knew that Beta opened up the seriousness of her past, while Alpha opened up her inner knowledge. She would have to work around this.

Ashleigh was stuck between a world she half lived in, didn't want to believe in, yet knew she had to continue living in.

She tried to swallow, but her mouth was dry. Suddenly, she found herself more cognizant of what the August Webster Regression Center was capable of, and how detrimental it could become to the government and its people.

This governmental ruling had only been devised to "regress" and "find," period. True, the purpose had been to scan the great picture and bring back our heroes. But in Webster's empire, along with the past came the nightmares and the suicides.

For some reason, that last contingency worried Ashleigh. It seemed that no matter how hard she tried, she proved unsuccessful in doing enough. She certainly wasn't able to prevent all the suicides, nor did she do Kayla Smith any good. And now, Kayla seemed to be at the end of her rope. Ashleigh felt she wasn't doing the job she was trained and hired for. It was like walking a tight rope on that fine line between sanity and insanity.

Downing the last of her drink, she took the glass to the kitchen. Sometimes, she hated leaving her apartment and going into that cold, reality-filled world. This apartment reflected the true personality of Ashleigh Bennett.

Her softness showed in the flowers and lace of her furniture. Her sensitivity could be seen in the pastel colors of the wallpaper and carpet. Sometimes, she wanted to wrap herself into this apartment and pretend like nothing ever happened at all. What she didn't see or hear, she didn't know.

When Ashleigh passed through the living room to get some water, she caught a glimpse of herself in the hall mirror. It certainly wasn't a pretty sight. She looked exhausted. All the strain of the last twenty-four hours had shown up in her face, and not just subtle hints of stress. These were lines of a weary woman. Her ordinarily curly, strawberry blonde hair had turned stringy since this morning's shower, and her gray-green eyes were surrounded by whites that had small wiry red lines of fatigue running through them. She felt much older than her thirty years. Had the mirror betrayed her into looking it?

Groaning, she spoke right into the mirror at her reflection. "Look at you," she whispered. "You look like a foolish old lady, but you're acting like a young teenager with the wild notion that you can cure the world by nonsensical jumble. You're no counselor. You're a fake. And one hell of a lunatic too."

She shook her head. Was it lunacy or ego? *Are we playing where God never intended us to play*?

After getting the glass of water, she returned to the sofa, this time, avoiding the mirror that she passed.

She knew that her subconscious already had the movie scripts of her past lives. All she had to do was turn a knob and run the projector. So, she stood up, removed her shoes and situated herself in a reclining position. She was ready. She was ready to self-regress and put herself back into the life that she had visited so many times before.

Although she told no one, she was a man in that life and the founder of a group called SPR, Society for Psychical Research. Her name was FWH Myers and he had died in the year 1901.

It was here that she drew her strength to work from. Hopefully, the information that she gathered at these sessions would help her in this life with her patients.

Ashleigh began to enter her Alpha level. Almost immediately—it had taken her much longer to relax in the past—she could feel that level pulling her into a flowing, rhythmic sensation within herself.

She began focusing her attention on her breathing. Just that one simple step acted as a tranquilizer. Breathe in relaxation; breathe out the tension. Breathe in the quiet; breathe out disorder.

Soon, all her muscles began to relax as she fell into a state of meditation. She reveled in the feeling of being calm, serene and free.

The subconscious stairs were there somewhere for her. She always used them in her regressions. These stairs took her to her favorite place. Her quiet place.

At the bottom of these stairs stood someone she'd felt safe with throughout her lifetime. And so she descended towards her father one step at a time.

With each step she felt calmer. There was a distinct feeling of astro-projection, although she knew she was intact with her body. She felt a floating sensation, as if she weighed no more than a feather.

Once she stepped into his arms, she let her body go and slip so naturally, as she had done so many times before, back into the life of FWH Myers to draw out a little more knowledge from one great psychologist to one struggling counselor.

Spending enough time with FWH Myers would surely help to bring some closure to Kayla Smith's torment.

Kayla was locked into a two-dimensional world that she had

no control of. And, while Ashleigh was trying so hard for success in her meetings with Myers, Kayla Smith's life was hanging heavily over her head.

Six

David felt anxious as he drove the three miles to Ashleigh's house in the middle of what started out as a small rainstorm soon turned into whipping winds and torrential downpours.

It was hard to see through the windshield, and it forced him, along with dozens of other drivers, to pull over onto the side of the road and wait it out.

David didn't mind. In fact, he got out of his car and energetically faced the vicious demanding storm that loomed on the horizon. The wind, a groaning wail over the city, was announcing itself with angry, gray, thunderous clouds.

Whiplashes of lightning lit the river, illuminating the droplets of rain bouncing off the water. The whole Hudson was now a thick, black assemblage of quivering, supernatural matter.

Despite the storm, David stood quite comfortable with it all. He felt omnipresent. Boundless.

The wind lashed out at him like a forked tongue. He laughed back.

The lightening seemed to play with him, teasing him as it displayed, with each bright shaft of light, the spray of salt water high into the air. This storm was a perfect machine of infinity, and a similar storm was brewing within David Wilder.

Laughing, he wiped the rain from his face and pushed back his hair. He felt exhilarated, angry, and sad all at the same time. He thought of Ashleigh. They had known each other most of their lives and it was through a multitude of conversations on the subject of life after death that pummeled them toward the same goals and into the same direction.

It was almost as if they had peeked in on God one evening, as they grew deep in colloquy. So deep, in fact, that they occasionally terrified themselves into laughter. "Stop," she would cry. "You're scaring me, David."

David knew then that he had found a partner in the world beyond. Someone who took him seriously, yet could lighten it up at the precise moment that it got too heavy.

They both knew that nothing was funny. Reality could make one hysterical, they agreed, but the joke was on them.

Tonight there would be no joking. The task they had ahead of them was a grave and dangerous one. Ashleigh didn't know what David had in mind. Ashleigh didn't even know David would be visiting.

The torrential rainstorm wasn't the single incident that contributed to David's elation and excitement. It was the decoder. It was this decoder that brought the most amazing thought to him as he sat in his lab. If this young woman, Kayla Smith, was in such trouble, and Patrick designed the decoder, why then shouldn't that wonderful piece of equipment be used to decode Kayla's chip?

Now was the time for Kayla to forget that life and all the inconsequential ones before or after it and live this one out in peace. He was anxious to pass this by Ashleigh.

David felt alert and in command. Although the storm outside his car was abating, the one within him was growing more intense.

Ashleigh was told a little about this decoder when it was in its infancy stages, but was not told the intricacies of it. Since then, it had never been further discussed. Therefore, this evening's business would be new and would deliver some unbelievable information.

Ashleigh's townhouse also bordered the Hudson. It was once in an area of domestic ruins. Now, many people had a need to keep busy, so they improved on the construction of their homes, adding glass, stone, brink, and landscaping. This indeed added to the city a vision of some prosperity.

Pulling his car directly in front of her door, he sensed the unusual loudness of silence. Although the hour was late, if the lights were on, the music usually was on as well. His first feeling of trepidation crept in.

The side door opened into a laundry room with white and mauve checked tile floors, a laundry sink, washer and dryer, and rows and rows of shelving loaded with detergents and softeners of all brands and scents.

He walked through the beautiful pure white tiled kitchen where he remembered their first long talk. Neither had wanted the evening end. There was more laughter and exchange of true emotion than he had ever experienced before in his life.

He hadn't been back since.

There were voices coming from the living room. A large circular rug with a Navajo design covered the entire floor. It seemed that every light in the house had been on.

Although the voices were numerous, they had the same incantation about them. Something about each voice was familiar with the other.

He climbed the three stairs to the bedroom level and pushed opened the door, quietly stepping inside. He called out her name.

Ashleigh didn't answer.

He repeatedly called out to her so as not to startle her. But still, no answer.

David remained where he stood, listening intently. The room was dark. There was no other sound in the room other than the low murmuring of her voice. He could barely make out a figure lying on the sofa. His heart began to pound.

What was she saying? He thought.

The sounds were becoming more and more distinct. But, the harder he listened, the less sense they made. Why was it that there was only one person on the sofa? By a glint of light, he could see the red in her hair. He was sure it was Ashleigh. One person. Two voices.

Suddenly, the figure on the sofa stood up and walked over to him. It was Ashleigh.

"My God!" David whispered. "Where *are* you, Ash?"

The two voices were definitely distinct from one another; yet, they were coming from Ashleigh. One was Ashleigh's voice, but the other? He couldn't understand it. He couldn't make out if it was a man or a woman.

Slowly backing toward the door, David slipped out. He was afraid of waking her and startling her. But, just as slowly as she got up, she turned and slowly went back to the sofa and lay down again. Immediately, she fell into a deep sleep.

There was a chair by the door. David sat down on it, fearing that his legs could take him no further.

It wasn't but a few minutes later that a slight sigh escaped Ashleigh's lips and her eyes fluttered open.

David watched from where he sat. Then he stood up and walked over to the sofa. Reaching down, he gently shook her shoulder. "My God! What in the blazes are you doing to yourself, Ashleigh?" he stammered in fear.

As if just awakening from an ordinary sleep, she simply opened her eyes and smiled at him. "Regressing myself. Why?"

Taking his hand, she lifted herself from the sofa. "How long have you been here?"

"You scared me, Ash. You scared me. That's why."

"You act as if you've never witnessed me regress before," she said. "Besides, what are you doing here at this ungodly hour of the night? Or should I say morning?" She looked down at the folder in his hand. "What's that?"

"I've a profound idea that I wanted to pass by you," he said, still shaky from what he'd experienced. Yes, he had seen her regress before, but she seemed to be speaking another language this time. He shook his head. This time it was different.

He scanned the room. "It looks like you haven't been able to get much sleep either."

She nodded and once again looked at the folder in his hand. "What's that?"

"This, my dear," he said handing it to her, "is Kayla Smith."

Just the mention of the girl's name sparked Ashleigh's interest. "What kind of profound idea?" she asked cocking her head to one side in curiosity.

David stood awkwardly and shuffled his feet. "Well, actually, it was Patrick's idea."

She looked at him, studied his face, and a small smile started at the corners of her mouth. "So where's Patrick with this idea? Does he even know you're here?"

David shook his head. "Not unless you called him."

Ashleigh laughed. "In the event you find the time to clue Patrick in, I'd like to . . ."

"Of course I'm going to tell him," he interrupted. "I just thought I'd run it by you first for all the right reasons."

"Why me?"

"Because you're the psychologist, aren't you?" he asked.

Ashleigh turned around with the folder still in her hand and went to the small dining table in the corner of the room. She sat down slowly and pushed the hair back from her face. She was drained. "I sometimes question that, David," she said, tapping the folder with her fingers. "What does this folder have to do with Kayla?"

David joined her at the table. He sat down heavily, examining her carefully as he did. "Are you all right?"

Nodding, she touched his hand. "Just tired and worried, David."

"It's what you told me about Kayla. How her past was causing her so much anguish. I need to know more . . ."

Ashleigh drew back. "I only told you that I was counseling her. I wasn't obligated to tell you more than that."

David smiled. "No one asked you to, Ash. I understand about your confidences. That's why we had to go in and find things out for ourselves."

She looked at him sharply. "What do you mean, 'go in and Webster's office? Both of you?"

"We broke into Webster's office a couple of days ago. We *borrowed* some of his files. Patrick and I"

Ashleigh sat with her mouth agape in shock. "How? Everything he has is under lock and key?"

A smug smile crossed his face. "We were lucky. Obviously, his nurse put them in her bottom draw for filing the next day. We took about fifteen files."

"Fifteen?" Ashleigh was mortified. "Didn't you even copy them?"

"Hadn't even thought of that," David stated. "No."

"Shit, David, when Webster finds out, there's going to be hell to pay."

David gently pulled the file from under Ashleigh's fingers. "Yeah. And unfortunately, it will be directed at his nurse. Sorry about that."

Sighing heavily, Ashleigh said. "Yeah. I'll bet."

"Look. We knew you were counseling her and that you were even making some progress to a certain extent. Right?" He tilted his head, squinted, and looked at her. "But, not enough. Am I right again?"

"On two counts. I just can't seem to break through." She gestured to the folder. "Can I see it?"

"Most of it, you already know," he said handing it to her.

"I know. But I can only hope that there's something in here that I might have missed. I'm sure Webster's notes are a lot more in depth than my own."

She hungrily scanned through the notes. "There has to be something here that can give me a hint as to what I'm doing or not doing to help her."

David reached over and pushed Ashleigh's hair from her face. "Don't ever doubt yourself Ash. You're doing an exceptional job at the center. But, there's only so much one human can do for another, especially in a case like this.

"Kayla's mind is stuck in the past. It expresses itself particularly in her dreams. But," he lifted her chin for eye to eye contact, "who's to say that we can't wash that past right out of her mind?"

Ashleigh smiled at the narration of an old song that he made resemblance to. "I don't suppose you know what you're talking about, do you?"

David's eyes flicked away from the confused look in hers. Reaching into his pocket, he pulled out a long, narrow, velvet box, similar to a watchcase. "This is what I'm talking about."

Ashleigh brushed the mysterious box with her fingertips. "What is it, David?"

"A decoder."

For a few seconds, they stood staring at each other. Then Ashleigh pulled her hand away, as if the box grew suddenly hot. She walked into the living room with David following. "Want a drink?" she asked as if he had said nothing to astonish her.

It seemed odd to be drinking in the middle of the night, although they both knew that there would be no sleep for either of them anyway.

Ashleigh fixed him a scotch, and refilled her Bloody Mary. Then she took a deep breath and sat back down opposite David. "Okay. What's a decoder?" She noticed him closing his eyes as if in pain. "Are you all right?"

David took a thoughtful sip of his drink, rotated his head, and brought his hand up to his neck. "Tell you the truth, this old body of mine is tight as a drum."

Putting her drink down, she walked around behind him and put her hands on his shoulders. "Close your eyes and put your head back, and take a deep breath," she said softly.

"I'll give you two hours to stop this, Ash," David crooned lazily.

"You got it. But, while I'm doing this, tell me about this decoder."

David sat up straight. "To make this as simple as I can, Ash, it decodes the microchip. It erases all past memory . . . not of this life . . . but what the chip has activated."

"David," Ashleigh bit her lips and lowered her voice almost to a whisper. "That's absurd."

"You may think so. And so may I. But after knowing Patrick the way we do, I'd say we hit a home run this time."

"But erasing the memory can be done through hypnosis. And isn't this the object d'art that Patrick tried to tell us about a few months ago?"

"Yes, one and the same. And to answer your first question, hypnosis can and sometimes does erase memory. Webster isn't doing that at the center either and probably never will expunge their memories. Even after they have served their purpose." David shook his head. "We probably don't realize half of what could be going on out there in that center."

"Wouldn't he just regress them again?"

"How would he find out we're doing it?" David gently touched the box the decoder was in, as if it were sacred. "Besides, by the time he finds out about us, we'll have him hog tied and tagged, in jail."

Ashleigh closed her eyes and half turned away. "You know, this all seems so overwhelming at times. I'm talking about Webster. What he's doing. How he's doing it. Where it all begins and where it will all end. It makes me tired, David."

She looked tired. It was an effort for her to keep going . . . to keep thinking . . . to keep fighting.

"I'm so pathetic, David. I can't help anymore. I can't even help myself." Tears stung in her eyes.

"We've been through this before Ash. You are not pathetic. We are not pathetic. We need to put a stop to all of this and we need to do it soon."

Ashleigh looked at the man opposite her. Here was a man who did what needed to be done, and did what was right without thinking about it. And he was a man who did it without stirring up too much trouble and demands about what may happen tomorrow. Here was a man who had learned to deal with today. The moment. The hour.

The tears flowed from Ashleigh's eyes. "I feel pathetic. I don't like to feel pathetic. I won't put up with it."

"When I look at you . . ."

"I don't care what you or anyone else sees when you look at me. I'm pathetic in my own mind. So screw you, David."

After a short battle of wills, he stood up. "You're not going to do me a damn bit of good with this attitude, Ashleigh. Now, I know you're tired. But, we'll get through this."

"How David? Are you and your little band of merry men going to go around detonating microchips for a living?"

David nodded, ignoring her sarcasm. "As a matter of fact, that's exactly what we're going to do. Starting with Kayla Smith." He stood up. "And we're not going to save everyone, Ash. But, we'll get to those we can. If we can detonate on a steady basis, we can do a lot of good in this city. We can save a lot of lives."

"How do you propose to get near them?"

"Remote control." He inhaled deeply and let the air out slowly. "Ash, there are people all over the place who haven't reached their activation dates yet. We can get into schools, hospitals, and all kinds of places with scores of people."

Ashleigh noticed the sun coming up. She looked out the window towards the trees. Trees that seemed so much closer to the house than they did before. "And the shame of it is that as we do the decoding, that bastard's doing the regressing." She pointed to the narrow box between them. "And that's it, isn't it?"

"Yup. That's it," he said pushing it towards her. "Its technical name is the RM2 Effacer."

She opened the box and looked at the rectangular control. It looked similar to the remote of a television set.

"That baby can detonate a chip up to a distance of one hundred yards." He continued. "That means that we can do this from the street. As long as the person is in full view, we can even detonate through a window, if need be."

"How can you be sure it will work at all?"

"It's been successfully tested on monkeys. Patrick's premise is that if it can detonate a chip outside of the human cavity, why not within it? So instead of asking and wondering, we tried it. It worked.

The temperament of the animal had been drastically changed upon activation and just as dramatically returned to its normal emotional level upon detonation. You see, Ash, even a monkey has lived before."

There was dead silence in the room.

Then David continued. "You know, Ash, my grandfather had a saying. 'Never give the wind the chance to turn your umbrella inside out.' When you've been given the opportunity to do something you know is right, go for it." He picked up the box and stood up. "When's your next session with Kayla?"

"Tomorrow morning. Ten o'clock. Why?"

"Because at ten o'clock, Miss Bennett," he pulled her gently to her feet. "You may have no one to counsel. Grab your coat, it's raining."

She looked up at David with wide, bewildered eyes. "I know you're kidding." What a funny thought she had at that moment. Why hadn't they ever gotten together? Why hadn't they ever pursued a relationship between them? Surely they were attracted to one another. She guessed it just wasn't in the cards, and if it was, there wasn't anyone dealing at the present time. Still, he was handsome and gentle and . . .

David pushed her out the door interrupting, the thoughts that were so similar to his own. "Let's go."

"Where are we going?" She asked walking the narrow sidewalk ahead of him.

"You're going to lead the way to Kayla Smith's house."

Ashleigh pulled her coat together against the rain. "Why, David? Why Kayla's house?"

David stopped and looked at her with a silly grin on his face. "Why, to detonate, of course . . ."

Standing outside the car door waiting for him to unlock it she said, "Something very odd is going on here. It's inexplicable. It's terrible. It's great. It can't be happening."

"Shut up." He helped her into the car and slammed the door, shutting out the wind and rain.

When David got into the driver's side, he found her staring at him intensely, apprehensively.

"But, it is happening, isn't it David?"

David started the car and pulled away from the curb. Once they were on the road, he reached over and touched one of her strawberry curls. "Are you okay?"

Ashleigh nodded, took his hand and pressed her face into it. "Let's do it!"

Seven

When her courage said, "now," Ashleigh inhaled and knocked on Kayla Smith's door. It seemed a lengthy time before she turned to David and shrugged, looking at her watch. From over David's head, she could see the sun just peaking over the horizon.

"What do you say the chances are that she's still sleeping like every other normal person in this city?"

"Yes, but Kayla isn't normal and this isn't a normal situation." David knocked on the door himself.

Perhaps, they were slow in their planning, because it seemed the door was readily pushed open with the pressure of his knuckles.

Ashleigh called for Kayla, but there had been no response. David didn't wait for an invitation. Instead, he strolled right in as if invited.

Ashleigh had been a little more apprehensive to being so courageous. She waited in the foyer, not quite sure if she should immediately follow him into the dimly lit living room or wait until he called. "David?" she whispered loudly.

He turned around. "I'm sorry honey. Just follow closely behind."

She sighed and shook her head. They should never have come.

This is immoral. She felt as if they were invading someone's privacy or listening in on a secret. But, why was the door open?

"Do you think she's sleeping?" she whispered.

Kayla's apartment was a haven of comfort. There was the good smell of home cooking, even though she lived alone. Ashleigh knew through her sessions that domesticity was the real world for Kayla, after living all day in a world of strangers at the bank.

Ashleigh could recall the pain in Kayla's voice when she spoke of her lonely times. Those were the times she would think of her John and what it would have been like had he lived and given her children.

"Kayla?" Ashleigh called out again. "Kayla, it's Ashleigh Bennett! I've brought a friend with me."

The door to the bedroom was opened. David gestured her toward it, afraid Kayla might have fallen asleep undressed.

But Ashleigh had a bad feeling, and a second sense about going in first and nudged David toward the door instead.

***

David saw her first.

Kayla was sprawled across her bed wearing a thin nightgown, which showed what a lovely, frail body she had. Her eyes were opened wide and her mouth agape. She was dead, and it appeared to be suicide.

"Oh my God!" Ashleigh cried, turning her head away. "Oh my God!" Was she going crazy? Was this the girl that sat in her office only yesterday morning?

David turned quickly and enfolded Ashleigh into his arms, rocking her from side to side. "Shh. It's all right, honey. She's finally at peace and in her right world."

"I'm so sorry, David. I'm so sorry."

In death, Kayla Smith was not a pretty sight. Her long blonde hair seemed a muddy color, her complexion a dusky gray, her arms and legs stiff from the onset of rigor mortis, and she had what appeared to be burn marks around her mouth.

"Cyanide." David said bluntly, releasing Ashleigh.

Ashleigh lifted her head to look. "How do you know?"

He pointed. "Her mouth. From the way it looks, she must have shoved the stuff in." He looked around the bedroom. What could have caused her to take her life so spontaneously? Or was it planned? Where did she get the cyanide?

As if reading his mind, Ashleigh said, "This must have been planned. The intention must have been there when she acquired the cyanide, David." Once again she turned from the body.

"Look, David." She pointed to a tumbler that was on the bed, not a foot from Kayla.

Bending down, he sniffed it. The unmistakable bitter, almond scent of cyanide stung his nostrils. "Is there a note?"

Ashleigh went to lift a book from the night table.

"Don't touch anything!" he yelled.

Startled, she dropped the book, giving him a stabbing look of hurt and anger.

"Call the police, Ashleigh." He looked at her and immediately realized how he sounded. "I didn't mean to yell, Ash. But the police make it a point not to touch anything."

"We're not in the movies, David. If there's a note, we should look for it, unless . . ."

"Unless what?"

"Unless she was murdered."

Neither thought of that. Murdered? Could Kayla have been murdered, David thought, *and if so, by whom?*

Ashleigh quickly left the bedroom and went into the dining room. She plopped down on one of the chairs at the table, put her head down and sobbed.

Moments later, she felt a warm hand upon her shoulder. "Come on, Ash. I'll take you home."

She looked up at him with huge, tear filled eyes. They were so pathetic and mournful that his throat constricted with tears of his own. He didn't know Kayla Smith, but he knew Ashleigh Bennett.

"It wasn't murder, David," she said between large sobs and gasps of breath. "It was suicide. I'd stake my own life on that."

David touched the top of her head and then pulled out the chair next to hers. "Why are you so sure of this, Ash?"

"Because," she pushed her hair back from her face and inhaled with a shudder. "Because it's so terrible. This whole thing is so terrible."

David didn't pursue the subject. He could see that she was decisively upset. But she continued on regardless of his own repose.

"She was so miserable, David. She couldn't live with the nightmares any longer. She couldn't handle having a past life. Never mind one that she presently kept living. She couldn't handle knowing that there would be another one after this one and always having the never-ending question, what will I be? Who will I be?" Ashleigh placed her hand on his. "And where is she now, David? Are we ever at peace? Is she an embryo? Is she floating somewhere unsure of whether she is dead or not? Is she fighting the bondage between this life and the next? Because now, David, every one of us is cognizant, perhaps even in death, of the fact that we're a never ending process."

David stood up, still holding onto her hand. "I don't' know much about the other worlds out there, Ash. I just know we have to fix the one we're in so that there won't be many more Kayla's out there anymore." He reached for the phone and called the police.

David knew that Ashleigh felt responsible for this woman's death. "Are you with me on this, Ash?"

There was a tentative pause. And then she took his hand and nodded. "I'm with you, David. And I'll be with you when we take down Webster."

She sighed as she looked back toward Kayla's bedroom. "For Kayla."

Eight

The funeral service for Kayla was held on Long Island that Friday morning at nine thirty in the small chapel of St. Vincent De Paul.

David felt sure that her funeral would be monitored. Webster would attempt to identify those who attended and run histories on them. He would probably have conversations taped to ascertain inquisitors. But, no one questioned her death. Not family, nor friends.

The day was chilly, but the bright sunlight contradicted a day for a funeral. The church was full and the atmosphere somber.

David's heart ached for Ashleigh as well as for Kayla's parents and brother. Their muffled sobs assaulted him like gunshots. Where was truth? Was it somewhere in the middle?

"ROCK OF AGES CLEFT FOR ME . . ." The tenor's voice filled the chapel. Five years ago, just around this time, David's mother and younger brother died in an air crash. He could still smell the flowers. So when he entered the church, the memories hit him square in the face. It was that same scent that brought back those horrendous memories. Memories that he thought he tucked way back in his mind. Only at times like this did they surface and bring upon him a grievance that was much too unbearable to withstand.

"LET ME HIDE MYSELF IN THEE." He thought of Ashleigh. How must she be feeling with all that's been happening? How many more of her clients would end up this way?

And then he thought about the real Ashleigh. The one he had known so many years ago. The one who helped him through his family's tragedy, his failure of his final exam at State University, and the death of his retriever, Lobo.

She was the one who helped him through at least seven major setbacks in his life and what had he done for her? *What have I ever done for her?*

Had he ever told her how he really felt about her? Had he ever allowed her to tell him how she felt? He knew. They both knew, but it ended right there at the knowing. Not another step was taken.

Once back in the car, Ashleigh began to compose herself. "I hate funerals and cemeteries," she said matter-of-factly.

David looked over at her and watched her wipe away at her tears. "Let's not talk," she sighed.

She's beautiful, he thought.

"Let's just drive." She rested her head back against the seat and unbuckled her seatbelt.

He looked at this act with genuine affection and feeling for her. He was feeling something he hadn't felt in years and thought he might not be capable of again. "We won't talk. I've plenty of gas and I'll just keep driving until you cry uncle."

Ashleigh smiled. "Thanks."

It wasn't just another stretch of road, David speculated, as he looked out the car window at the scenery passing. It seemed to be an entire city with a distant horizon of lights.

As they approached Manhattan, the sections that usually were comprised of car washes, auto repair shops, and beauty salons began to disappear, becoming rapidly replaced by tacky blocks of town homes, each with scruffy little spots of lawn and sometimes a spray of mums or artificial flowers in small clay pots bordering walkways.

At one time, the houses in the neighborhood had been so well cared for. Yet, now, they were beginning to look dilapidated and beaten. The streets were looking decayed, cracked, and jagged. Gangly weeds popped up in exposed rivulets of dirt.

David sped up. He was anxious to get into the city and closer to home.

Where some people detested the crowded city life, he found it comforting and safe.

Once in his own surroundings, he braked a little. It was impossible to get anywhere in a hurry because each cross street had a stop sign.

He watched as a pair of teenage lovers leaned on the side of a battered car, and a blind man and his dog sat close to each other on the ground against an abandoned building. It made him wonder where he had gotten the dog. He knew they were costly; yet, here was this poor man who obviously had no home and begged for his supper, with a seeing-eye dog.

What was his past? What was his last life? And how had he been affected by it today?

David glanced over at Ashleigh. Her eyes were closed, but he knew she wasn't asleep. He kept driving.

Down a narrow side street he sighted fire trucks and heavy activity. Curious, he made a quick left turn.

An old wooden apartment building was aflame, rainbows of fire shooting out of every window on the top floor.

A fireman clambered onto the roof with a poleax in one hand and a shielded drill saw in the other. He was climbing like an experienced bobcat after his prey, edging his way forward until he was directly over his victim. Hefting the poleax high in the air, he slammed it against the roof again and again until the square that he cut into showered him with smoke and sparks. Why they were trying to save the old building, he didn't know.

All these buildings were to be torn down by September, anyway. David would have just contained it and let it go.

"How about a cup of coffee?" He asked, looking over at a very quiet Ashleigh. "There's a Greek diner at the corner. Ash?"

She nodded. "I don't want to go home yet." Her voice seemed to plunge down a descending scale.

David nodded and pulled into the parking lot just across the road. He stopped the car and turned off the ignition. "If you want to talk and be alone, we can go to my apartment."

Ashleigh shook her head and looked at her hands. "No. I want to be with a lot of people, David. People who are living some kind of a life on this earth. People who are laughing and taking each day one at a time.

"Right now I don't feel very real and this whole thing is beginning to get out of hand." She shook her head again, this time looking at him. "I hope you understand.

"This whole thing has been out of hand for some time now, Ash. It would have just grown until someone was smart enough to figure it out and stop it. Now, I just hope it's not too late."

Ashleigh opened her door and lifted herself out. "I do too."

Walking through the small diner they searched for an empty booth and found one in the back corner. The room was as loud as any convivial business restaurant at the height of lunch hour, and still, above all the noise, Ashleigh could hear the din of the air-conditioner and the slight hum of the fluorescent lighting above them. It was a very comforting feeling. She was beginning to feel much better.

David gestured to the waitress and she came and filled up their cups. It also smelled comforting and brought with it a touch of reality. And it was good, even though the pot looked like it hadn't been cleaned for weeks.

"David, I want to tell you something." Her voice quivered slightly. "I want you to know," she looked straight into his eyes to show sincerity, "that I am going to help you get to the very bottom of this and carry it out to the very end."

David smiled and looked back into her eyes. "Thank you, Ash. I was hoping you'd say that. Patrick and I need your help badly."

"Now tell me something," she asked suddenly very businesslike. "I know the answer. I just need it explained precisely to me. Just what is really supposed to become of this earth with the Regression Act? How are the other centers doing?"

David took a sip of coffee. "Well, as you already know, because of the drop in the environment level and rise in the pollution level, this planet seems to be going backwards instead of forward. So, what the government has in mind is to pick the brains of the people who have the foresight, if you will, to pull us together and gain some control of the planet."

"And we're talking hundreds of years of people?"

"Hundreds of years, Ash. All we were instructed to do was regress a human back to his first lifetime, and if there was anything or anyone that could help this planet through those years, we were to ask the vital questions and then erase all that they told us."

"Is this what they're doing in the other parts of the country?"

David nodded and began folding his napkin over and over again. "Science is just not going fast enough for us, Ash. And it certainly isn't going fast enough for August Webster. He doesn't believe that once you're regressed and relive your past life that it's done and over with. He believes that more memories will evolve with familiarity. Therefore, place these humans in a job-related position to their past and they'll come up with more and more facts for him."

Ashleigh nodded. She seemed to be in deep thought as she ran her finger around and around the rim of her cup.

"And he has a point, Ash. That would be the perfect way to solve our planet's problems. But our humans can't take the strain, as you can see with Kayla and James Proud."

Ashleigh sighed. "So what you're telling me is that the government intends to go slower to get to the end results and not hurt our people, but Webster is working toward being the hero."

"Right." David's napkin now sat in little pieces by his cup. "Imagine, if you will, that you came upon Dr. Elliot Humlich, one of the discoverers of the ozone layer. If you recall from his journal, when he died, he was just touching upon how this layer somehow affects the idiosyncrasies of our personalities. This is strictly hypothetical of course, but today, his answer could alter the whole course of history.

"Don't forget, we're dealing with past geniuses, Ash." He gulped another mouthful of coffee. "All we would have to do is ask him just the few questions necessary to complete our investigation and dismiss him. His present body would never remember, and could then proceed with the natural events of his life."

Ashleigh had a smile on her face as David talked.

"What's the grin for?"

She put another sugar in her coffee and more cream. "Oh, I was just wondering if August Webster has ever been regressed himself. "

David laughed. "Yeah, he was probably a prehistoric animal."

"You know," she said seriously. "That might be the key we're looking for. What kind of life or lives *has* he led?" She shook her head as if struggling to get back to sanity, and signaled the waitress for more coffee. "I want to get that man. And the first step should probably be building up enough statistics to put him away for a very long time. We need a game plan, David. And we need one fast."

David paid the bill and they left the noise of the diner. Ashleigh looked and felt better. David had one more person on his team who believed in him.

Tonight, he would stay with her in her apartment. She didn't want to be alone. Tomorrow, they would try to initiate a plan that would help save a planet that was slowly being destroyed.

Oh, how foolish that sounded. . . .

Nine

Jeffrey Mitchell

Case number 343533

He laughed at himself in the mirror. The butterflies in his stomach had worked their way up into his chest and were currently trapped inside his ribcage and playing havoc on his heart. This wasn't the Jeffrey Mitchell that he knew. This was a washed up, beaten down Jeffrey Mitchell. He turned from the mirror and plopped down on the sofa.

It had begun almost a year ago. His regression was a long and painful one. What made him kill all those women then? What made him disembowel them and place their organs on a table beside them? He certainly wasn't capable of that now.

He was aware of tears falling down his cheek. He realized that he was afraid . . . and Jeffrey was never afraid. At least, if he ever was, no one ever knew. He looked helplessly around the room. Once again he turned and gazed into the mirror. Had he suffered any penance for the deeds he committed? Had he been punished in any way?

He didn't know. He just knew that he needed to be punished. It was only right.

Jeffrey's eyes remained locked on his face. Slowly, his lips moved to form a word. "Murderer," he said picking up the 45-colt revolver. He pointed it at the mirror, and pulled the trigger. The glass shattered, reflecting his face as tiny slivers of flesh. That's what he should look like, a cut up, broken man. That should be his punishment, a horrible looking man who could never have a woman ever again, a man shunned by the opposite sex. That way, he could never ever hurt another woman.

    Jeffrey put the gun down and removed a thick sliver of glass from the sink. The blood ran down his arm as he lifted it to his eyes. It was pointed and sharp. He put it to the face that had loved so many women and earned a place in almost every one of their hearts. And he sliced . . . And he sliced again. . . .

Ten

When August Webster woke that unseasonably cool Saturday morning, he had a foreboding, almost unalterable feeling that something was wrong. For a few minutes, he stood staring out the window of his lavish Fifth Avenue apartment. An apartment that he never in his life thought he would own, considering the conditions he was raised in.

As he scanned the city, just awakening itself, he remembered himself as that little boy playing in the streets with the other children on a hot summer's day. He remembered watching the older kids pulling the cap off the fire hydrant so they could all get cool. The excitement of getting caught was probably the best part of it. But, everyone knew that on a hot summer's day, releasing the fire hydrant water into the street was an all too common occurrence for children. They would never get caught. The poorer folks were exempt from trouble in situations such as these.

He remembered scavenging through the garbage for crusts of bread and candy. Anything that wouldn't go bad overnight because he had a squeamish feeling for rotted and molded things. Maybe because it smelled all too much like his mother's breath as she lay sprawled on the couch in a deadly drunken stupor, snoring loudly with her mouth opened and exposing large rotted teeth. God, he hated his mother.

And, who was his father? At first, it was told to him that he was a serviceman across the ocean. Webster bought that for a little while, and even followed the news at night to see when he would be coming home. But, before long, he caught on to the game and just nodded in agreement as they told him he was traveling from country to country in his nation's honor. He even shed a tear or two when they told him he died in an act of war in some small country in Asia.

But, all that lay behind him. In fact, he hardly thought about who his father was anymore. He had his own life to live.

Through hard work and determination, his resolution began to pay off only a year out of grad school. And then when he got the contract with the government for the regression center, three years ago, everything began to soar.

Maybe he wasn't doing things exactly as they instructed, but whatever the difference was, they should only be concerned about the end results being exactly what they requested. For some uncanny reason, he felt he had to always have that extra inch of control. Always.

Webster had had these uneasy feelings or inklings in the past, and through the trusting of his own instincts, he had learned to become alert to them. He didn't claim that he was psychic, just careful.

This morning was one of those rare days when he felt an uneasy presentiment. It was as if someone out there was looking right back at him through his own window and making plans for him. And whatever those plans were, they somehow promised they would destroy him.

Webster shook those icy thoughts from his head and went back into the kitchen to refill his coffee. He tried not to wake Wendy what's her name, the high-class call girl they offered at the private club he attended last evening.

He didn't need to hear her irritating nasal whine this early in the morning. He made a disgusting face as he looked at her. Today's women were not like they use to be when he was growing up. Today they were all too independent, making their own money, doing their own thing. They didn't want to be tied down to kids and laundry. "Tsk, tsk," he clucked as he stirred his coffee and went back into the living room to drink it and scan the newspaper. "How things change."

But Webster couldn't concentrate on the newspaper no matter how hard he tried to take his mind off his premonition. He tried to ferret out the reason for the trembling in his fingers and the feeling of fear in the pit of his stomach but he drew a blank. Unless, of course, it had something to do with the only world he knew right now . . . his agency.

Although it was Saturday, Webster reluctantly prepared to go to the office. He had so many things to do today, so many visitations.

He yawned, wondering when that Wendy woman would get her rump out of his bed and out of his house. He should be slowing down sexually anyway. At fifty-three, he was acting like a twenty-year-old, and preferred twenty-year-olds in his bed.

Yet, today, his fifty three-year-old body felt wiry and achy. Almost as if his bones and muscles had shifted through the night.

He inhaled and stretched laboriously. He needed a good hot shower to clear the cobwebs and cotton from his mind.

On the way to the bathroom, he slapped the woman's rump hard enough to awaken her and then slipped into the shower.

***

It was another brisk morning for May. More like October, he thought as he wrapped his blazer closer to him. He decided to walk to the office this morning instead of calling for a car, but the cool air caused him to regret it before he reached the end of the first block.

Sandwiched in between two six-story buildings, stood his building. The structure was only two stories high with an odd sort of brick, making it stick out among the rest. Its appearance wasn't the only thing unusual. The fact that it was used as an office building stood out, too, as all the other buildings were apartment complexes. Actually, his building had once been an apartment building, too, but the variety of rooms within it enticed him to buy it for his business instead.

Webster felt the warmth from the moment he opened the door. It seemed for the past few years, the summer months had been cooler than he remembered as a kid. Could the atmosphere be changing?

Sitting at his desk, he plowed head on into his paperwork, not noticing the obituary notice in the newspaper that he had taken along with him.

Only after a steady hour of working, when he leaned back in his chair and pulled out a cigarette, did he see the paper in front of him.

Unconsciously, he looked around as he lit the cigarette. Smoking wasn't allowed in offices anymore. Actually, smoking wasn't allowed period. You had to have real power to even be able to get your hands on a pack today. They banned them in grocery markets and convenient stores, as well as gas stations and restaurants. In fact, there were very few places that carried them and those that did, carried them at outrageous prices.

Just the moment the light hit the tip of the cigarette, his eyes hit the paper:

A body identified as twenty-seven-year old Kayla Jean Smith was found Wednesday evening at her home in New York City. Funeral services were held for Miss Smith on Saturday the twenty-first of May at 9:30 in the morning. Miss Smith's family wishes to thank all those who were kind enough to attend.

Webster's mouth fell open, and he jumped as the butt of the cigarette burned his hand. "What the hell?" he whispered as he brought the paper closer to his failing eyes. "Kayla . . ."

He finished reading the article and rubbed his chin. Wasn't she the young woman who just recently pleaded with him to let her live her first life out? No. No, he thought. That was Mary. No. He rubbed his chin again as if the gesture would sharpen his memory. Kayla. Kayla Smith.

Webster went to his desk index that contained his significant clients and found her name. She was filed along with his latest resumes, which meant that she had indeed lived many lives before.

Quickly, he pulled the index card and went immediately to the file room to pull her chart.

"Sa . . ." he said aloud as he searched. "Scamander, Serbia, Smith . . . Smith!" He pulled out the forty or fifty files with that familiar last name and started again with the A's. No Kayla. No Kayla Jean Smith.

But he knew he had a Kayla Smith in here. Here, he thought shaking the card in his hand. Here's proof! Here's her card! He knew that he had spoken with her not more than a month ago.

Where was it? What had he done with it?

Panic struck at him, like a snake attack, slowly at first, then quick and vicious. He was very, very careful about his files and all his paperwork. The only explanation imaginable was that someone had been in his office tampering with his business. Someone had taken Kayla Smith's file.

Webster paced back and forth in front of his desk, dragging at the newly lit cigarette between his fingers, his thin frame tall against the shadows on the wall. Suddenly, all his pacing stopped. For now, he knew for sure that someone had been in his office. His eyes picked it up instantly.

Walking slowly to the window next to the file cabinet, he kept his eyes on the object that rested half against the cabinet and half on the floor. It was a shiny object, gold in color and long. "A pen!" He whispered.

Webster stood over the object for a few minutes before bending and picking it up.

Smiling, yet half-crazed with panic, he turned the slim pen in his hand over. Inscribed at the center, just before the separation of the top and bottom, were the letters P.T.

But that could be anyone, he thought, resuming his pacing. It could be a number of his patients or colleagues; it could be anyone's pen. But, the important thing was this. It wasn't his. That he was sure of.

And, it had to be a recent loss for the owner. Although Webster hadn't been in the office yesterday, it wasn't here the day before. All he had to do was go through his appointment book and find the patient or the visitor with the initials P.T. Then he would have him, right in the palm of his hand.

It was all August Webster could do to maintain a countenance of detachment while trying to concentrate on all the possibilities running through his mind.

His hands were shaking so much that at one point, the card he held in his right one actually began to rustle against his course fingers.

"Well, of course. Of course," he said softly. "I am a threat to someone. Another agency perhaps." With a face full of fascination and albeit, fear, Webster tried to create a scenario in his mind whereby this P.T. was brought before him, threatening to have Webster's agency brought down so that his could reign.

Aha, thought Webster, coyly. P.T. is a man that must be admired for his ingenuity and ambitions. He must be admired for his bravery at actually stepping into this office. He must be destroyed. . . .

Very effective scenario, he thought smiling, his fears eased. He put the pen down and went to the bar to pour himself a drink. He smiled again. "Yes," he said aloud. "Very effective."

But then, August Webster was a very effective man.

***

At eleven thirty five, Stephanie Ludlum arrived for her appointment at the Webster Center. She was just eighteen years old, today.

Today, Stephanie wasn't feeling well. It could very well have been emotional, but, nonetheless, as with everyone else, she had a fear of her chip activating in public. She wouldn't be able to take the humiliation. And though that was one fear, the very fact that she was in activation today, was in itself the other.

Not that the chip ordinarily activated itself. But it was so undeveloped. And really, she wondered, how much was actually known about it once it was implanted into the human body. Its primary focus was regression; it did its job quite well in that field, but . . .

Webster had the young woman recline on the large settee, one that he chose to go along with the old fashion lamp and draperies in the small room adjoining his office. Antiquated meant security in his field. He had always believed that.

The room itself provided a feeling of comfort and warmth, both necessary in the process of regression. It was important for the subject to feel relaxed, although nervousness was not a deterrent to hypnosis, only a hindrance. It was clear that only a senseless person could not be hypnotized.

It was Webster who grew anxious when one of his clients was apprehensive. It made him uneasy. It made him feel as though they could see right through him . . . feel as though they could guess everything that he was thinking; everything that he was doing.

Webster left Stephanie alone for a while to adjust to the situation and surroundings. Besides, he needed a little time to himself before the session.

Wearily, he let the tap water run cold in the bathroom sink as he struggled with the cap to the prescription medication. He had been nursing a migraine since earlier that morning; he presumed it was right about the time he found the gold-initialed pen. But regardless, it was agonizing and touched at his stomach. If it didn't start up on the other side of his head, this one last pill ought to do the trick.

Webster walked out of the bathroom and scanned his office space. Just outside his door were the reception area, file rooms, and waiting rooms. It was uncanny how hypnotism was taken so seriously today, enabling the regression centers to operate so efficiently. Not to mention the grant the government had allowed to run the centers.

At one time, to be hypnotized was considered a parlor trick or black magic. Now, it was definitely legitimate psychological phenomenon. Webster would kill to find Sigmund Freud in one of his sessions. But in all the sessions that he had held, there was not one particularly striking development or individual who held a memorable existence with which he could really derive essential information.

He often wondered which center it would be, if any, across the nation or world that would come across someone as sensational and significant as a Freud.

Unfortunately, Webster really never knew where he stood in comparison to other centers. Information from one to another was not allowed or available.

Inhaling deeply and intensely, the cottony, cobwebby feeling he had experienced earlier this morning swept through his brain again. He didn't feel quite alert enough. He didn't feel quite *there*. It was the headache, he was sure, along with the pen, the foreboding feelings, the woman in his apartment that he hoped was gone by now, and the general stress of his life.

Exhaling just as intensely, he walked into the regression room hoping desperately, this time, to have a breakthrough.

"Good morning, Miss Ludlum," he said calmly as he entered the room. He hid well his shaking hands and quivering voice from the pain and nausea of the headache.

On the sofa was a lovely young woman reclining quite comfortably. Her honey-colored hair was fanned about the pillow, almost as though she had purposely arranged it that way, and her hazel eyes were opened wide in anticipation.

Stephanie Ludlum was probably the most beautiful, sensual, and sweetest young woman he had ever laid eyes upon, and inadvertently his heart began to leap and pound and his intimidating manner disseminated almost entirely.

"I want you to relax, Stephanie," he said smoothly, sitting next to her chair. "You don't' mind if I call you Stephanie, do you?"

The young woman shook her head. She was truly frightened by this new experience, although she had heard of it being done many times before.

"Let's talk about your Karma, Stephanie. Do you know what Karma is?"

Once again she slightly shook her head.

"Karma is a Sanskrit word meaning 'action.' Your actions

in your past lives are reflected in your experiences in your present life." He paused to help her absorb what he had said. "And, depending on what you've done in your past life, your Karma can either be positive or negative." Webster relaxed back into his chair, reached for the stereo and turned on soft, classical music. "Are you ready?"

Stephanie nodded and barely breathed the word, "Yes."

"We're first going to get you into your Alpha level, so I want you to relax. You can begin doing that by breathing deeply and slowly."

Webster could see Stephanie's chest rising higher with each breath. Her eyes were closed and her fists were relaxed, banishing the whitening of her knuckles not five minutes before.

"Take a deep breath now and let it out very slowly." He watched her perform this simple task. "Now, focus on that breathing. Notice how the simple act of breathing is beginning to relax you. Listen to the sound of your breathing as you inhale . . . as you exhale. Imagine that you are inhaling a sense of relaxation and exhaling tension and negativity.

Breathe in relaxation . . . breathe out tension . . . breathe in solitude . . . breathe out noise . . . breathe in relaxation again, and now, start to feel your muscles relax. Feel your feet relax, your ankles, all of your bones, all of your nerve endings, arteries, cells, and fibers. They are all beginning to come in touch with your mind. They are relaxing you. And you can feel them, Stephanie, one at a time. Enjoy this feeling, Stephanie. Enjoy your Alpha level."

***

An hour into this session, Webster was totally drained, and just as he had anticipated, his migraine attacked the other side of his head. But he had gotten her through her Alpha level into her rainbow and back into a past lifetime.

It was minimal, but that was all he expected on her first session. She was a good candidate and that encouraged him.

"Stephanie, you will awaken now and remember absolutely everything. You will feel free of stress, absolutely happy and anxious for the regression sessions ahead. Soon, we will be able to fit you into a job that is related to an important life you have lived in the past, and eventually you will enjoy prosperous and effective living. Along with that, you will be dramatically helping our government with their planetary expectations. You will be a very important person, Stephanie."

Opening her eyes, Stephanie smiled. She was relaxed, yet she had a gnawing feeling at the back of her mind. She didn't like what she was feeling, but she felt as if she had just awakened and her mind was muddled. He told her she would feel relaxed and happy. But, instead, she felt tense, and although she was happy, there was something nagging at her.

"When shall I come back?" she asked. These few words were some of the only that she had spoken since she arrived, outside of her hypnotic state.

Webster thought she had a voice like an angel. He thought of Wendy what's her name, and realized that he was just settling. There was no reason why he couldn't have a woman like this Stephanie. He was rich and powerful and he still had a youthful look. Why then, shouldn't he focus on quality rather than whores?

Was he capable of loving someone more than himself, though? That was a good question, he thought.

"Let's make it again, next Tuesday. Same time. Is that convenient for you?" He flipped through his appointment book. Briefly, a flash of the initials P.T. passed through his mind, but his headache and rush to dismiss this young woman overshadowed that problem for the moment.

"Yes, absolutely, Dr. Webster," she said shyly.

Webster himself smiled at that. He reminded himself of the times he went to an optician and everyone called that man, Doctor. The man wasn't a *real* doctor, not a M.D., but he enjoyed the usage of the term, Webster gathered. And so did Webster, a Ph.D.

She swung her legs off the sofa and straightened her clothing.

Then, she simply stood up and left the room.

***

Webster let out a long aggrieved sigh when she left. He pulled off his glasses and rubbed his forehead in agony as he stared at the floor. Standing up slowly, for now he was becoming dizzy as well, he rang his house.

No answer. Good, he thought. Wendy what's her name was gone. He could go on home and climb into bed for a few hours and hopefully sleep away his pain. Later, he would tackle the problems he had faced earlier in the day, with a clear mind.

Webster phoned for a cab and closed down his office for the rest of the morning. He indeed had more visitations, but knowing he could never get through them, he immediately called and canceled them all, leaving messages to call his secretary to reschedule.

The cool breeze felt good against his face. But it didn't alleviate the pain. August Webster was angered by this migraine. He didn't have time for headaches and aggravation. He was an important man with important things to do. This migraine was setting him back and not making him as effective as he needed to be. And the most important thing that had to be accomplished right now was to figure out who had such an interest in his work. Whose initials were on that gold pen and who broke into his office?

Webster's house was warm and dark when he entered. Wendy what's her name left by the back door, but not without leaving a whiney note questioning him when she would be seeing him again. They never give up, these kind of women. They're always looking for a free meal or a free ride. But he had made it known to all of them that they were not to contact him. Ever! He would be the one to do the contacting. He would be the one to initiate the next meal ticket.

After sliding his drapes closed and setting his alarm for four o'clock, Webster drifted in and out of a disturbed sleep. His pounding head mingled in with his dreams, causing him nightmares. He jumped up in fear two or three times, and was so disoriented that, for seconds, he couldn't focus on where he was. He dreamed of P.T., and an attempt to take over his center.

There was no more sleeping for Webster. But he did stay in the bed until four o'clock. He lay there trying to align his forces, straighten out his thinking process, and initiate action. His headache had subsided by that time and he was beginning to feel more strength.

But, the one thing that Webster felt sure of in all his haziness was that P.T. would sooner or later be dealt with, and Webster couldn't wait.

Eleven

The meeting the next morning went better than expected, given such short notice. It was obvious to all three of them that they were facing a very serious matter exposing Webster.

Patrick and Ashleigh were fast becoming inseparable, and the conversation waved between just the two of them for a while. Then, the meat of the matter was taken into hand.

Patrick sat on a wooden bench near a landing. From here, he could see the whole warehouse where David so often stood and mentally redecorated.

He then started with the statistics of the people who had died unexpectedly within the last three months or so. He extracted these from the computer printout he'd *mistakenly* taken from Webster's office along with a few files.

"Doesn't it seem odd," he reported, "that not one of these people died a violent death. Not one of these people had a heart attack or accident. Every one of these people died in the hospital of natural causes." He slapped at the pages. "I'm talking eighteen year olds."

"How many?" Ashleigh asked sullenly.

"Six hundred or more," Patrick said. "Six hundred young people dying natural deaths in New York City." He gave a hysterical little whimper. "Hey! That's more than the statistics show for the last forty years on natural deaths!"

David looked at Patrick as if in disbelief. "This is a bummer, Patrick. This is a Goddamn bummer and we're right at the verge of exposing this bastard." He slammed his hand down hard on the desk. "And we're going to expose him! We're going to get this son-of-a-bitch and fry his ass off."

Ashleigh and David looked at each other. It was true the statistics were unreal. But it, too, was as if Patrick had a personal vendetta against the man.

"Patrick, calm down," Ashleigh said patting his arm. Then, on a whim, she asked. "How many are in your family, Pat?"

Pat looked at her and squinted. "Why?"

Ashleigh shrugged. "Oh, just wondering, I guess."

"Four." He hesitated. "Well, there used to be four. My younger sister died recently."

Ashleigh lowered her eyes. "A statistic, Patrick?"

There was sudden silence between the three of them for a few minutes. Then David grabbed the files from in front of Pat and opened them. "Let's see, Casey Spritz, Dale Abernathy, and Kathy Lee Hayes. These are the three files you picked up, Pat. These are the three people we'll be decoding tonight." He looked at the two of them. "We're going to have to get more files, guys."

"No problem," Pat said, composing himself instantly. "Do you have those blueprints we were talking about last night?"

David nodded and pulled a box out from under his credenza. From the looks of the box, it was as old as the furniture, which was as old as the building. Inside were a number of papers, yellowed from age and what looked like journals. "These are the blueprints of Webster's building," he said, holding the yellowed pages in his hand. He opened them very carefully and laid them out on his desk. "Here, my dear friends, is what we now know as the August Webster Regression Center."

David smoothed down the bubbles and bumps and pointed to an area heavily written upon. There were figures and equations that none of them could figure out, but what they were looking at brought a smile to each one of their faces.

"Well, lookee, lookee," Ashleigh sighed softly. "If this ain't what mama's been callin her baby . . ."

"A passageway straight into Webster's heart," Pat said smiling.

David threw his head back and laughed. "This, I never expected guys. Believe me." He put his hands behind his head and rested back into his chair. "When great grandpa designed this building, I had no idea that he had us in mind."

Everyone laughed.

"Seriously though," he continued, pointing at a small squared spot on the blueprint. "This area here will be the best way into his office." David continued scanning the papers, his eyes traveling the length and width of it. "It's an opening from the roof, but it will get you right into the place."

"I could give it a try tomorrow," Ashleigh said quickly, before she could change her mind.

David sat down heavily at his desk. "I wouldn't let you do that, Ash," he said with an exaggerated sigh.

"What do you mean you wouldn't let me do that? Who's the better man for the job?"

"Ash, it dangerous!"

Ashleigh plopped down on an old crate in the huge empty room. "Dangerous! What's the worst scenario? I get caught?"

David looked directly into her eyes. "Yeah! You could get caught."

Ashleigh shook her head in defiance. "But if someone gets caught, who would be better than a woman? He wouldn't hurt me, David."

The color had drained from David's face. "You're underestimating him, Ash. He's a cruel, vindictive, implacable man who would go to any ends to reach his means, even if that meant murder. You should know that just by the records here, or by the number of deaths out there," he pointed his index finger toward the window, "in that somewhat insane city of ours."

Ashleigh closed her eyes in frustration and blew an exasperated breath. "I'm going. There's no two ways about it.

You can't tell me not to, David." She looked over at Patrick. "Neither can you, Pat." Then she began folding the blueprints and spoke firmly, yet softly. "I'm going in tomorrow. There's no negotiation about it."

The two men looked at each other in shock. Here's this little bit of a girl just new to their project, throwing her weight around as if she were their boss, and they were sitting there like two jerks taking it. Everything they were trying to say to her to dispute her actions just sounded like a blubbering mass of verbal Jell-O. They were putty in her hands. She would be going in tomorrow.

"You wanna tell me just what the hell you are thinking?" asked David.

Ashleigh sighed. "I told you. I'm going in myself. It's that simple."

"Nothing's that simple," David growled. On the old file cabinet next to where Patrick was sitting was a tall, insulated coffee mug with a plastic seal top. He knew it was old, probably a couple weeks. But his thirst for a cup of coffee was tremendous.

"It's insane."

"I won't argue that, but do you have a better idea?"

Patrick just took in the conversation. Nothing he could say would make a difference anyway.

David slapped the table. "He's a fucking magician, Ash. He'll catch you. He's like . . ." He stuttered.

"He's like what David? He's cunning? He's evil? What is he? He's getting into everyone's bones and causing a lot of deaths and unhappiness. That's what he is." She patted the folders in front of her in place and straightened out the blueprints. "I'm the only one who can pull this off and I mean to try."

"Then I'm going with you." David stated calmly.

"No, you're not. The only way I could possibly allow that would be if you waited in the car." Ashleigh smiled sweetly at him. "Just in case . . ."

Plans were made. Ashleigh would retrieve the rest of the files.

That, she knew, probably wouldn't be the case. If her luck were at its best, she would be able to grab just a few. There would be more trips to contend with. She wouldn't let them see her fear.

David looked at Patrick in defeat. He shrugged, remembering the pain on his face at the mention of his sister. Why hadn't Patrick said anything about her before? Why was he so secretive about his personal life? David was there to help him, why didn't he accept the friendship?

As he watched Patrick's pain, the answer to all the unpleasant questions suddenly came into sharp ugly focus. His sister died at August Webster's hands.

Twelve

Sunday evening brought with it humidity and mosquitoes. Ashleigh kept slapping at her legs as she sat in her car in front of the center, waiting for David and Patrick to arrive.

Where the hell are they? she wondered nervously. She knew she should have come alone. Though the men were right in assuming she could get into Webster's office much easier than they could to retrieve his files, she hated to admit that they were also right in assuming that Webster was definitely capable of anything erratic if she were caught. For that reason, they wanted to be there to protect her, to be the "watchdogs" so to speak. So where were they?

She shut off her car and glanced curiously at the building. She hoped that the blueprints stood as they had been written years ago, and that nothing was built over the hole that she was to climb into to reach Webster's office. Too many years had passed and there was no way to check it out.

It was silent inside her car. The only sounds heard were the crickets in the high grass around the edge of the building and the sound of the sprinkler watering the lawn.

To this, add the sound of traffic heading south and the muffled sound of a dog somewhere in the distance.

It was nothing like the sounds of the past with its usual

squeal of breaks, shouting curses of taxi drivers, chattering of pedestrians, horns blaring and other city noises. The nights were now silent while the city slowly took on the face of the rest of the country, and of the rest of the world.

She didn't scream. The scream merely rested in her throat. And she didn't dare let it out because the unfamiliar face staring through the window at her froze it. Canceled it! Her mind was racing wildly with unthinkable thoughts bubbling their way to the surface. Her rational thoughts were working a fast shuffle. Her heart was racing, mouth as dry as cotton. It wasn't icy fear in her belly now. It was a sick, black fist of horror.

"Hey lady, want to move your car?" A dirty looking man in blue-collar clothing made her take notice that she was parked in front of the alley between the two buildings. He obviously wanted to get through.

"Yes, yes I'll pull up," she said gesturing to him, her heart winding down from the heavy plunging it was doing inside her chest.

He tipped his hand to her in a salute and walked back to his car. She really prayed that David and Patrick would come soon before she lost her nerve, regretful that she had exploited her own bravery as she had. Every noise began to startle her.

Ashleigh looked at her watch. It was a little after eight. Maybe she'd better go on up, get the files, and get the hell out of here. She didn't like the eerie feeling she was beginning to experience. Where was the safety of her apartment? *I'll be there soon*, she chanted to herself. *I'll be there soon.*

Quietly, she stepped out of the car. Pressing the door against the frame, she pushed it into place to avoid slamming it. Checking to see that her gloves were in her pocket, she headed through the alley to the rear fire escape.

She looked around for signs of meddlers, peddlers, and the like, but it seemed that everyone was minding their own business tonight. Lucky for her, she thought. But, on the other hand, if she needed some help, there would be no one around to hear her call.

Looking up the long flight of wrought iron stairs that led to the roof, she began her ascent.

A slight wave of dizziness from the height passed through her as she stepped onto the roof. She had to bend over and wait it out before proceeding further.

When she did, she noticed black tar paper beneath her feet. Ashleigh's mind was working furiously. Where was the opening that was supposed to be here? Could it have been covered up with this tar? She scanned the entire roof. David said that it should be located about . . . one . . . two . . . three steps to the right, and it should be located about . . . there!

There it was! Enclosed in a wooden structure. Yes! She was halfway home.

**

The door was the sort that swung back and forth. She opened it easily, stepped through to the other side, and reached behind her to rake it shut, being careful not to lock herself in.

And there was the grate! The huge grate that she would have to crawl through.

Ashleigh closed her eyes in weariness and fear. Sometimes she could just kick herself.

The grate wouldn't move as easily as she thought it would. It was rusted and dried and instead of pulling it off the opening, she was breaking off pieces of it little by little. The rust ended up as dust particles in her hands, as she feverishly worked to make the opening big enough to slip her body through.

By the time she finished peeling and cracking, her watch showed nine thirty. One hour and a half, so far, it took her to get from the car through the grate. What a pro, she thought wearily. She also thought about David and Patrick who should have been here by now.

Ashleigh climbed in. She donned her jacket, which was far too short in the arms, making it difficult for her to stretch, and proceeded downward. Slipping and sliding made the trip relatively quicker, although more painful, than she had anticipated, and within seconds her face was pressed against another grate. This time, she could see that it lead her to the hall between the reception room and August Webster's office.

Turning herself around, she pressed her feet against the covering and felt it give immediately. Her luck was holding out.

The small aluminum grappling hook on the edge of the grate gave her some trouble. But, by the third try, she was able to hoist herself up and swing herself into the hall. This was as much trouble as she would have so far. Webster's office was directly to the left. It should be a breeze from here.

As Ashleigh assumed, the building was deserted at this time of night. It was just like Webster to have the place as secured as Fort Knox, therefore, if she didn't run into a security guard, she would have to presume that the security alarm system was nothing less than the best.

From the direction of her entrance, this system shouldn't activate itself. Hopefully, she was safe.

A brief flick of her flashlight revealed that the floor in this area was carpeted. There would be no noise at least.

She checked her watch; it was nine forty-five. Only minutes since she climbed down the grate. She was beginning to make better time and that made her feel more at ease.

From the deserted hall, she made her way into Webster's office. She was breathing hard, which was more from anxiety than from exertion. So, when she leaned against the door to rest, she took the opportunity to put on her gloves.

It was dark in the room, but her eyes adapted quickly so that she was able to find her way swiftly through the unfamiliar territory.

She moved into the alcove, past the bathroom, noticing an empty pill bottle lying on its side on the basin, and reminded herself to take a look at it later. Every bit of information about Webster was valuable.

In front of her was a set of double doors with a dangling sign, much like those in a hotel that read, "Do not disturb."

This, undoubtedly, was the regression room. Next to that, was the file room with file cabinets that looked so incredibly easy to get into, it was sinful.

She hurried on, having no trouble imagining tabloid headlines summoning up her fate:

"Young woman found dead in the August Webster Regression Center . . . killed in self defense by owner . . ."

***

Ashleigh opened the file drawers one-by-one with a letter opener, which seemed ridiculously stupid to her, but it worked. She pulled out the files that she would be taking with her. They were dated back four to six months ago, so there would be no immediate cause for Webster to be looking for them.

At the moment, according to her records, he was working with new cases, the latest two months old. He had already secured jobs for the files in her hand, and the rest of the clients were dead.

It was kind of scary to think of . . .

What was that? There was a noise as plain as the nose on her face.

***

Ashleigh stood frozen to the floor. She wasn't expecting this.

Yes. Yes, she was. Of course she was. She just wasn't prepared for it. She told David she was, but suddenly she was tongue-tied. What would she say? Why was she here? Who was in the office with her?

Starting to panic, her breath came in short gasps. Which way out? "Oh, God," she moaned silently.

Holding the files close to her, she moved quietly toward the door and stood behind it. Waiting. Her breath became irregular and she felt faint.

The noise came closer. Her heart beat harder. A scratch at the door made her suck in a ragged breath as she waited.

There was the courageous side of Ashleigh who was overcome by the desire to run out and face her aggressor. She wanted to rush past him and take him completely off guard. But, the scared, more sensible Ashleigh pushed tighter up against the door and prayed that she could make it by him and back into the hole in which she had entered.

For a brief moment, she visualized herself as Alice in Wonderland being chased down the hole by a rabbit. *No time, no time for silly, silly thoughts*, she mused half crazily.

For some uncanny reason, her rational mind kept her in place. Waiting. Waiting.

She wasn't aware of the exact moment of breaking the paralysis that was holding her occurred. At one moment she was standing frozen by the door, and the next, she was on her knees trying to peek under it, fearing that the intruder would smash open the door hitting her square in the face:

"Young woman found dead, with broken nose . . ."

Ashleigh couldn't stand the suspense any longer. She could see nothing from this angle, and she couldn't stay there all night. And the worse thing would be for Patrick and David to come looking for her right now. They would all find themselves in jeopardy.

She quickly opened the door and started to run.

But, halfway across the room, Ashleigh took a spill. One of her legs came down hard against Webster's desk, painfully forcing the pointed corner to stab at her hip. The other went out in front of her, sending her sprawling on her side, hurting her left breast.

She cried out, covering her mouth with her hands. She was caught. Surely the other intruder had heard her scream. Surely, he would be come running.

Ashleigh lifted her face and winced in pain and fear as she realized she was lying face to face with the predator.

It was even worse than she had imagined.

Their eyes met and steadfastly bonded. His chest was pumping in fear as hard as hers, and then, in a flash of a second, he was gone.

Ashleigh dropped her head into her hands and gulped at the air. Then, as quickly as the fear started to recede, the laughter came flooding in. Or was she crying?

Here she was on a Sunday evening—when she should be home reading a good book or watching a good movie—in August Webster's office, on the floor writhing in pain, and all for the fear of another intruder with just as much guts.

All for the fear of a mouse!

***

Lifting herself painfully up, she could envision the ugly black and blue bruise that was forming on her hip. And it was hard to breathe from the bang to her ribs. Yet, her relief gave her the added incentive and desire to get the hell out of there now!

Finding her way back to the first grate, she tossed the files in ahead of her and started her ascent. But just before her climb, she realized that she had forgotten something that could be vital to their case. Webster's prescription bottle.

Stepping back into the room, she made her way to the bathroom. There, she picked up the bottle and turned it around as she read aloud. "Megatrixene 25mg. Take one capsule every four hours as needed for migraine pain."

She tried to remember if Rita had mentioned to her that he had suffered from migraine headaches. She didn't think so. If she had, it was only in passing. Not knowing if it could be important or not, she slipped the empty bottle into her pocket.

It was harder getting back up toward the roof, not only due to her injuries, but because the rusted dust particles that she scraped off made the flooring slippery.

She shone the flashlight on her watch. It was ten-o-five. Her dilemma only lasted fifteen minutes, yet it seemed like an eternity.

A giggle threatened to surface, but she suppressed it. Would she tell the men about this? She supposed so. But she would change the story a little. She would tell them how afraid the mouse was of *her*.

Looking up, she could see the moon. Excitement surged

through her. "The beautiful moon," she whispered in the darkness. She could also see movement, which once again froze her to the spot.

"Ashleigh?" The voice was familiar.

"David? I'm coming, David." She extended her arms. "Here," she called. "Grab the files." He was waiting, she thought. She was home free.

Ashleigh didn't realize how tense she was. When she saw David, she had the compulsion to cry in relief. She wanted to hold him and feel the acquaintance and safeness of his body.

Tears filled her eyes and she swallowed hard as she reached up to him. His hand grasped at her wrist and she was pulled from the hole. She could finally breathe in the fresh night air. She was free.

Ashleigh smiled. She looked at Patrick who was standing by the fire escape waiting for them. He winked at her.

No, she wouldn't tell them of the man who scared the be-Jesus out of her in the car. Nor would she tell them about the mouse and the bruised hip and breast.

"How'd it go?" Patrick asked with a smile.

"It was a cinch, guys!" she said as they walked to the car. "A real cinch!"

Thirteen

Ashleigh and Pat were in David's living room sorting out the information they would need to be documented. They were totally exhausted. It had been a long day in preparation, and a long evening.

But now, files in hand and mission completed, they began to relax in the soft lighting of the lamp and the third bottle of wine. Ashleigh sipped at hers and began to tell Patrick, in more detail, her role at the center. "Not only can past life experience therapy help this earth from forwarding itself again, but it can do wonders for the mental health of the subject. Your fears and attractions all come from events in your past life, even this life.

"All we were intended to do is be a mediator between the subject and the past. The regression centers were to guide the subject to there past in order to reveal what possible work they could do to bring us all together again as a productive planet in the future."

Ashleigh looked at David and Patrick, noticing that they were totally immersed in what she was telling them. Her phraseology must be charming, she thought, losing herself for a moment in amusement. It was as if she were a kindergarten teacher telling a spellbinding story to a bunch of children.

David and Patrick shared a quick glance and turned their

attention back to Ashleigh.

"What exactly is reincarnation all about," Patrick asked. "I mean, clear it up once and for all. All you counselors and psychics must have some sound facts to offer."

Ashleigh picked up a powdered sugar doughnut, took a bite, returned it to the napkin next to her coffee, and then ran her finger around her mouth to remove any leftover sugar. She didn't much like sugar doughnuts, so she had to smother the taste with a gulp of coffee. "No one really knows, I'll have to admit," she said, still licking at her lips. "Transmigrating from one life to the other is usually understood only metaphorically. There are plenty out there who believe that reincarnation is the outcome of karmic morality. It's the way we are punished for evil doings in the previous life."

David laughed. "I have to say, whatever I did then, I'm sure working on penance today."

Ashleigh looked at him and shook her head. "You know, David, you can't believe that the earth is in this kind of shape because you lied or stole candy in a past life?"

David was embarrassed. "I didn't quite mean that, Ash."

"What I mean is there are such terrible things still going on out there, that we have been caught up in a planetary complication. It really has nothing to do with whether we were good or bad in a past life."

David remained quiet. He could see now that Ashleigh took this very seriously, as he and Patrick did, but she lived it day after day through Webster's center.

"It would be interesting to know if we continue to reincarnate with the same people, wouldn't it?" Pat asked.

"I think we do," Ashleigh stated. "I think we switch roles with each reincarnation. Some people may reincarnate as friends or lovers and others reincarnate in power struggles. I believe that those are the ones, the power struggles that continue on lifetime after lifetime, playing those struggles out because of such emotions as guilt, fear, or anger carried over and over from one or more lives."

"Whew!" David exhaled. "That was a mouthful and scary as

hell. There are some people I really wouldn't want following me around life after life, if you know what I mean."

"August Webster," Patrick and Ashleigh both chimed in and answered the question.

"Let's get back to work," Patrick suggested.

***

By late evening, the trio had almost completed the majority of files. There was the rustle of paper in the room, the whir of the air conditioning, the ping of soft rain against the window, and soft, steady breathing.

"Perfect!" David said straightening up and getting to his feet. He began to pace, his face taking on an odd sheen of excitement. "You couldn't have picked better files if you read through each one of them and hand picked them, Ash."

"Holy good Christ!" David said, the shock apparent in his voice. "Look at this, will ya?" He handed Patrick the file he was reading. "Thomas Paul Wilson. Subject regressed back into 1782. This was traced back to his first and only life. Age four. Ultimately dying at the hands of his own mother." David stopped his pacing and looked directly at Ashleigh. "Now why do you suppose Webster allowed this poor man to retain his memories? What else did he expect to extract from the poor guy?"

Ashleigh shrugged. "Does it say where he works?"

David shook his head. "No. Webster told him he couldn't place him. Too under-qualified, I guess." David stopped in front of Patrick and squatted. "He died two and a half months ago of natural causes," he said softly.

This angered Patrick who was still skimming the pages, his hands shaking. "Poor soul," he muttered. "Why the hell is this happening?" He looked up at David. "I can figure Webster's motives to an extent. But none of this makes any sense.

"Wilson made three appointments in which he begged Webster to erase his memories. Says here that Wilson couldn't live knowing his own mother could perform such an act . . . and more than that . . ." Patrick looked up at David and Ashleigh. "The woman followed him to this day. She's his mother now." Patrick put down the file. "And he knew it. So he had questions that couldn't be answered by her. . . . It's a tragedy."

Ashleigh gave a low whistle in disbelief. How sad, she thought, that one man could cause such pain. "Well I know one thing," she said, pouring herself more wine, "these are the people that need decoding. These are the people who resort to suicide and that's where you get those high statistics, like poor Mr. Wilson and Mr. Proud and . . ." She stopped and ran her finger around the rim of her glass slowly. "And Kayla . . ."

David nodded, sitting next to her on the sofa, and patted her hand. "I agree with you. And don't forget the people with the malfunctions. They're another breed altogether." He looked through the files to see if there was a special code for the patients with the malfunctions. There had to be. Surely, once or twice upon regression there was a slip up somewhere, a stuttering, an alien language indescribable to Webster, or anything the chip may have set off unpredictably. "I feel that anything computerized can malfunction, therefore, what we should do is read through these files and pick out the three or four that are in most serious need. Then we can go to the rest," David said, slapping his legs and bending forward to pour himself a glass of wine. "In the meantime, I'll call and book a trip to Washington. It may be time to have a little chat with Mario Prisero, the leader of the assholes handling this."

"What good's that going to do us?" Patrick asked, still scanning through the files.

"Gonna get us heard. That's a beginning, isn't it?"

"Right now, my friend, you have nothing to tell but a hypothesis. I think it's too soon."

David nodded, his voice suddenly coming alive. "That may well be true. But a hypothesis has some base to it, doesn't it? And that's just what I'm going to give them. Point is, I'm going to stick them with a heady ending too. Food for thought"

There was silence in the room for a few minutes. Then Ashleigh stretched and stood up. "Well guys, I'm going home.

I'm too exhausted to make heads or tails out of this anymore tonight. If you want, tomorrow we can meet at my apartment. And, if you come early enough, I'll make you both breakfast before we all head for work and start out the day."

David smiled and helped her from the sofa. "Sounds good to me." He looked at Patrick. "Want to call it an evening, or do you want to hang around and go through some more of this stuff?"

Patrick shook his head and downed the rest of his drink. "Naw. I'm going to go on home." He lifted himself heavily from his chair and tucked in his shirt. "Come on Ashleigh. I'll walk you out."

For a second, David felt a stab of jealousy . . . a feeling he hadn't felt for years . . . hadn't wanted to feel for years. A brief flash of memory swept through his mind as he pictured Suzanne, a girl a very long time ago, throwing the engagement ring he gave her in his face. Her face was terse and angry, her eyes full of pain. If he didn't stop working on this Homeosis project, she wouldn't stay with him, she had stated simply. She was scared. It was too dangerous being near that kind of virus with all the people that were dying from it. And he couldn't blame her. The project kept him working very long hours. Sometimes, he had stayed at the lab for days at a time. And if he caught a cold or sniffle, she immediately stayed away from him, fearing it was something he may have picked up from one of his viruses.

So, David made the easy choice for her, but the hardest one for himself. One he especially didn't want to make. But he had already put too much of himself into the project to give it up. He chose his work, and she chose to leave.

"What time, Ash?" David asked, pushing himself from the memory.

"Early. Around six thirty, seven?"

David nodded. "We'll be there."

Not one minute after they left, David found himself staring out the window after them, watching them laugh together. Somehow, he felt the butt of their jokes. Stupid. He was being paranoid. They were his dearest friends. He knew where his heart was going, and he was scared. Now wasn't the time to let emotions get in the way. He had to get to Washington. He had files to sort and phone calls to make. He had no time for silliness like love.

He looked out over the city. Millions of people were out there relaxing, reading, some with problems, and some facing their own demise. Most of the young people were out there facing regression, worrying how they would handle it, wondering who they were.

Of course, the biggest fear they had would be regressing before their time. Once eighteen, within fifteen days the notice went out for them to make their appointment at the Webster Center. If they failed to do so, they could regress anywhere. Those who did, either found themselves quietly at home facing their past lives, or in public becoming maniacal.

Because of the uncertainty of where it would happen and the certainty of it happening, when the eighteenth birthday approached, not one New York resident failed to make his or her appointment at the center.

David anxiously gathered the files up for his morning meeting. If they didn't do something about this quickly, the outcome would be devastating. He was as sure of that as he was sure he was in love with Ashleigh Bennett. Two things he didn't want to admit.

Smiling, he walked around the apartment shutting off the lights. He picked up her glass and brought it to the kitchen sink, touching her lipstick print with his own lips.

His life seemed so complex lately. There were too many things to worry about and so many things to do. He didn't want his lab work to suffer because of Webster, yet look at the other suffering he could prevent. With Ashleigh and Patrick's help, it could well be over soon. Then, he could pursue his other interests avidly.

There was a chill in the house, but preoccupied with the task at hand, David was oblivious to it. There were times, such as these where he wished he could close his eyes and make his dreams reality. Was Noah Webster's definition of dreams fantasy or nightmare? He wondered.

***

The alarm woke him promptly at five o'clock. David switched on the bedside lamp and adjusted his eyes to the light to check the time. He had wanted to get to Ashleigh's before Patrick this morning, yet, scrupulously sensitive and guarded, he tempered his tendency to admit why.

Rolling over and out of bed, he went to the window and pulled up the shade. The pane was a sheet of water as the rain cascaded down in layers. David groaned and stretched. Rain made him tired.

He went into the bathroom and turned on the shower. So many things rushed through his mind, his life suddenly seeming critically complicated. His enthusiasm for the project was high, and with the added help of Patrick and Ashleigh, there was more of a chance of bringing Webster to his knees.

It seemed that he went to bed with these problems weighing on his mind. He woke up with them, and sometimes during the daytime hours they would hit him like a ton of bricks, a never-ending story. A constant drain on his mental state.

The coolness felt good waving down the length of his body. He held his face under the shooting water as if to drown out all the unpleasant events taking place in his life at that moment, but he knew that such a thing would be impossible. Nothing would ever rid him of his discomforts unless he took positive, drastic action.

David stepped out of the shower and ran a comb quickly through his hair. He then gargled and went into the kitchen to fix coffee. He knew Ashleigh was going to make some with breakfast, but he couldn't function without a shower and that first cup in his system.

While he drank, he stood at the window observing the weather and scanning the sullen sky. Grim clouds clothed a deep flannel canvas. There was a fine hint of sun bleeding through the gloom, but not enough to avoid casting the day as dismal.

The rain had a rhythmic beat lapping in currents as it tumbled down. David hated driving in this weather, but he was already running later than he planned.

It seemed more like evening than morning, David thought, straining his eyes to see the road. He mentally went over his notes and felt beside him for the files from which they would be gathering their information.

Biting on his lower lip he realized he had left his wallet and money at home. He was closer to his apartment than to Ashleigh's, making it worthwhile to turn back. The five extra minutes or so wouldn't make much of a difference compared to the problems of not having these personal articles with him. He argued with himself for all of the two minutes that it took for him to make up his mind to turn around. He could always go back after breakfast. He did want to be alone with Ashleigh for a little while.

No, the wallet was important. Damn.

But it wasn't just the five minutes out of his life that he had to worry about at the moment, it was his life, indeed, that was in trouble. The sudden increase in speed, as he accelerated to make a u-turn, made the car fishtail on the wet road. His heart seemed to leap from his chest. "Oh, no!" He yelled as he gripped the wheel, hoping to control the car. But, it spun around as if it had a mind of its own.

It was still dark, and from the corner of his eyes, he could see the lights of an oncoming car. He turned the wheel into the skid and careened onto the shoulder. Like a skier, the car stretched forward as if in a crouch. The front wheels lifting as it slammed down at an angle. Then, almost as if in slow motion, it began to roll. He felt every twist as he flopped around powerless and insubstantial. . . . He couldn't see . . . couldn't think.

David could feel the sickening crunch of steel as the car slammed into a tree, his body forced against the roof. He raised his arms in front of his face as the splinters of glass imploded from the windshield, the glistening mass lunging at him . . . leaping at him . . . tearing at him. He felt immobile, suffocating under the weight.

Darkness was closing over him as his mind tried to will himself conscious. He could hear voices. One, he was sure, was Tom Hale, his attorney. He knew that voice anywhere.

"He's hurt badly, I think," Tom said to someone. "He's unconscious."

David tried to speak; to tell him he wasn't unconscious, but his lips wouldn't form the words. His eyes wouldn't open.

"There's blood coming from a gash in his head," someone else said. "Has someone called an ambulance?"

The voices spoke to one another as they tried freeing him from the wreckage.

The files, he couldn't let them get the files. "There may be other injuries. Internal injuries." A different voice spoke this time.

Floating . . . drifting. *I can't reach you, Tom.*

Hands grabbed at him gently from beneath his armpits and began to tug.

"Gas is dripping. Let's get him out of there!"

Fire. The car's going to explode. The files. From a distant fog, he could hear sirens. Hands lifted him onto a stretcher. Doors opened and closed. He felt movement. Then, even with his eyes closed, he could see a bright flash. Then a whoof! An explosion.

David drifted deeper and deeper into unconsciousness. *The files . . .*

Fourteen

Vinny (Slammer) Picone

Case number 1223

Slammer looked in the mirror at the handsome dark-haired man that looked back. He had it all. Damn, he had the looks, the charm, and the ambition to be the greatest name on Broadway.

Slammer, whose real name was Vincent J. Picone, wondered why he still couldn't get an audition, try as he would. Even as a stand in or background person, he just couldn't get a break.

His agent told him he had to change his image. He was too tough looking. He was too street wise. But Slammer didn't know how to change.

He wondered about it often, though. He wondered why on earth he walked around with that damn chip on his shoulder like he was Mr. Mafioso or something. He wondered why he had to act so tough, even around his friends, especially around his friends.

Was it because he was small? Did he have a Napoleon complex? That's what his mother use to tell him. Small people were louder people. Just like those little dogs that barked more and nipped at people's feet. They had to think they could trick everyone around them into thinking that they were much bigger than they actually were.

But no one was fooled, he thought. Everyone knew Slammer for what he was. That's where he got his nickname. In order to get attention, he would slam his hand on a table or desk or whatever was closest by him. Whenever he wanted to speak and it didn't seem as though anyone was paying attention, he would start slamming.

But all tough guys have a nickname, he thought. He must have some notoriety and influence to have been given one, too.

And now, he needed the notoriety on Broadway. He needed to land himself a part that would knock the socks off everyone. Show them who he really was. A star. He would be a great Broadway star, and fuck 'em all.

Slammer gave one last pat to his hair, picked up his keys, and headed out to his agent's office. Maybe this time there would be something for him when he got there.

Vinnie Slammer Picone would be twenty-nine years old next week. The last year before he hit his thirties. That sickened him. It sickened him because he still was nowhere in life. He had no trades, no schooling and no cash. Except for acting skills, he had nothing.

The phone rang just as he was locking the door. Slammer knew never to ignore a ringing phone. You never knew when someone would be calling about a part. So he quickly opened the door and ran for the phone.

Slammer stood with the phone in his hand and his mouth hung opened. "What're you talking about Jimbo? What do ya mean, dead? How?"

There was silence for a few minutes. Then, "I see. Yeah, yeah. Cripes, does anyone know where she is? I don't." Slammer hung up.

"Shit," he said slamming his hand on the counter. Picking up the phone, he dialed his friend Tony. "Hey Tone. Hear about Dominick?" The affirmative answer spurred him on. "We got some big troubles, right? None of us knows where the girl is. Dom told us that he grabbed her as she came out of the bank.

He was only gonna pay her old man back for repo-ing his car. Just a couple of days, he said. Daddy would think she was kidnapped and go hog wild and Dom would get his satisfaction. Payback, ya know?" Slammer tried to control his voice from shaking. He hated sounding scared of anything. "Now we're accessories to this scumbag's tricks, and he goes and gets himself killed. I don't know where the fuckin' girl is, do you?" His voice went up a whole scale. "But we gotta find her, Tone. We gotta find her, and fast!"

Slammer hung up the phone and threw his keys on the table. He didn't feel like going to his agent's now. He wasn't in the mood to act, because he was damn scared right now. If he had to be scared in an audition, this would be the perfect time. He would surely get the job.

Dominick, Jimbo, Tony, and Slammer were four friends from grammar school who never lost contact. Some people considered them a small gang, but that just wasn't so. Sure they were into mischief lots of times, but it was kid stuff. Nothing like what Dom pulled now. In fact, he told no one of what he was up to. Only after the incident did they find out that he had kidnapped the girl, who was seventeen years old, and he didn't ever tell them where he put her. And then, to top it off, the scumbag gets into a motorcycle accident and kicks the bucket. "Fuckin' scumbag," Slammer said, nearly in tears.

***

The morning of the funeral, Slammer wasn't looking as good as usual. This time, when he looked into the mirror, it wasn't the same handsome man he saw every morning of his life. This time, he was looking at someone who seemed to have aged overnight. He had bags under his eyes from lack of sleep and he had lost at least ten pounds that he just couldn't afford to lose because he was so worried that he was going to get involved in something he had no control over. But, just because they knew about it, just because Dom told them about it, made it look as though they were involved.

Just that afternoon, the afternoon that Dom got killed, the friggin' police came around asking questions about this broad. They were anxious to question Dominick, but nobody knew that he had been killed yet. So they told the cops that he'd be back later and it might be better if they would come back then because they knew nothing. They really couldn't help. That's when the cops told them that the girl was missing and the father suspected Dominick Russo.

It's funny, he thought, how just being friends with someone can get you in all sorts of trouble. But this was the kind of trouble he didn't need at this stage of his life.

The funeral parlor was filled to capacity. He knew most of the people there because he had grown up with Dominick's family as well as the other's families. So here were all the brothers and sisters, their kids and cousins, aunts and uncles, friends, and who knew whom else that had come out of the woodwork. God, these Italians loved a good funeral.

"I don't want to go up to the casket," Jimbo whined to Slammer.

"Come on," Slammer hissed. "We have to go. He was our friend."

"It's spooky. I don't like dead people."

Slammer grabbed Jimbo by the shirtsleeve and pulled him toward the front of the room. "Come on. No one like's dead people."

Dominick Russo even looked dead, Slammer thought. He never wore makeup in his life. He would be mortified if he could see himself now. He'd get up and run. How could his mother allow this?

"Hard to believe he's dead, ain't it, Jimbo?" He stated. But, when he turned to Jimbo, the big guy was gone. All two hundred pounds of him had vanished.

Suddenly, it grew cold in the room, and Slammer had developed a clicking sound in his ears. Rubbing at them to try to clear the canal, it only got worse. Click. Click.

"The girl's in the old mill down by Scranton Creek Road."

Slammer looked around, but no one was near him. Did he

hear something or did he just pick up on a conversation nearby?

"*Tell the cop standing by the door where the girl is, Vinnie.*"

Slammer almost collapsed. Dominick was the only one who called him Vinnie. Everyone else used Slammer. But it couldn't be.

Wanting to leave, but not being able to rise from his knees, Slammer's heart began to race. *How can it be him*? he thought. *It's his voice, but how can it be? Someone must be playing a trick on me.*

His eyes moved to where the coffin met the huge potted flower vase. He saw no one hiding there.

"*It's me, Vinnie,*" the voice whispered in answer to his question. "*No one is playing a trick on you.*"

Slammer closed his eyes. I'm snapping. I'm friggin' snappin'.

"*You're not snapping, Vinnie. I can't rest if you don't tell them where the girl is.*"

Why me? Slammer asked. *Why did you come to me? You can read my mind*?

"*I **can** read your mind. But only because you allow me to.*"

I'm not allowing a damn thing, Dom. I don't like this one damn bit.

"*Listen,*" said Dom. "*We are speaking through the minds. I chose you because your mind is more open than the rest of them. You, being artistic, are more opened to this kind of thing, and you are more apt to take me seriously. There's a cop in the corner of the room. He's a friend of the family. Tell him where she is. He's my friend, Vinnie. He was there when I died. I told him I took the girl and that you guys had nothing to do with it. I started to tell him where she was when they came and took me. They wouldn't even let me finish my sentence, so I had to get back here to tell him.*"

There was a pause. "*You have to go to him and tell him that you know the body is in the mill.*"

He'll think I'm crazy. Where would I get this information?

"*Tell him I gave you the information just now. He'll believe you. Tell him what I just said. Tell him I told you that his little girl is safe and happy. Her name is Tamara and she's here with me now. No one knows he had a little girl. It was a long time ago in another town. Once you tell him that, he'll believe you."*

Geez, Dom. I don't . . .

"Do it!"

***

Slammer was finally able to get up. Glancing at the clock above the exit door, he realized he was only kneeling there for minutes, yet he thought he was there for much longer than that.

It was hard controlling the knocking of his knees and the chattering of his teeth. It was very difficult trying to figure out what had just happened to him and the only way he was going to know for sure, would be to tell the cop just what Dominick had said. If what Dominick told him was true, then the cop would know it.

"I'm Slammer," he said to the officer, stuttering the two words out. "Actually my name is Vincent Picone, but everyone calls me Slammer."

The officer looked at him and pointed to his badge. It said Russo, Officer Russo. Slammer looked at him again. He looked like Dom. He was a relative, not just a friend. Dom had lied to him. Maybe the whole thing was in his imagination. Why would an officer be at Dom's funeral anyway, unless he was related?

"Know the kid?" The officer asked.

Slammer nodded. "Yeah. He was a good friend."

"He's been in some trouble in the past, but he's a good kid."

Slammer nodded again. "Yeah. I know. I've known him since grade school. I notice you have the same name. Relative?"

"On his father's side. Third cousin. Never seen each other much before I came to this town eight months or so ago."

Slammer took a deep breath. Here goes, he thought. "Dominick just told me where the girl is."

The officer looked around and then grabbed Slammer by the

shoulder. "What are you talking about?"

"He just told me to tell you that she's in the mill over by Scranton Creek Road."

"Kid, you're crazy." The officer turned his face. "Now get lost."

"Dom said you needed to know and you're going to know," Slammer's said, his voice rising.

"I said get outta here, kid. Dom's dead. Dom's dead and you're a piece of shit for making a joke out of his Goddamn funeral."

"He said to tell you that your little girl is just fine and she's with him right now."

Now he went too far. He saw the officer's face turn pasty white and he clenched his teeth in anger.

Slammer hurried on with the rest of the message. "Your little girl's name was Tamara. Tamara Russo. Wasn't it?"

Slammer took the officer's hand off his jacket. "He just told me that. I don't know how, but I heard it as plain as day. Maybe you ought to call it in to the station. Someone has to go out there to the mill and get that girl."

But Officer Russo didn't hear what Slammer was saying. Officer Russo was crying. Crying so hard that he couldn't catch his breath.

Slammer grabbed a chair and eased the officer down. "I'm sorry, sir. Really."

"The name's Frank. Frank Russo." He wiped at his eyes and blew his nose. "I'm sorry to break down like this, but I believe you. I really believe you because no one could have known about my little girl. Not even Dom." He began to cry again. "Not even Dom."

Slammer wanted to get out of there. The clicking in his ear was extremely loud. He couldn't imagine where it was coming from.

And then he closed his eyes and could hear someone calling him, but the name did not come clear. The name didn't sound right. He could swear that they were calling him, though they seemed to be calling, "Nostradomus . . ."

Fifteen

Someone was calling his name. "David. It's Tom Hale. Can you open your eyes?"

I'm trying . . . I can hear you . . .

"Do you know where you are, David?"

The question, so easy to answer, he thought. He could feel his head being stitched. Why would Tom still be here? Unless . . . the files.

"David," Tom continued speaking. "I've called Patrick Tuchman for you. He's on his way. We're all worried about you, Pal. Try to move your hand if you can hear me. Don't leave us here worrying."

I can hear you, Tom. I can move my hand, too, but when I try to show you, it doesn't budge.

He tried not to wince at the pain of the needle making stitches.

"Probably swelling of the brain that's causing the coma," the doctor was saying to someone.

What coma? I'm right here. I can hear you. Can't you hear me? Drifting . . . floating.

"He's a chemist. A damn good one too. I've represented him a number of times in small matters." Tom was talking as the doctors worked. "I was driving in the opposite direction when I saw a car trying to get out of a skid. I didn't know it was David until I saw his car take the first roll. Poor guy was probably trying to get out of my way."

David was imagining Tom speaking nervously over him. He was always nervous and irritable. David imagined his wide framed body and heavily jowled face moving frantically as he spoke with his hands gesturing wildly, as if combining sign language in with his words.

Tom had a mass of curly hair and a bulbous nose. He was comical to look at, but he was a good friend, and a damn good attorney.

David could feel himself being wheeled into a room. Bottles were rattling as the stretcher rolled over each crack of tile. He could smell the antiseptic odor of the room as they approached.

Please hear me. Listen to me. Watch my eyes. Why can't I open my mouth? Why can I only speak with my mind?

David could hear the doctor ordering oxygen from the nurse. He ordered more IV fluids, EEG monitoring, and 4 mg. of morphine to be given intravenously immediately.

No! No morphine! It will cloud my thinking. I'm not in pain!

It wasn't long before he could hear the EEG machine spew paper out onto the floor. David had never in his entire life felt so vulnerable.

"We're going to keep him in Intensive Care," the doctor said. "Everything should be okay, and hopefully, he should be showing signs of improvement within twenty four hours."

***

Patrick parked his car in the parking space closest to the emergency room entrance. He ran toward the automatic doors and, once inside, looked around for a sign of where David might be.

"May I help you," a voice said from behind him. He turned to see a pretty red-headed nurse that didn't look old enough to be out of high school, much less be a head nurse as it indicated on her name tag.

"I'm looking for David Wilder. He's been in a car accident, and I was told he was taken to this hospital."

The nurse went behind the round desk and tapped into the computer. "Ah, yes. Dr. Wilder was just taken into ICU."

"ICU?" Patrick could hardly control his shaking voice. "Why? How bad is it?"

The young nurse looked quite sympathetic. "I'm afraid he's slipped into a coma."

"A coma?" Patrick was fighting for composure. What he really wanted to do was scream how impossible this all was. "What are his chances?"

The nurse shook her head. "I'm sorry, but the doctor will have to tell you that. I have no records or charts here."

"Patrick!" Ashleigh came running toward him. "Patrick is it true?" She was sobbing, and from the look on her face she had been crying all the way here.

Patrick put his arms around her. "Yes. He's in the Intensive Care Unit, Ash. How did you find out?"

"Tom Hale." She wiped at her nose with the back of her sleeve like a little girl. Patrick wanted to hold her. "He was the one that David tried to avoid hitting."

Patrick nodded. "Yeah. I know, poor man. He must feel terrible about this."

"It wasn't his fault, Pat."

Patrick nodded. "Yea. But who's going to tell him that?"

Ashleigh turned to the nurse. "Can we see him?"

She nodded. "I'm sure you can. But in Intensive Care, there's only two allowed at a time and only for five minutes. And I believe he has a visitor now." Smiling, she pointed to the elevators. "Third floor, 6C. I hope your friend pulls through."

Patrick nodded. "Thanks." He pulled at Ashleigh's arm. "Come on, Ash. David's waiting."

**

David couldn't remember ever having been frightened . . . or ever being nervous, for that matter. Tense maybe, but never nervous. But, he thrived on being tense. He lived for it. Always ready for action. Always ready for a challenge. That's how he wanted it to be. That's the way he wanted to live out his life.

But now, he was not only tense, he was frightened. He had no power. He had no control over his own life. They picked at him, they stuck needles in him, they shot him up with morphine and stuck tubes up his nose. Everything that could set fire to a man's dignity and reduce it to ashes happened to him in the short time he was here.

Now he was frightened. Why couldn't he open his eyes and talk with them? Why was it that he could hear them, feel their fingers and hands moving over his body, yet couldn't respond to their touch? He was as still as a corpse. Why was he screaming inside his head so loud that the dead could hear him, and yet, his friends couldn't? The doctors and nurses couldn't. He could hear himself. How had he lost so much control?

He felt his head being moved this way and that. They were putting cream or something all over his scalp. It was warm.

"What's that?" Tom Hale asked.

"EEG," the nurse replied curtly. "Helps us read the brain waves. See if there's any activity going on."

David panicked as he thought about the consequences one would suffer from a malfunction in the EEG machine. Suppose it told them he was brain dead, yet he wasn't? Suppose the wave lines were flat? Death. They could give him up for dead! His heart beat faster. Didn't they notice?

David mentally closed his eyes and thought about courage. Thought about how far he had come. The chip. The detonator. He was fortunate he didn't lose control of his mind. Yet, maybe this was worse. To have control of your thoughts and mind and not your body was worse than being brain dead.

If he didn't fight, he would surely die. He would fail Ashleigh, and she didn't deserve that after all she'd gone through. He would fail Patrick. How could he leave them in such a mess?

And they would be compelled to go on despite the fact that

there was no David. They would take matters into their own hands and finish the project . . . put Webster behind bars. They could surely do it without him. But . . . but he didn't want them to.

"How long has he been this way, Tom?"

It was Ashleigh's voice.

I can hear you, Ash. Come closer. Hear me.

"A few hours now." Tom looked around the room. "Where's Patrick?" He asked.

Ashleigh nodded toward the door. "He's waiting outside. They said only two were allowed at a time."

Tom quickly moved away from the bed. "Here, let me get out of here. I'll tell him to come on in and take my place."

"No. That's okay. I'll only visit for a few minutes."

But Tom left anyway and gestured Patrick inside. He had been with David most of the morning and was getting nauseated by the smells around him.

"How are you doing?" Patrick asked, grasping Ashleigh's arm but watching the EEG screen. He knew something about these things. He knew that a flat line meant death.

"Not great," she said, tears threatening to spill over her cheeks. "He looks so still. So sick."

The nurse patted her hand. "He's in no pain, my dear. We gave him something to make him comfortable and this test is just a precaution." The nurse adjusted one of the prongs on the EEG patches. She was a burly woman of close to two hundred fifty pounds. Her hair was curly and the way it framed her face, it made her look twice as large.

"Then why is he in a coma?" Ashleigh sat down in the chair closest the bed.

"He probably has swelling to his brain. The way I understand it, his car rolled down an embankment. That could answer for the way his head was hit. Probably hit it on the roof of the car."

"When will he wake up?" Ashleigh asked.

The nurse shrugged, her big shoulders heaving with fat. "Can't say . . . maybe by morning. Soon as the swelling goes down, and we're giving him medication for that."

Ashleigh didn't respond. Neither did Patrick. He was watching his friend's face as he lay in sleep. Just yesterday, he let David know how disappointed he was that he chose to decode Kayla Smith alone. It hurt. He felt betrayed. But, by this morning, all was forgiven and he was waiting at Ashleigh's for him. Now he wouldn't be able to tell him he wasn't angry anymore.

Patrick closed his eyes and wondered why it was that he was always one step too late for everything. When his sister died, he was within seconds of finding her. She breathed her last breath in his arms and shuddered her last words to him. How was it he never caught on to her pain?

Where was he when she cried? Why didn't she talk to him about it? Had he arrived minutes sooner, he would have been able to talk with her. Get her some help. Stop her from dying.

And this morning, he was within thirty minutes of letting David know that he wasn't angry with him. Within thirty minutes, David would have known he was forgiven and there were no hard feelings. Now, David was on a bed in Intensive Care fighting for his life.

What was going on in his mind? Patrick wondered. He was sure that David could hear everything that was going on around him. They had proven that a person in a coma more often hears everything, and that his cure certainly had a lot to do with the conversation that went on around him, and the will to live.

Patrick leaned forward. "David. I know you can hear me."

I can. I can.

"I want you to fight. Fight to open those eyes and come back to us. We need you to help us finish what we started."

I can hear you, Patrick. I just can't reach you. But I'm trying. I'm coming up. Talk me up, Patrick. You know how we do it . . . talk me up!

"You're deep in sleep David," Patrick continued to speak. "But you're lifting yourself up to the top level of consciousness now. Come up a little further. That's right. Up . . . up . . ."

I'm coming. I can feel myself rise. I'm becoming more aware of sounds around me. There! Someone coughed. I heard that. Bring me up, Pat.

"That's right. Higher. Pretty soon you'll be to the top and able to open your eyes . . . Up . . . Up."

I'm coming to the surface. Keep talking. Please Pat. Don't quit now. Keep talking.

Ashleigh cut in. "Patrick. He can't hear you."

Yes! Yes I can. Please don't stop him, Ash. Don't listen to her Patrick. Please. I'm almost there. David was frantic now. He was sure that he was to the top . . . just a little more. Patrick had to keep it going.

Please, nobody interrupt his train of thought. Leave him alone! Leave him to me!

Patrick didn't answer Ashleigh. Instead, he put his efforts into extreme concentration. "Come on, pal, let's go. Rise higher. Higher. You're almost here with us."

By now, a crowd of nurses, orderlies, and visitors were standing in the doorway not daring to make a sound to disturb him. Somehow, it seemed an unwritten law that there should be no talking, walking, movement, or sound of any kind.

"You're here. Now all you have to do is open your eyes. Just open them slowly. No one's rushing you."

Okay, Pat. I'm here. I'm here. I'll open my eyes. I'm up. I'm trying . . . trying . . .

Patrick shook David hard. "David! David! There you go. Open your eyes! Come on . . ."

The room suddenly became very quiet. It seemed as if it lasted for minutes. Maybe hours. Yet, it was only a matter of seconds. But no one dare move. They were all waiting for the fluttering eyes of David Wilder to open completely.

Ashleigh stood up, leaned over him, and took his hand. "David. If you can hear me, squeeze."

Suddenly her eyes brightened as she looked at everyone in the room. "He's squeezing. He can hear me."

"I can hear you, Ash." David's voice came through very weak, but everyone's ears were attuned to it. He held onto her hand tightly, and opened his eyes fully, allowing them to adjust to the light. He followed movement and then gazed at one smiling face at a time, until he saw Patrick. He nodded and grinned. "Thanks, pal."

Sixteen

Tom Hale pulled into the parking lot outside the hospital a few minutes before nine in the morning. He lingered in the car for a few minutes gathering his thoughts about the files he had found in David's car. This was the part of his job he hated most. The questioning. Always making people feel guilty before they could open their mouth to explain.

Tom had that knack. He could sit an unconditionally innocent person down in a chair at a deposition and have them walk away wondering if they were indeed as unblemished as when they walked into the room. It almost made him chuckle at his ability. Sometimes it was quite handy, but certainly not in this case.

He had known David Wilder for many years. He needed to present his questions in a non-accusing manner. That was providing of course, David was conscious and able to talk.

Tom Hale was a "good old boy" from Alabama, the first in his family to get any kind of education and the last of his family to remain alive. Even in his sleepy backwards town, where the people helped one another in need, but mostly kept to themselves, the virus had seeped in and ate away at the unaware and faultless. Everyone was gone except some old biddies that were trying desperately to die without using their own hands.

Tom left that sleepy town early in his life. He wanted to feel some life in him. He didn't want to grow as his father and his grandfather had, living in one town, marrying a childhood sweetheart, bearing many children, growing old quickly and dying. He needed the surge of excitement in his bones and the law assuredly was his thrill.

Hale worked himself out from the steering wheel, due to his fat belly, and wondered as he walked toward the hospital, not for the first time, if he should just retire. He had saved enough money all these years to afford himself the life he had always wanted on the beaches of Miami and his long-wished-for sailboat.

But no, he still fought the cold weather, stayed up night after night reviewing court cases and ate himself into a frenzy. He knew he wasn't great looking, which was probably why he never married. He was told that he was a John Candy look alike. And although, John Candy was appealing to most women, he certainly couldn't have been considered sexy. It was his personality that did a lot for him.

But not to Tom. Tom really didn't have that cute as a teddy bear personality. And to him, there was something about approaching a woman and waiting for the fall that made him not do the approaching at all. He was fine this way. He was the type to be alone.

And after he told himself that lie, because there was nothing more he wanted in this world than to have someone to love who loved him in return, he faced the fact that someday he would be here in this hospital fighting a heart attack, or worse, due to his obsessive eating. But did it stop him? No. He didn't care enough, he guessed. Food was his love. And second best would just have to do for now.

Hale checked his watch. The nurses got the patients up early in the hospital. If David continued to improve as he had last evening, then Tom was sure he'd be up now.

***

"You thought you could out drive me, didn't you?"

David lifted his head sharply and winced. "Of course!" He stared at Hale who sat himself heavily in the chair opposite the bed. "And I will next time."

Hale laughed. "There won't be a next time, my friend." He patted his huge stomach. "I'm surprised at myself at the dexterity I had in getting out of your way. A head on could have been much more devastating than a rollover."

David shook his head. "I can't believe it was you, Tom. I could have killed you."

There were no words exchanged for the moment. Then Hale rubbed his hands over his face and asked, "What were you doing, David? I thought I saw you making a turn in the middle of the street."

David plopped back onto his pillow. "I was. I had forgotten my wallet at home, and seeing no one coming, I made a u-turn. I was on my way to Ashleigh's. I lost control."

Hale adjusted his bulk in the small wing chair. "I've got to go with my gut instinct on this, David. I just know you and your friends are up to something."

David's heart lurched to his throat. He closed his eyes. "The files?"

Hale nodded. "The files."

"How much do you know?"

"Enough," Hale said. "But, not enough." He coughed a vile wet cough. "I mean, I don't know all the ins and outs of what you say he's been up to, but if you've got proof, I'm inclined to go along with your theory, if I get the gist of what you're saying. But I can't buy that he alone is responsible for what's going on in the city."

"How much have you read, Tom? And why? What made you go through my files? You, of all people, should believe in confidentiality."

"I didn't think you'd make it, David. I felt responsible. I thought maybe I could help."

"You can, Tom," David said turning away from him. "You can help by staying out of it. Forget what you read."

Hale hung his head and was silent. He was offended, but

understood that some things were untouchable to him. "What did I read, David? I don't know what you're talking about." He stood up, straightened his clothing and walked toward the door. "But if you need me," he waved his hand, "for whatever reason, call me."

When he left, David felt misgivings about not confiding in Tom. However, he knew it was the right thing to do. Too many people involved could only lead to a mass knowledge and eventually lead to Webster himself. He need not be warned of his fall, or he would take serious precautions to watch his footing.

***

Ashleigh arrived at the hospital at exactly ten past twelve. She could see him as she walked toward his room from the hall. He was sitting up in bed waving to get her attention. She looked appealing in a long, pale blue sweater and black tights. Her fresh young innocent appearance amazed him, especially after all she'd been through.

She waved back, picking up her pace. Smiling brightly, she hurried to his side. "Sorry I'm late for your lunch. But I couldn't find a parking space in the whole lot." She squinched up her nose. "I hate hospital smells."

Roosevelt Hospital, although completely renovated, still had that medicinal smell that the older structure carried. It was as if the building was built around the smell instead of the smell being contained within the building.

At first, the only odor was the paint and the newness of wood and plastic and glass, but within days of occupancy, the medicinal and antiseptic smell took over.

David agreed with her readily about the smell, but had other things on his mind. "Last night I realized there was something I didn't ask you but it's been on my mind since the accident," he said.

Ashleigh looked disconcerted. "What is it, David?"

"I was worried about the files. Where are they?"

"Locked up," she stated.

"Locked up where?"

Ashleigh sat at the edge of his bed. "Tom Hale had them locked up in the hospital safe. He thought they might be important to you and he didn't want to take any chances on them getting into the wrong hands."

David looked relieved. "Did he ask any questions about them?"

She laughed. "The only thing he said was that the files were safe, and he wouldn't ask one thing about them because he's known you too long."

David laughed. "He's quite a guy."

"I'll say. He stayed with you from the moment the ambulance arrived, until the time you opened your eyes."

David smiled. "He knows what's in the files, Ash. He was here this morning."

Ashleigh's face showed grave concern. "He wouldn't stop us, would he? I mean, what right did he have looking through the files in the first place, David. I can't believe . . ."

David interrupted her. "He didn't think I was going to live, Ash. He wanted to see if he could help me. He needed clues as to where I was rushing to so early in the morning."

"How did you explain it?"

"I simply asked that he stay out of it and forget what he saw."

"And?"

"And he forgot."

Ashleigh's voice softened as she pulled the sheets up around him. "Tom's car is the car you swerved to avoid, you know."

David nodded. "I know." He sighed heavily. "And I can just imagine how he must feel, Ash. I know I'd feel just as badly." He looked up at her. "But, does he know it wasn't his fault?"

Ashleigh nodded and touched his face. "Yes, he knows, David." She suddenly brightened. "Now! When did they say they were going to spring you from this place?"

"Maybe tomorrow."

"So soon?" she asked. She unconsciously brushed his hair

away from his face with her fingers.

"I love you," he said.

Ashleigh looked at him in astonishment. "What?"

"I said I love you."

Ashleigh was speechless. "What in the world made you say that?"

David sunk deep into his pillow and shrugged. "It had to be said, and so I said it. I said it because it's true. I love you, and if truth be known, I've probably loved you right from the very start, but was too pigheaded to realize it."

She began to say something, but he waved it down. "I'm not asking for you to commit yourself to me. I'm not asking you to feel the same way. All . . ."

"But I want to."

There was silence. Then David spoke quietly. "What?"

"I said," she lowered her eyes shyly, "I want to say the same to you. I want to commit myself. Don't you see, I feel the same way?"

David laughed sarcastically, shaking his head. "Great . . ."

"What?"

"I mean, this is really great." He picked up his hands and flopped them down by his sides. "I mean, here we are a couple of headstrong people, not really knowing our asses from our elbows, and we sit here like two dopes afraid to say what we really feel."

"What's wrong with that?"

"Nobody said anything was wrong with it, Ash. It's just . . . well, why didn't we tell each other before? Why all of a sudden do we spill our guts?"

Ashleigh shrugged, leaned forward, and laid her head on his chest. "I don't know, David. I guess we were both a little afraid of rejection, even though it would have only taken one of us to say it first."

David stroked her hair. "I'm glad I said it first. Looks like I'm the one with all the balls."

"David!" She laughed, slapping his chest with her hand and then bending over to kiss where she slapped. She felt good in his arms. He had wanted to do this for so long, but wouldn't dare risk their friendship.

It was much the same for her. When he touched her hair, or nudged her out the door before him with his hands on her waist, she wanted so much for him to keep them there. She wanted to feel his closeness and smell his manly scent. She felt protected and cared for.

"So now what do we do?" He asked.

"I guess we just take it from here. Start all over again. But maybe it's best if we wait until you get home to say more."

David smiled and kissed the top of her head. "Okay."

After a very brief moment of silence, she said, "I have to go to my office for a while. I've scheduled a one-thirty appointment."

"Okay."

But, she didn't move.

"When will you be back?"

"This evening."

"Okay."

Finally, she pulled herself away from him, kissed him gently on the cheek, and left the room.

David lay back into his pillow and sighed. He had something to look forward to now. He was so glad he had the nerve to tell her, although he didn't intend to do it quite like that. He never intended to just burst right out and say it.

There was no indication that she felt the same way about him. She certainly gave nothing away. Therefore, he took quite a chance. But, in a worst-case scenario, they would have continued being friends, and he would have suffered a little uneasiness and embarrassment.

***

Thankfully, David suffered very little from his injuries. There was no headache from the concussion, no soreness from his bumps and bruises, and no broken bones. In fact, his doctor had already given him the okay to be discharged in the morning.

Maybe it was pushing it a bit and maybe David insisted upon the discharge, but he needed to continue his part in the investigation.

David always had the compulsion to protect Ashleigh, although, there was very little need to. She had certainly done a good job of taking care of herself before he came along. Maybe that's what triggered his compulsion to speak up. She belonged to him now. It was possessiveness, a sense of oneness. Taking care of her and protecting her was now his job.

His thoughts were disturbed by Patrick, who came into the room with stacks of files, pencils, and a calculator.

"What the hell is all that?" David asked.

"Work," David answered.

"Work, my ass. I'm a sick man."

"The hell you are," Pat retorted. "Look at you. You look well enough to tackle this stuff."

"Pat. I was in a car accident yesterday. Remember?"

He remembered too well the scare they all had when they were told of the accident. He remembered the fear when he looked at his buddy deep in a coma and thought how he would never make it through this.

Whatever possessed Patrick to try and talk David out of the coma was no mystery to him. When his sister died, he was sure that if enough time was given, he could have talked her out of her own death. It was all in the mind. The mind could do anything. It controlled all.

And so it was with David. Patrick knew he could talk him up from the deep sleep heading for death. He was positively sure. He had it in his mind for so long now that if given the opportunity, he wouldn't ever let another person die without at least trying to lead them back.

"If you think I'm going to spend my much deserved sick time in bed doing paperwork, you're absolutely crazy," David screeched.

Patrick threw the paperwork on David's lap. "You're going to do this work, pal. I'm not going to be stuck in the house all day doing this. I've other things to do. This was what you were supposed to go over in your office today. And you'll do it today."

David groaned. "Okay. Okay. What is it?"

"It's the report you asked me to do for the government."

"You've got it done?"

Patrick nodded. "Worked on it all night." He flipped through some of the pages. "I think I've got it all here. I went through every file, picked out all the deaths and their causes which, as we assumed, were either through suicide or natural causes."

David shook his head as he read. "It seems as if no one dies from cancer these days. Or a good old fashion heart attack. Does it?"

"Not only that," Patrick continued. "Most of them have been activated for a period of six months to a year before their deaths. It leads me to believe that their activation was the primal cause." He looked at David. "Is that what it says to you?"

David nodded emphatically. "Yes sir. That's just what it tells me. But can we convince this Mario Prisero of that?"

Patrick sat down on the wing back chair in the corner of the room and looked directly into David's eyes. "What do you think Webster has in mind with all this? Is it just control or madness, or a slow, nervous breakdown?"

David raised his eyebrows, surprised at Patrick's sudden serious mood. "Both," he admitted. "But, obviously we don't know Dr. August Webster that well. He is a very private man. Extraordinarily professional and deliberate and whatever he knows, he carries around, up here." He tapped his temple.

There was a moment of silence and then David continued. "But do you know what comes with being extraordinarily professional, deliberate, and private, Patrick?"

Patrick shook his head.

"A false sense of power, which is something he's drawn to like a magnet. And along with that comes something else."

Patrick twitched unwillingly. "What?"

David inhaled deeply and released an incredibly audible sigh. "Extraordinary danger . . ."

Seventeen

August Webster had an appointment at twelve o'clock sharp. He had set this appointment during his client's lunch hour so that he could be assured to get her back at precisely one o'clock. After all, wasn't he the one who was instrumental in securing this position for her? Hadn't he secured positions for most of his clients?

Webster skimmed through his appointment book. Things were improving. Last week, for instance, he regressed fifteen people. Only five of which had no past lives. Six months from now, those five people would be well on their way into their second lifetime. They would die quietly. Peacefully.

Once they came in for their last visit, he'd give them a shot of declytrozine zampozene. The effects would make them a little disoriented. Then, they would become tired and either go directly to bed from fatigue and die quietly in their sleep, or fight it until they become increasingly nauseous. Then the discomfort would usually become so grave that they'd drive to the nearest hospital to get some relief.

By this time, this undetectable medication would have seeped into the blood stream, and before any physician could perform his magic, the patient would be dead. That easy. The only explanation? Cardiac arrest.

His center brought with it each day, more and more excitement for him. His thoughts encompassed all that he saw in the future. Today, New York, he thought, tomorrow the world.

The phone jarred him back into reality. "Yes," he said softly. "Yes, I understand. And when was he admitted?" He nodded and rolled his eyes as if this phone call was disrupting his whole day. "I'll be there as soon as I can."

Webster slammed down the phone. "Damn!" He muttered. The patient admitted was Julian Verde. He had seen him this morning and administered the heady injection of DZ.

It looked as if Mr. Verde had fought against it a little too hard. His heart refused to give out and he was admitted to the Roosevelt Hospital where he was being sustained on life support.

Webster had his secretary call and reschedule his twelve o'clock and he headed for the hospital.

On his way to the hospital, Webster concentrated on his own thoughts instead of the road. If he hadn't prided himself as an intelligent man, he'd have probably convinced himself that there were guardian angels directing him to his intended destinations when he was in a trance such as this.

What was it that separated the mind from the other working parts of the brain? He wondered. His mind watched all the stop signs and lights, watched all the surrounding obstacles, knew the direction in which he had to go, and before he knew it, he was there. It was like someone else took over entirely.

Webster shook his head again and lifted himself out of his car. "Incredible," he muttered.

He went right in through the doctors entrance, and he would have parked in doctor's parking had there been a space close enough. He walked with command to the front desk. He knew that the staff gave him carte blanche to do whatever he felt was necessary in this hospital. He was treated as a physician. The thought of that still amazed Webster, considering his past. It sent hormonal fluids surging through his body that captivated the ego part of his substance. He was important. He looked important. They, most definitely, thought he was important.

At the four-cornered wall of the Coronary Care Unit was a waiting room filled with blue plastic chairs, plastic plants, and plastic ashtrays. The room looked like a picnic ground, cold and unfriendly. He would make sure he mentioned this disgusting sight to the Chief of Staff. At last, he had the position that, when he spoke, they sat up and took notice.

Sitting alone in the corner, staring out the window was Mrs. Verde. She had been crying. When she stood up to greet him, he could see the terrible pain in her face. Webster recognized the familiar precursor to death and grief. Her red-rimmed eyes pleaded with him to help her understand what was going on with her husband.

"He was fine this morning, doctor," she said struggling for composure.

Webster smiled, but not out of pity. It was the way they all called him doctor, like a real physician.

"I don't understand it," she continued.

Webster guided her back to her seat. "Have you spoken with his doctor yet?"

She nodded quickly. "He gave him a clean bill of health just this morning. Just before he met with you." She began to cry again. "I just don't understand it."

Webster's face grew ashen at the mention of his appointment with Julian Verdi. He sighed, letting his breath out. His narrow shoulders sagged forward a bit and his anger faded. In its place, he allowed a face of crushing sadness. When he spoke to her, his voice was quivering. "This is not an uncommon thing, Mrs. Verdi. Many times people come directly from the doctor's office with a report of perfect health, only to drop of a heart attack a few hours later. It could well be from the anxiety of going to the appointment in the first place. It's still a mystery to us doctors." He tried to get her attention away from the fact that he had an appointment with her husband that day also. "I know you are hurting now, Mrs. Verdi. We all are. I've come to know your husband as a friend. And I'm going to go in there and do all that I can possibly do to save his life."

"So it's bad . . ." her voice began to break.

"I'm afraid it is, from what they told me over the phone."

The color drained from her face and she covered her eyes with her hands. "I can't believe it. Thirty-five years we're married. I can't believe it."

Webster patted her gently on the hand. "There, there. We'll get through this together." This scene disgusted him. How he hated when things got emotional. It was such a waste of time and energy. He quickly left her side and sought out the treatment room Verdi was in.

As soon as he reached the room, Dr. Hargraves appeared at the door. "Hello," he said, extending his hand. "Dr. Webster, I presume. I'm Julian Verdi's physician. Please follow me."

The doctor ushered him into the room full of nurses, bottles, equipment and everything necessary to save Verdi's life.

"Mr. Verdi was in grave pain when he came into the hospital," the doctor explained.

"Are you sure it's his heart?" Webster asked, thinking his injection shouldn't have caused actual pain.

Hargraves nodded emphatically. "Most definitely, sir."

Webster smiled inadvertently at the word, 'sir.'

"We're going to move him to progressive care," Hargraves said. "He'll need to be watched carefully for the next twenty four hours."

Webster nodded. "Of course."

It was going to be a very long day. He couldn't take the chance of leaving now. Somehow, unless Verdi died soon, he would have to give him another injection. He couldn't take the chance of him regaining consciousness, as remote as that seemed at this point.

"I'll just wait outside with Mrs. Verdi until you get the room ready," he told Hargraves. Then he left and went back to the waiting room. He hated this part. He hated this charade.

Just as he was about to do some more consoling, his phone rang.

"Dr. Webster? I found out whose initials are on the pen you found in your office." It was Jim Foster, a private detective that Webster hired to find the man who owned the pen. "A Patrick

Tuchman." Then he hung up.

Webster sat staring at the phone, bewildered. "Patrick Tuchman," he whispered. "Who the hell is he?"

In short, slow steps he proceeded toward Mrs. Verdi. He felt a twinge behind his left eye. "Damn," he muttered. He just couldn't handle another migraine.

***

After about an hour of careful conversation with the woman, Hargraves appeared at the door. Just the way he stood told him what he wanted to hear.

"I'm sorry," he apologized. "There's nothing more we can do. Mr. Verdi has expired."

Mrs. Verdi covered her face with her hands. For a moment, Webster thought she might faint. But instead, she picked up her purse, stood up, and quietly left the hospital. She didn't even ask to see her dead husband.

"I'm sorry," Webster said to Hargraves. "I know how hard it is when you lose someone."

Hargraves nodded. "Yes, but, it's your loss too, Dr. Webster."

Webster smiled sullenly. "Yes, doctor. Yes, it is."

After papers were signed and releases were documented, Webster called the mortician he used in these cases, and told him to come pick up the body. He didn't want it hanging around the hospital any longer than was necessary. Years ago, it was the family of the diseased who had him or her picked up and taken to their choice of funeral parlors. Now, the doctor of record made the arrangements. Webster made sure in all cases, that he was the doctor of record.

Feeling safe and more at ease, he left the hospital with a happier gait than when he had come in. His business was finished. It was good to have control. He had control over everyone. He knew where they were at all times. He monitored practically their every breath.

He smelled the fresh air of May. He hoped it wouldn't be a

hot summer. He hated heat. It made him feel all closed in. Tight. Cornered. And, although he didn't like the feeling of being cornered, he reveled in the idea of doing the cornering.

Eighteen

Once again the morning air was surprisingly cool, not warm and muggy as the Mays in the past, but with a definite chill permeating the house.

David closed his eyes and tried to relax. He kept his mind clear and tried to focus on the headache he endured for the last twelve hours. There was no sign of it.

The sunlight came filtering into his bedroom window through the verticals. He had a lot to do today and it felt so good to be able to get up to sunshine without pain. Optimism rapidly set in.

The phone ringing jarred him back into reality. "David?" It was Ashleigh. "Did I wake you?"

David smiled. "No, honey, I was already awake. I feel good. No headache, finally."

He could hear a sigh of relief escape her lips. "I was worried."

"Well don't. Look, Ash, I know we've been taking ourselves from our jobs for the past week or so but bear in mind how important this is. I was thinking that maybe we should consider taking a four or five-week sabbatical. If we're lucky, we might be able to put Webster away by then."

There was silence at the other end of the phone. David felt

sure she would agree with his suggestion. They could both afford the time from work. He had his rental income and she had her inheritance from her old Alfred Hitchcock spinster aunt in Maine. She only used the money in emergencies, which thankfully had been few. He was sure this would constitute an emergency to Ashleigh.

"Ash?" He called.

"I'm here, David. Maybe you're right. We certainly can't do both, so the jobs should be the ones on hold. If not, we're only going to be working in our spare hours and not that efficiently, I'm afraid. What does Patrick say?"

"I don't know, I didn't ask him." David chuckled. "Besides, what does he do for a living anyway?"

Ashleigh laughed. "You're right. He plays with his computers for Synco, in his own home, at his own pace. One way or the other, a sabbatical wouldn't affect him."

"I've made my plane reservation, Ash." He said, hearing her sigh.

"I know. When?"

"Tomorrow morning. Seven o'clock," he said. "You have to be sure to work with me while I'm out there, Ash. Keep yourself as close to a phone as you can and make sure your portable is always with you. I'll be calling you frequently to let you know the progress I am or am not making. And you may be able to facilitate me with pertinent information in the meantime."

"Fine. What time do you want me over? I've Kayla Smith's files for you. It documents the anguish she had been going through just before her death. I've Ted Williamson's also. He was a first timer. Never lived before."

"Why did he need counseling?"

"Actually, he didn't. He called me just to talk one evening and I set up a file for him. I always do that whether they become clients or not."

"What did he want to talk about, Ash?" David asked.

"Oh, he was confused as to why he hadn't lived before, yet he had a few episodes of déjà vu. I explained to him that the feeling of déjà vu sometimes came with association."

"How long did he see you?"

"Six months. Then he died suddenly, in his sleep. Natural causes, the coroner said." She snickered. "Ha."

David changed the subject quickly. "Are you dressed?"

"Yes."

"Then come on over. I'll put a pot of coffee on."

"I'm on my way."

***

David had just gotten out of the shower when Patrick arrived. He brought doughnuts, a large paper bag filled with pencils, pads, cold cuts, bread, tomatoes and soda.

"I've got the day's supply of food and drink if you've got the coffee made," he said, plopping everything down on the table.

David laughed. "Just made it. Ash is on her way too."

Patrick smiled cunningly. "Hey. What's going on with you two anyway?"

David gave a bewildered look. "Why? What makes you ask that?"

Patrick sat down, leaned forward, and placed his wrists on his knees. "Are you going to stand there and tell me that there's nothing going on between the two of you?"

"No, I'm not going to stand here and tell you anything." David rubbed the towel through his hair. "Listen. Mind your own business. She'll be here shortly and I'm not even dressed yet."

Patrick laughed. "Okay, okay. But, I'm going to have my suspicions regardless." He waved at him with his hand. "Go. Get dressed."

Patrick smiled as David left the room. Too obvious, pal, he thought. Much too obvious.

***

By twelve o'clock, the three of them were well into their work.

"You both understand what I'm going to Washington for, don't you?" David asked.

Patrick shook his head. "I think it's too soon. What do you really have to show for proof, David? What did Webster do so bad that the government is going to march right to his door and deposit him into a jail cell?" he asked. "At least, what did he do that you can prove?"

David took his cue. "I was hoping you'd ask that." He stood up and began to walk back and forth as he spoke. "Understand that the problem lies with only one man thus far. A man who wants total control of the city of New York, or maybe even the world, as I can see it." He looked at them both. "Am I correct?"

Ashleigh and Patrick nodded.

"One out of every ten files that Ashleigh has, contains documentation of a soul not being able to handle the situation in their past life."

Patrick interrupted. "Ashleigh. Maybe I've missed something here. But, have you ever met August Webster?"

"Never," she stated.

"Then, how did you get the files on these people?"

"Through Rita, his secretary." She could see he looked confused. "You see, I was assigned to his agency to help counsel those having a tough time handling the anticipation of their regressions. Of course, the only way I can help anyone is to study their files. So, I pick them up once a week from Rita and return them when I'm through.

"She has the microfilm, but I've always delivered them back to the center within a week. And . . ." She looked sheepish. "Not before I make copies." She received no response from the two men, so she continued. "Through these sessions, I'm finding out about their fears and despairs, which seem to be numerous. I know that Webster knows about me, because that's part of the center's set up. I don't believe, though, that Webster ever spoke of me nor has he ever seen me. If he's doing anything shady, I'm sure even Rita doesn't know, poor dear, she is playing by the rules. This, I think, is something that Webster is overlooking, which could be the eventual cause of his demise."

"What do you mean, he doesn't know?" Patrick asked.

"Well, like I said, when these centers are set up, they're set up by certain rules and regulations." She swallowed hard, her throat dry from talking. "One of which is as I've mentioned. A counselor is brought in and files of the clients given to her or him, in which case, the counselor reviews the files, chooses the ones that need help and returns the rest to the agencies. It's standard operating procedure in all centers. In fact, Rita does that automatically without even reporting it to Webster."

"So why are we continually breaking into his office to steal files?" Patrick asked.

"Because," David cut in, "the files in his office are the ones that Webster is particularly afraid will somehow get loose. Those files are the ones that can, and will, put him away."

There were a few moments of silence before they continued, all three seeking a necessary solution to all of this.

"So," David continued, "What's in those files is enough to put Big Bird away for life, folks."

Patrick stood up and ran his fingers through his hair. "Jesus Christ," he said. "You'll pardon me if I tell you this is a little difficult to swallow. I mean, you're talking about a man who's a persuasion all in himself."

"Crazy, isn't it?" David said. "But remember, it's his craziness, not ours."

Nineteen

The prettiest sight that David had ever seen was the burnt orange sun with rims of yellow that hovered over the earth and splattered across the metal of the aircraft. It was as if an artist grew impatient with his work and flung the palette in anger.

From the seat just behind the wing, the sight was incredibly preternatural. The orange glow filtered in one side of the plane and exited out the other. It highlighted the coffee cups, the red in the little girl's hair that sat across from him, the glitter of the makeup that the stewardess had on, which was a little excessive, and the dust particles that danced in the air, right in its own rays. Somehow, David felt God.

He didn't bother opening the files to work on board because he had just about enough of the Webster situation for the moment, and he was determined to relax and enjoy the thirty-five minute trip. By the time they were up, they were down.

***

The lightening of the plane as they descended touched at his stomach for a second churning acid in his gut. Swallowing hard, with effort, he took in deep, full gulps of breath and let them out slowly. By the time they touched down, it had eased up. He felt better.

The plane accelerated and sped down the runway, leaving the dried balls of grass and loose dirt to do their own ballet with the earth. Its force picked up objects that had lay dormant for days, scattered birds in all directions and caused a whirlwind of death to anything that came near it. It was a complete change of course for the aircraft. In the sky, the universe was its ruler. It was a small, trifle object captivated by vast space. Yet, on the ground, it reigned king, its Herculean configuration standing boldly among all that crossed its path.

Much like Webster, David thought. In the face of the world, he was but a mere speck, not even noticed. But, in the city of New York, he was rapidly becoming that Herculean figure beginning his own whirlwind. Someone had to clip his wings.

***

As soon as David entered the terminal, he picked up the scent of cinnamon and coffee. This scent was mixed in with the leather of luggage, ink of the newspapers, and indistinguishable men and woman's cologne. If one could sit and concentrate, he could probably pick out each scent individually.

It was a huge airport. David had never before landed at the Baltimore Washington Airport. The last time he was in town, he took a small aircraft and landed in an executive airport about two miles from here. It was interesting to see how many politicians arrived and departed. By sitting in one of the seats by any gate, one couldn't help but see secret service men guarding some diplomat here and there. Since 2003, all government officials in all capacities were to have at least one secret service man.

After picking up his luggage, he slipped into a cab and registered at the Sheraton, three miles away. His appointment was already made with Tony Antonelli for one o'clock and David wanted to go over his files and opening statements.

When he entered his room, the message light on the phone as blinking. David called the front desk and the message was from Ashleigh. He immediately called her.

"Ash?" he said, lifting his feet and reclining on the bed. "Is everything okay?"

"That's what I called you about. I wanted to know if all was well with you. Have a good flight?"

"Incredible. Haven't flown for so long that it was like a new experience for me. Short trip, but good."

"Good. Well, are you ready for your meeting?" she asked.

"I'm trying not to think about it. If I do, I'll start proofing the paperwork over and over and before you know it, I'll change things without any more satisfaction than I have now." His voice went up a pitch and he seemed to be yelling. "Christ, Ash, I don't feel prepared at all, and I'm going to look like a fool. It's sort of like trying to prove a God to an atheist." His voice was hurried.

"Goodness, don't worry so much!"

"I'm not. Just a bit nervous, I guess."

"Well, you're going to be all right, David," Ashleigh said. "Call me when you get back?"

"Right. I love you, Ash." This was the second time he'd said those words to her. They were beginning to feel good.

"I know." She threw him a kiss and hung up.

David quickly jumped into the shower, taking thoughts, schedules, meetings, and rehearsals with him as the hot water covered his body. He was going to have to sell this Antonelli a bill of goods if he was ever going to seem credible. He was going to have to convince him the first time over, or it would be twice as hard afterwards.

He towel dried his hair, grabbed a fresh shirt and a clean pair of underwear from his luggage, and called for another cab.

David gave the driver the address and sat back, avoiding thoughts of the pending meeting. Traffic was getting heavier as they neared the city and all around them; about thirty feet above their heads were monorails taking tourists, business people, and residents to their destinations.

Predictably, the cab driver started talking about the weather. David looked out the window distractedly, bored with the conversation.

After "yes-ing" the driver to death, the talk abruptly stopped. From outside his window, David could see a green exit sign approaching. They were in the city.

Buildings surrounded him. Some very, very old and some recently constructed. The mix suited the old city well. There were people slowly walking from building to building of the Smithsonian Institute, reading brochures, eating popcorn, drinking beer and coke.

There was tremendous activity in front of the White House and surrounding buildings. Perhaps some foreign diplomats were enjoying a visit with Madam President.

His destination soon loomed up before him as the driver pulled up to the curb. The building was antiquated in style, a dusty gray with spots of white cement peeking out from the aged finish. The windows were small and closely set to one another, and there had to be thirty-five steps up to the entrance.

David looked at the stairs and shuddered. Already he felt the onset of a headache hiding somewhere inside his skull. He searched for an elevator, thinking twice before climbing the steep flight of stairs ahead of him.

***

David stood in front of the door that said A. Antonelli, Investigator. He was an official government investigator working out of the state offices. David was told that he was a no nonsense man that wouldn't give you the time of day unless you had documented proof of everything you were privileged to tell him. David was as prepared as he would ever be.

"Come in Dr. Wilder. We've been expecting you," Tony Antonelli said, gesturing to a chair. "I trust you had a pleasant trip."

"Yes, thank you." David took a seat on the opposite side of the desk. In front of him stood a man of about forty-five years of age, an over-exaggerated rib cage, which gave him the appearance of looking heavier than he actually was, and very intense green eyes. He stood about five feet ten.

"How can I help you?" He said taking a seat himself.

"Well," David said, shuffling his feet. "Actually, I'm here representing a few people in a cause that I hope you will patiently listen to and look at with an open mind."

"I look at everything objectively, Dr. Wilder. You will soon see that." He poured himself a scotch, not offering David one. "I go by pure fact, not supposition, and I guess you could say that's my trademark."

"Uh, hmm, yes, I've heard that." David was growing increasingly more uncomfortable as the time went on. "I've documented everything that I could and based all my findings on pure fact, sir."

David was concentrating hard on what he wanted to say, but the magnetism radiating from Tony Antonelli was making it difficult to put his thoughts into words. The man was intimidating and had a pair of half glasses on that made his face hard and antagonistic.

"Dr. Wilder." Antonelli stated. "I do have a meeting at the White House in about an hour, and I do realize that you came a long way to see me. So, let's not waste the time we have. Let's get right to the point."

David nodded. "Sure . . . Uh . . ." He opened his briefcase and the files fell to the floor. He was growing angry with himself. He never let anyone intimidate him this way. If it meant him getting thrown out of this office, he was going to say his piece without trepidation. He had nothing to lose.

Picking up the first file, and leaving the rest on the floor where they fell, David carried on.

"These are the files of the client's from the August Webster Regression Center on East Fifty Sixth Street in New York City."

Antonelli brightened. "Ah, Dr. Webster," he said warmly. "Good center. One of our best."

This threw David off guard for a few seconds, as his heart raced in subtle defeat at those words. "When you read through them, you will begin to see a certain pattern. This follows through file after file and after studying it and speaking with several key people involved, I've come to the realization that we have a criminal act going on here and all I ask is that you investigate it."

"Investigations are costly, Dr. Wilder," Antonelli said sipping on his drink and resting back into his chair. He lifted his legs and swung them on the corner of his desk and smiled. "Unless you have some positive proof, there is nothing I can do."

"This is the pattern, Mr. Antonelli. You take it from there." David opened the file. "A soul reaches his eighteenth birthday and/or his inoculation date expires. He makes an appointment at the center to help with his regression and finds a very warm, amiable place in which he can place his trust and his life."

Tony Antonelli nodded and lit a cigar. "Go on."

"Once he is regressed, one of two things happens. He either has a past life, or he doesn't. If he doesn't, he is considered a new soul. If he has a past life, depending on where, when, and what he was, Webster will take the most important of them and find a job relating to that life." David watched for expression on Antonelli's face. "You see, Dr. Webster also runs an employment agency out of there. If the man or woman is already employed, he raises their pay schedule and coerces them to accept what he has to offer instead. Believe me, Mr. Antonelli, it is enticing enough that no one says no."

Tony Antonelli was a good audience to David. He listened attentively to what he was saying and outside of lighting his cigar or pouring himself more scotch, he didn't once waiver from the conversation.

"He will not erase their memories, as the government tells him to. Instead, he has a session with them once a month, encouraging memory to coincide with job, which helps the subject to remember more. Everything is documented.

If the subject has had a very bad past experience, you will note that suicide follows within a six month to one-year period. Once you read the files, you'll notice every suicide that has occurred had a devastating past life." David was on a roll. He kept on talking.

"The second scenario is the man or woman with no past life. This new soul is not allowed to carry out his first life. He is put in a menial job, still at good pay, and after six months is somehow murdered by the hands of August Webster. All of these subjects have died of *'natural causes.'* I still have yet to figure out how they really died."

Tony Antonelli sat with his mouth open. "This is absolutely preposterous," he said finally. "There hasn't been one complaint against the Webster Center. In fact, it's one of our best centers."

David shook his head. "Not true. He's one of your more careful centers. But, he's slipped up. His secretary goes by the books. She gives the counselor all the files and the counselor does her job of counseling, period. In fact, she's the one who noticed this pattern first and came to me. Her name is Ashleigh Bennett." David was losing ground. "One of her subjects was Kayla Smith. She recently took cyanide poisoning because she couldn't live with the nightmares of the burnings of a Salem witch. This witch was she, herself."

David was becoming incensed. Was he whining? Pointing to the files, he said. "You have to read through these Mr. Antonelli. It's all here. Every last piece of smut you can imagine. This August Webster has unleashed rapist and murderers from long ago back into our streets. Isn't that one of the reasons the government wanted all memories erased? So as not to provoke the undesirable?"

David cleared his throat. "I think this is where he slipped up. He . . ."

Tony Antonelli sat up straight in his chair and interrupted. "You are an incredibly stupid young man, Dr. Wilder. No one should go to the lengths that you've gone through, if they want to live." His eyes bore into David's. "If what you say is true, don't think this August Webster won't find you. You will *also* slip up sometime and it will probably cost you your life." He took a deep drag on his cigar. "But, what you say seems a little far fetched. I'm not ignoring it, mind you, and I am going to read your files this evening and then make my decision. Again, if what you say is true, Dr. Wilder. You and your friends are playing a very serious game."

David gathered up his files and placed them on Tony Antonelli's desk. "When can we meet again, sir?"

"The only time available would be tomorrow at ten. Is that good for you?"

David nodded. "Fine. I'll be back."

Tony Antonelli stood up as David took his leave. "Oh, Dr. Wilder."

David turned around, hand on the doorknob. "Yes?"

"You're on the brink of disaster. I hope you know what you and your Scotland Yard friends have gotten yourselves into."

David closed the door behind him. He was miserable.

Twenty

"How'd it go?" Ashleigh asked.

"Not good, Ash." David was in bed, lights out, resting the phone on his pillow. He was trying to make some sense out of what had happened during the day. "I can't understand it. The man thinks I'm crazy. I can tell."

"Why?"

David shook his head. "You know when you can tell something? A gut feeling? I'm telling you Ash."

Ashleigh was bewildered. "You have documented proof of everything, David. What else does he want? Did he read the files?"

David's lips twisted into a distorted grin. "No. He's going to read them this evening. But it was like he was protecting Webster's center. Maybe that's his job. But, he has to give us a chance."

"Does he know anything about Webster?"

"No. In fact, he said the center is one of his best. No complaints." He laughed. "I guess I'm the first."

There was silence. Then . . . "Once he reads, David, he'll look at things with a different perspective. You'll see."

David sighed audibly. "Ash. One thing he said worries me."

"What's that?" She asked.

"He said that we were playing a foolish game, so to speak. He said that if what we say were true, Webster would stop at nothing to kill us, too, Ash. I'm almost sorry I got you into this. I'm worried about you."

"Look, David," she said softly, comfortingly. "At the moment, Webster doesn't even know we exist. He has never asked who I was and he could never connect me to this. He doesn't know who Patrick is or who you are. Right now, we have nothing to concern ourselves with."

"Except for one thing."

Ashleigh voice tightened. "What's that?"

"He has Patrick's gold pen with his initials on it. If he's smart enough to print it, he could find out who Patrick is."

"His pen?" Ashleigh panicked.

"Don't worry about it. I doubt if he could pick up Patrick's prints. His own must be on it, too. Probably wiped Pat's off when he examined it."

Ashleigh inhaled deeply. "I hope so, David."

"Listen. You give me a call in the morning. I'm going down for a bite to eat and then I'm going to hit the sack." His voice softened into a whisper. "I wish you were here, Ash."

"So do I." She threw him a kiss and hung up.

**

Darkness had fallen and he could feel the first chill of the evening. He really did wish Ashleigh were there. He missed her and worried about her . . . and Patrick.

Antonelli's words rang deeply in his mind, over and over again. They could all be in danger. This was not what he had anticipated. The thought hadn't even crossed his mind.

It wasn't a very good night. Every time David closed his eyes, he saw Webster before him. Judging him.

He tossed and turned, looking for a comfort zone. But he had been moved out of his comfort zone and so he needed a place to stabilize for a while. Just until this thing was cleared up.

After the fourth time at trying to fall asleep, David finally got up. It was ten o'clock and he was hungry. He craved something light accompanied by a little wine. That should at least put him to sleep.

So he ordered white fish cooked in garlic and olive oil and a bottle of white chilled wine to take the edge off the evening. While he waited, he picked up the Gideon Bible and started to read.

The first part of the book served as a review in religion. David was familiar with the beginning and the word. But further on in, it got more complicated and he had a hard time following the scripture.

He closed the book briefly and looked again at the cover. King James Version. It wasn't a Gideon after all. He concentrated on who begat who and who was the father of whom. It didn't work. His mind wasn't on the Bible or anything else other than Tony Antonelli and August Webster. Antonelli's words stinging at his brain.

David's dull headache earlier this morning was beginning to turn into a disturbance. The wine should calm the roaring beast, he thought. The wine should put an end to his miserable insomnia and pathetic misery.

***

About forty-five minutes later, room service had arrived. Everything was flavorsome and cooked to a distinction and the wine was perfectly chilled. David poured himself a glass.

This time, instead of picking up the Bible, he picked up a book of recombinant DNA that he had taken along. This he grew interested in immediately. One case study was the splicing together the DNA's of two different species of rats and forming a new life, a combination of both. Particular areas of the DNA were called genes and the new life had the equivalent amount of both species.

David took a sip of wine. He was becoming unattached. His headache was winding down again. This little book was very well written and easy to conceive, but he wasn't even into reading at this point, as interesting as it was.

Putting the book down, he walked to the window of his eighth floor room. He looked out onto the bustling city below and thought how amazingly close it looked to his own city. Absent mindedly, he fondled his hour-shaped glass and thought about Ashleigh. The idea that she might be in danger bit at him like an ice-cold bullet. He should have taken her with him where he could protect her. He shouldn't have left her to Patrick.

Placing the glass on the tray, he carried it to the door and placed it on the floor just outside the suite. Then, he immediately slipped back beneath the covers and fell into a deep, dreamless sleep.

***

David glanced obscurely at the clock once more. It was finally seven in the morning. By nine o'clock, he was in a cab, taking the same route, with the same talkative driver to Antonelli's office. His stomach tightened into a hard ball of tension as his eyes fixed upon the building. What did Antonelli read when he read the files? How did he interpret all that he read, and would it be in his or Webster's favor?

There were so many whys and why nots swimming through his head. Unfortunately, he could feel the ebbing away of peace, and the consistent drumming of a headache trying so hard to form in its place. And sometimes, like now, he wondered why he allowed himself to get involved with all of this. Why, when there were so many other people in this country that could be investigating Webster, would he be putting himself and all that he loved in jeopardy? And even if he proved Webster's corrupt strategy, what difference would it make? It could mean a lengthy lawsuit that could run into years and money. And who was going to pay for it? Nonetheless, he knew he was doing the right thing. He knew that, had he to do it over, he would do it again.

David looked up at the same stairs he'd seen yesterday, but this time elected the climb. His breath drew in sharply as he prepared himself for Antonelli's interrogation. He couldn't even predict what was going to happen in the next few hours.

Tony Antonelli was sitting at his desk when his secretary showed David in. He didn't get up.

"Dr. Wilder. Please," he gestured to the chair opposite him again. "Sit down."

David didn't speak. He wasn't in for pleasantries at the moment. He was merely interested in what Antonelli had to say about the files. Unfortunately, he was in a mood where no one could intimidate him. He was tired and scared for Ashleigh and Patrick. If this dumb shit wanted to give him trouble, so be it.

"I read over the files last night." He nodded and pushed them towards David. "Interesting, I must say."

David still didn't speak.

"But . . ."

David hated "buts." It was a word of rejection.

"I'm sorry to say that you have no hard evidence in this matter, Dr. Wilder."

He had to be kidding.

"If you could only get me some proof from, let's say, Dr. Webster's own mouth perhaps."

I can't believe this.

"Then, maybe we could view this in an entirely different prospective . . ."

"What the hell are you talking about?" David yelled. He stood up and leaned forward putting his hands on Antonelli's desk. His face was dramatically close to the man's own. "You got to be shittin', you asshole."

"Dr. Wilder!" Antonelli exclaimed.

"Dr. Wilder, my ass. You don't know what the hell you're talking about, Antonelli. You have a Goddamn problem on your hands here," he said pointing to the files, and frightfully close to tears. "I can't believe you're not even going to check on this."

Tony Antonelli stood up and faced David. "You little runt. I don't have all day to play your parlor games. I'm not out to close a regression center just because you don't like the guy in charge."

"I haven't even met the bastard!" David yelled. "What the hell's going on here? Webster paying you?"

"Dr. Wilder! If you don't cease your nonsense I'll have security here in a minute and remove you from my office."

At that moment, terror and anger gripped at David's heart along with a blinding headache. He flung himself across the desk and grabbed onto Antonelli's collar. "You bastard," he cried. "You bastard." The tears came readily. "You're not even going to give me a chance, are you? You're in on this. You're in with Webster, aren't you?"

Antonelli touched a button under his desk and four security guards came bursting into the room. Two of them grabbed David by the arms, restraining him, while the others slipped on handcuffs.

"Throw him in a cell until he cools off!" Antonelli yelled. "And charge him with assault!"

David struggled against the guards, screaming at Antonelli. His headache was now like thunderous cannons going off every few seconds. He felt as if he would pass out. A guttural sound escaped his lips distorting his words. "I have the right to an attorney!" He mumbled loudly. "You can't do this, Antonelli. You bastard. You can't do this!"

The guards dragged him down the hall, down the stairs and into the squad car waiting outside. A crowd was gathering. David tried to compose himself, but his emotional level was much too high. Ashleigh, he thought, tears running down his cheeks. How can I protect you if I can't protect myself?

Twenty-one

David's eyes opened. He couldn't believe it. He was lying on a bare, urine smelling cot in a dirty city cell and it was nearly seven o'clock in the morning.

Somehow, he had made it through the night. He looked out the small opening they called a window, at a sky only artists dream about, and it was hard to imagine that there were places like this among all that beauty.

He didn't remember much of what happened except that he'd lost his temper and lunged at Tony Antonelli.

David was feeling an incredible frustration. Like a poet looking for a rhyme, he had no other way to express his fears. Was this the price for intolerance?

Unable to escape from a constant evaluation of his behavior, he turned his anger inward. He made promises that he would never keep. He wouldn't rest, if it meant his death, until he put August Webster away.

David Wilder knew that there was no vindication in hatred. He knew that he was a product of his own devil. But with the circumstances getting so totally out of control, vindication was looking good.

Just outside the oblong room that housed him and three empty cells, David heard voices discussing his bail. "He could never afford such a sum," one voice said.

Another answered. "I won't drop the charges, Sal."

"You're being foolish, Mr. Antonelli. There's no possible reason for keeping him here."

David couldn't believe his ears. It was Tony Antonelli and someone else speaking about him.

"I'll add another charge," Antonelli said sardonically.

"It'll never hold."

"No. But it will stall justice, my friend," Antonelli said as he walked away. "It will stall justice. Talk to you later."

Another charge, David thought. What other charge? Added to assault, it could mean a long stay in the county jail.

"Guard!" David yelled. "Guard!"

The heavy-set man with the wire rim glasses approached him slowly. He was chewing on a chicken drumstick, his mouth and hands greasy from the fat.

This was Washington, for God's sake, he thought, not some little out of the way hick town where the guards were unmannered and loathsome.

"What was Antonelli talking about out there?" He yelled at the man. "What did he mean by added charges?"

The guard shrugged an indifference to the conversation. "Don't know, pal. But what Tony Antonelli says, Tony Antonelli does."

"But there are no added charges. All I did was jump at him for Christ sakes." David ran a shaky, embarrassed hand through his hair. "What the hell else does he have on me?"

"Dunno," the guard said with a mouthful of chicken. "Guess you'll just have to wait and see." He turned his fat body around and waddled out the door.

David spun around and slammed his hand against the cement wall. "Damn!" he screamed. "Why the hell is this all happening to me?"

"Because you're a trouble maker, Wilder." Antonelli was walking past the guard into the cell area. "You come in my office half cocked about something you know nothing about and then accuse me of being part of it." He leaned against the wall of the room. "Two cardinal sins in a city this size, Wilder."

"But it's all true."

"Not so." Antonelli shifted his feet and rubbed his face with his hands as if weary of his job. "I'm not part of anything you're fabricating in that mind of yours. You asked me to read the files. I read the files. You asked me to give it serious thought. I gave it serious thought. But you can't accuse me of the things you accused me of just because I don't agree with your theory."

David walked to the bars and gripped them with both hands, pressing his face against the iron. "But it isn't theory, Antonelli. It's positive proof. It's documented material. How can you just toss it aside like that?" He placed his head against the bars, eyes down. "Besides," he muttered. "I was speaking out of anger when I accused you of being in with Webster."

Antonelli chuckled. He loved being in command of a situation. "Well, Wilder. You lose. If I have to keep you here two months on phony charges, I'll do it."

David looked up at Antonelli with hatred in his eyes. "Why, Antonelli?" He asked. "Where will it get you?"

"Satisfaction, Wilder. Cheap cop satisfaction." He snickered. "Besides, if word got out of what you accused me of, I'd lose every ounce of dignity I've worked so hard for. You have no right."

Antonelli walked out of the room with a casual step, hands in pockets and whistling.

David spun around, tears in his eyes. *What can I say*, he thought. *I'm a lucky man.*

There was no going back. Instead of fighting what happened, he should open up to the experience. He should learn something from it. Because, for the first time in his life he had lost his temper to the point of being incarcerated. He had no way of controlling himself. The worse part is he didn't want to control himself. Once he took the dive across that desk, he wanted to do nothing less than kill the bastard that ignored every warning about Webster that he was presented with.

Who could he blame for this mess? His headache?

He remembered the pain then, the pain that seemed to ambush

him where he stood. He remembered the sharp, burning pain that caught his breath and caused him to mutter an indistinct curse.

The pain was only momentary, his body's reaction to an unaccustomed invasion. But, then it came again catching him off guard for the second time in minutes. Every sound that was made was like chalk screeching across a blackboard to him. Every word spoken, every door closing incited him enough to want to kill. It incited him enough to actually think he was going crazy.

He thought of Ashleigh and Patrick. Hopefully, they were in the process of getting him out of this place. Hopefully he had very little time left in this filthy hellhole.

He sat on the dirty cot for a very long time in the deepest of thought, until his leg muscles suddenly began to protest their prolonged tension, and knotted into cramps so vicious he almost cried out. Panting, he dug the heels of his hands into his leg and tried to knead the muscle into relaxing. But, the muscle just seemed to knot again and again. Just when it seemed as if it was easing up, he could feel the spasm come again like a wave, slowly at first, then hard and long.

Once, he had seen a runner rub a cramp out of his calf by rubbing with both hands, back and forth, back and forth. Taking both hands, he placed them around his calf and massaged the knotted muscle beneath his hand. Within seconds, the pain began to ebb. And David noticed that he began breathing again, realizing that must have been holding his breath through the pain.

Every time David looked around the cell, the severe episode of that morning and what put him here had left him feeling dazed and dopey. He walked around in that eight by eight square at least one hundred times, not expecting anyone to come by. Around sundown, he began to feel as though he couldn't stand being there another moment. His thought processes felt slow and clumsy, as if he had been drugged. He needed some fresh air. He wouldn't be getting any.

Sitting on the cot again, David put his head down and massaged his temples. If he could get rid of his headache, he would better be able to think of a solution to get out of this mess. But, instead of it growing weaker by the hour, it was progressively stronger. Stretching his long body out on the cot, his misery soon took over him and he fell into an uneasy sleep.

Twenty-two

Ashleigh stood at her window staring out at the early morning bustle of the street below.

She drew in a long sigh. Her mission was accomplished. The information she reported would be in this morning's paper, and Patrick would be over shortly to review it with her. Thankfully, the woman he knew at the press worked with him on the article.

She hated it when things that she planned didn't go well, and nothing so far was going right.

Patrick was there within ten minutes after he spoke to her and he could tell she wanted to be alone. "How are you?" he asked.

"I'll be all right," she lied, wishing he would go so she could cry. She missed David and she worried about him, especially his health.

He stood by her and put his arm around her shoulders. Ashleigh was stunned by his gesture for a moment, but within seconds the tears came and she found his arms comfortably folded around her.

"Things aren't going very well, are they Ash?" he asked sympathetically. "But, they are going to be fine. We'll get through this." He lifted her chin up and looked her in the eyes.

"Did you think this was going to be a piece of cake?"

She shook her head and smiled. "No, of course not. But I didn't expect that one of us would be in trouble. My thoughts were more on the line of us all together in or out of trouble."

He nodded. "Me too."

There was a thud at the door. Immediately they knew that the paper was delivered. It usually came much earlier, but this morning, because they were anxious, it was late. But that was par for the course these past weeks.

"I'll get it," Patrick suggested.

Ashleigh took the paper from him, went to the desk, turned on the lamp, lay the paper down and smooth away the crinkles as best as she could. She began to read.

> The August Webster regression center was been broken into sometime last Sunday evening. As of yet, there are no suspects. Data was taken from Dr. Webster's personal files, but nothing more was reported missing. Dr. Webster has no comments.

***

Ashleigh looked at Patrick. "This should blow his mind, my friend," she said smiling.

Patrick grinned. "He's going to find out about his own break-in from the newspapers."
He looked at his watch. "In fact, he's probably reading about it as we speak."

They both laughed.

"This article is suppose to be in the paper nationally, Ash, so our Detective Tony Antonelli should get a whiff of it today also."

"So should David, if he's allowed a paper."

They both wondered what David's reaction would be when

he read what they had done.

"Probably gloat at our sense of humor, Ash," Patrick said mischievously.

As far as they were concerned, the problem of David Wilder was solved.

Twenty-three

Walking home Webster pulled his coat tighter around him to buffer the slicing wind at his body. *It's not coming together fast enough*, he thought. *I'm not finding enough pertinent information for them.* He was worried. So worried that he wasn't sleeping, he was having more frequent headaches and he couldn't sit still for a minute. There were still so many people out there to regress, yet, if he didn't come up with the key people to present to the government, his utopia would forever be lost.

Webster felt desperation set in and the uneasy feeling was growing more urgent.

He reached the corner where the newspaper stand was. It was empty. He stopped, a great sadness welling in him, as he wondered if he would ever see it in operation again. *He was the one*, Webster thought sadly. *He was the one who lived a great many lives before.* He was just waiting for his regression date.

Webster looked around the stand. It looked as though it was closed for good. There were no papers or magazines locked up for the night. There were remnants of old newspaper articles that were torn off for some reason, and the old man's cigar butts in a coffee can underneath the counter. But no old man and no newspapers for today's edition. They should have been here by now.

"Hello, Dr. Webster," said a soft, hollow voice at his elbow.

Webster looked around and delight speared through him. "There you are," he said happily. "I thought you might be sick." He stopped talking, concern replacing delight.

"I'm not sick. Don't be worryin' about me." The sad eyes were etched with deep lines of despair.

Webster didn't say anything. He was studying the old man. He didn't want to say that he was anxious for his activation date. He didn't want to scare the old man away from him. "Is everything going all right for you?" He asked pointing to the stand. "It looks like you closed down."

The old man nodded. "Did."

Webster had to be careful. He had to gain this old man's trust. "May I ask why? Is there something I can do to help?"

Shaking his head, the old man began walking.

"Wait!" Webster called, catching up with him. "Is there something I can do to keep your stand going?" He laughed a nervous little laugh, afraid that the old man would catch on that whatever the reasons for keeping the stand opened, it certainly had all to do with Webster.

"Why, Dr. Webster?" the old man asked, stopping and facing Webster. "Why in the world would you be so interested in keeping that old stand opened?"

"We all want it opened. It's where we stop on our way to work or on our way home." Webster paused for a moment, then, "What will you do now?"

The old man shrugged. "Don't know. I just know that I'm going to be eighty-nine next week and I'd like to spend the rest of what I got left, in front of the tube, or fishing, or doing any damn thing I want."

Webster gave a short courtesy laughed. All he heard out of that statement was that the old man would be eighty-nine next week. That suited him just fine. He had to be coming to the center.

"Well, I'll probably see you next week then. Don't forget your regression session if it's your birthday. You don't want to take a chance of it activating on its own now." Webster patted the old man on the back, turned around and walked the other way. Suddenly, the chill was gone. He felt warm again. He was feeling much better.

The old man looked after him and picked something out of his teeth. "Dr. Webster," he said aloud. "It'll be a cold day in hell that you'll see me at your center."

***

It was past midnight, and the temperature had dropped greatly along with a heavy breeze that was stirring in the air. It had already started to rain, casting a gloomy feeling over the city.

A heaviness lay over the house, and as August Webster sat in his living room, he felt the air around him become oppressive and close, making it hard for him to breath.

He had been sitting there for hours. The evening paper was lying across his lap and his hands lay folded on the paper.

He reflected on the findings of the detective he hired. It didn't make sense. There was no sign of anyone by the name of Patrick Tuchman associated with his center or any other. Not as a patient, nor service coordinator. He was a total stranger who knew more about Webster than he had entitlement to.

He can't be far, he thought crossing to the bar and pouring himself a bourbon. Just the thought of someone wanting something from him so badly unnerved him. His anger was frustrating.

He picked up the phone and dialed. "I want you to find Patrick Tuchman, Jimbo. I don't know who the hell he is, but he sure in hell knows me. When you find him, bring him to me. I have some long range plans for him."

Webster knew that he had to be Patrick Tuchman that reported the break in. Who else would know about it? It was Tuchman's pen that was found in his office, wasn't it? Well, he smiled a little crazily; he had a trace on the man. He would be found shortly.

But the big question was why? And what was it that he wanted? Why *those* files? He couldn't help but feel that the man knew exactly what he was doing. That the man knew a whole lot more than Webster wanted to believe he did.

Webster stood up and mixed himself another drink. A double this time. He needed to calm down a little, he thought as he watched his hands shake when he poured the liquor into a glass. It was all going so good. Too good.

Taking his drink, he walked out onto the veranda. Water poured off him and he shivered as the breeze whipped around him. He tried to swallow the bile of fear that was resting in the base of his throat. What should he do?

Part of him wanted to flee. Take all records and burn them. Take the money out of the bank and vanish to another country and live his life out.

Another part of him told him to stay here and fight. It would all be worthwhile. Screwing up his courage, he took his drink and walked back into the living room. He had made the right decision.

After all, he didn't do anything wrong. He was only following directions from the government. Well, somewhat, he rationalized. He was actually doing the government a favor by taking some of the matters into his own hands. It would be wise for some of the other regression leaders to do the same.

For example, why keep a new soul around for an indefinite period of time? The faster they're born again, the faster they begin to develop multiple lifetimes. Therefore, in the event of another planetary crisis, they would be equipped with the means to be able to reverse the damage.

Webster's lips twisted into a smile. Where was the justice in it all, he wondered? Here he was trying to build an empire and someone was trying to shoot him down.

It was uncanny the way he thought about exterminating the new souls, uncanny and quite ingenious. He was paving the way for the future.

Maybe he wouldn't be around to see them all back, since no one knew how long a soul remained suspended before being reborn. But it insured they wouldn't be strangers in a strange land any longer. They wouldn't be aliens in a world full of old souls.

He wondered about his own demise. When he returned, what would his new life hold for him?

He hated the idea of giving up this life and all that he had built. It had been so prosperous. But progression was the key word here. He was, as all souls were, supposed to progress.

Webster's jaws suddenly tightened. His thoughts immediately went to James Proud. He was a suicide case about a month ago. Mr. Proud ended his own life because he couldn't handle the debasing of this life. Where he was supposed to progress, he instead degenerated.

If each life had something to do with the merits achieved in the last life, how would his present life be viewed? How could he be anything but praised for his work here? He was doing the earth a great deal of good. Yet, would he be judged on that or the deliverance of new souls to their demise? Murder was a crime. But, would his acts of good will be considered murder?

His failures had been so few. Only one in six years. Webster considered his program at the center a complete success. It was true, of course, that a few hiccups crossed his path every now and again, but he managed to shuffle them under the rug quite efficiently.

The phone ran like an explosion in the room, making him jump and spill his drink over his silk shirt.

"Hello," he said gruffly. "Yes. Yes." He listened for several seconds that seemed to stretch out for hours. "Good." He smiled. "Very good." He scratched some information down on the pad near the phone, his face being a mask of controlled indignation. "Thank you very much. If I need your services in the future, you can believe that I'll be calling you. Good bye."

Webster took in a heavy, deep breath and exhaled loudly. They found Patrick Tuchman, he thought. His pulse was jumping. It was all getting a little too crazy.

The room was in semidarkness, lit only by a small lamp on the sofa table. Somehow the darkness seemed saner than the brightness of the overhead lights. Webster poured himself another drink, sank into one of the armchairs and stared blankly at the wall.

His head ached. He'd had too much to drink, but hadn't realized it. He struggled to his feet thinking that a shower would do him good.

It did. But as the headache grew stronger, he realized that it was not an ache from alcohol, but another migraine coming on. Stress.

Maybe he could sleep. He was exhausted.

Naked and still a little wet from his shower, he pulled back the bedcovers and slipped in.

But, sleep came in waves. He bobbed back and forth from consciousness again and again. "They found Patrick Tuchman," he said aloud. His problems were over. He fell into a deep, exhausted sleep.

Twenty-four

The young man watched in amazement as the cars streamed across the causeway at this early morning work hour. His nostrils were burning from his last blast of cocaine, and he could feel his heart racing as a surge of euphoria hit him. He knew that it would only last about fifteen to twenty minutes but in that little time, he could dream he was king. And with each blast, he would make it through one more day of his life until that life was thankfully over.

Today it was unusually warm. He couldn't make heads or tails of the weather lately, but if it said warm, he undressed, if it said cold, he dressed. Today, he was to undress.

He peeled off the damp shirt that was clinging to his body. Beneath, he exposed a thin-framed chest that was totally hairless. He was about seventeen years old, with long dirty hair, the color of wheat, and he had a terrible odor to him. His name was Kevin Black and he was a junkie.

In some of his more lucid days, he'd reflect upon how he managed to get himself in such a jackpot. At one time, drugs were banned throughout the country. But because of the politicians who controlled it, the system lost its battle and had no choice but to legalize drugs and make them available to the public. This was only since 2030, but it was long enough to turn

Kevin into a burned out human specie. No future. Too many pasts.

Way back in his mind he visualized the day he took his first blast. It was the fourteenth of November, almost six months ago. It was a very cold day, and he had to hold his coat tightly together to prevent the winds from whipping through his thin body.

He lived in the village then, and although it had been mostly renovated and housed a higher class of people, there were still the unfortunates, like his family, residing in the lower hubbles of the buildings that haven't yet been fixed up.

On that particular day, his older brother had been drafted to the center for his regression. It wasn't a long session, because he was told he had only lived once before. But he had lived the life of an executioner. He was the one who dropped the blade onto the shaking head of a criminal. He was the one that had to watch as that shaking head was severed from its body plopping into the bucket awaiting it. He saw the body still twitching after the execution. Many times, the hands still reached out toward the neck's vacant spot before dropping to its side in death.

He hated his job, but he had thirteen children and the pay was good. He was what one would call a moron, in the year 1516, and such a job was appropriate for a simpleton. A simpleton didn't understand the impact of the job. The simpleton couldn't have the guilt and feelings of remorse.

But they were wrong. He later tied two large bags of cooking potatoes to his feet, clasped his hands behind him like a vice and toppled into the river behind his village. His guilt was no more.

Kevin's brother's name was Nathaniel. And Nathaniel never once thought he had a past life, and if he did, he never thought that all that guilt would come back to haunt him. He never even suspected that he would be removed from his suspended peace to live again in a world where memory paid you back. But after one month, he did the same thing, except this time with a razor.

Kevin ran the last two blocks to his home that day and called Nat's name from the landing. It was a great day to see the

Round Robin football game at the high school. Although Nat was two years older, he always went with Kevin to these games. He had just gotten out of school the year before, so he enjoyed the memories of the games and some of his old classmates.

It was unusual not to receive an answer from Nat when he called him from the landing. Nat always waited for this greeting and was there with an exact response at exactly the same time every day. Kevin's stomach churned. Something was wrong.

It's the heat, he decided as he descended the three steps to his apartment door. The heat gets to people after a while. Makes them imagine things. He shook his head.

He found Nathaniel on the sofa, eyes opened, blood crusted wrists, and the razor still clenched in his left hand.

There was no sound from Kevin's mouth, although it was opened in a scream. He fled the apartment and never returned.

Two weeks and ten days after Nathaniel's death, Kevin took his first blast. It was his first blast of amnesia. He learned to forget about that awful day, and he learned to make a habit of it.

Kevin leaned against his brother's ten-year old car. This was the only thing that he had that belonged to Nathaniel. Reality seeped through his dazed mind this morning. If it hadn't been for the August Webster Regression Center, his brother would still be alive today. No one should have to be regressed. No one should be forced to do something that will endanger him.

How could he stop it? He wondered. How could he stop all these suicides? He knew at least three people that had taken their lives because of the memories. He never expected his own brother to be the fourth. But, you didn't fight August Webster.

Kevin Black made a decision that morning. He was going to protest against the Webster Center. He was going to get the whole high school campus to strike against it too.

There would never be another Nathaniel Black to come home to again. What did he have to lose beating Webster at his own game . . .?

Twenty-five

Ashleigh pulled up to the light in front of James Madison High School, on Bedford Avenue. She hadn't intended to be in this part of the city today, but a client from Webster's Center seemed to be in trouble. She received the call at seven o'clock this morning.

As she looked at the structure, she thought about how tradition carried on in the world, regardless of the sad, pained, troubled planet.

This high school was attended by her parents, their parents and on back through the generations. It had once been marked with graffiti, etched with initials, ladened with dirt and still, after all those years of weariness it went on.

At the end of the twentieth century, the tired old building was torn down. Portable classrooms were constructed right on the grounds and the faithful students watched as bricks were laid for the new multi-leveled structure.

Now, it was called the New Madison High School. Ashleigh smiled as she passed the structure. It was already more than forty years old, this new structure, yet the word 'new' was just part of its name now.

This school was constructed of solid, shatterproof glass. It had underground parking for the upperclassmen and teachers and the once six-story building was now twice that, and housed more than eighteen thousand students.

Ashleigh, herself, had attended James Madison High. Although nothing about this new building was familiar, the happy memories danced crazily in her mind.

***

Standing against the school, feet crossed and puffing on a cigarette, was a young man. He was clad in torn blue jeans, laceless sneakers and an opened plaid shirt revealing a dirty undershirt beneath.

Immediately, Ashleigh recognized him. His brother was Nathaniel Black. She had attended his funeral not too long ago.

This boy's name was Kevin, as she recalled, although she had only seen his pictures since he didn't attend his brother's funeral. In fact, the parents say he left the day of Nat's death and had never returned.

Ashleigh swung right, into the parking lot of the school, and weaved her car around the curved lane to the front entrance. She didn't acknowledge him for fear he would run. Instead, she pulled to a stop, shut off the engine and casually stepped from the car.

He saw her, but he didn't move. Taking a deep drag on his cigarette, he uncrossed his feet and crossed them the opposite way. He had no intention of leaving.

Ashleigh walked toward the young man and smiled. He didn't seem worried or scared. She remained as casual as she could and directed a question to him. "You're Nat's brother, aren't you?"

"Ain't got no brother," he replied.

Ashleigh was taken off guard. "Well, yes," she stammered embarrassed. "I know you have no brother now . . . Kevin . . . isn't it?"

The young man didn't reply.

"But you did have a few months ago, didn't you?"

The young man tilted his head to the side and squinted his

eyes. "So what's it to you?"

"I want to help you, Kevin. I know you're in pain, but . . ."

Kevin stood straight up and away from the building. "Listen. I don't know who you are and I'm not sure that I even give a shit. But you better be somebody important enough to get involved in my business." He flicked his cigarette to the side and leaned back against the building again.

For a few seconds, Ashleigh was speechless. Then, very calmly and quietly she told him who she was. "I'm Ashleigh Bennett, Kevin. I was your brother's counselor while he was going through regression. I heard what happened to him and they told me about you. I want to help."

Kevin snickered, some spittle dripping down his chin. "Like you helped Nat?"

Ashleigh smiled and lowered her eyes. "I tried to help him, Kevin. But his memories were much too powerful. Now, I have something that would have erased that memory all together, but I didn't have it then."

"Sure," he kicked at a stone spraying loose dirt on his already dirty sneaker.

"I just want to know what you're feeling, Kevin," she stated. "Maybe it's something that we've all been feeling for a long time."

"Do you believe that this regression law is going to fix our planet?" he asked.

Ashleigh raised her eyebrows and answered as carefully as possible. "Well, it has worked to some extent, Kevin. For example, we did find some leading scientists and mathematicians. We've learned from them what we could about advancing our space program. We learned what the past generation, before the one we lost to the virus, was setting their goals to. So, although we did lose some quality people, we have found some also."

"So you agree with the program." Kevin stated glumly.

"I can't say that I actually agree with all of it. No. But for the most part, the intentions were commendable."

Suddenly, Kevin shot a crude look at Ashleigh and all his anger and pain poured out. "Well, I don't! I didn't have to lose my brother. It was that Webster asshole. He forced it all on him." He was sobbing now, as he wiped at his eyes in embarrassment. "I'm not going to let them do that to me."

"It doesn't have to happen to you Kevin. I can take care of all of that now. We can beat this Webster at his own game. But, I need your help." She touched his arm. She had to be able to read what he was thinking. "I've a decoder, Kevin. It can decode and detonate that chip instantaneously. Want to give it a try?"

"Where'd you get it, lady?"

"I have some physicist friends who invented it. It works, Kevin. Let me decode your chip." Ashleigh stooped down to see if she could see his face. 'We intend to decode as many people as we can Kevin. We're going to get Webster.

Kevin's head dropped onto his chest and his shoulders shook as he wept. All the pain. All the anguish was emptying itself right there in the school yard, and he couldn't speak. Kevin nodded his approval.

"Okay then," Ashleigh said. "In my car, I have the decoder. You stay here and I will detonate your chip from there. You'll feel nothing but a tiny pop and then you won't have to worry about a thing from there on. Without the chip activated, Webster can't demand that you hold on to a memory you don't want to hold on to."

"But suppose I'm drafted in?"

"You will be. And that's when good acting abilities come in to play. That's when you fake it! Become someone that he wants you to become. You have time to think about it and read about it. Study the personality and mannerism of someone important and make sure, by all that's holy, Kevin, just make sure that it isn't your first life. You must have lived at least once before this one." Ashleigh touched his arm gently. "Are you ready? Do you trust me?"

Kevin nodded. "I'm ready and I ain't got much choice but to trust you."

Ashleigh smiled tightly. "Okay. Here goes." She walked quickly to her car, opened the door and sat in the passenger side. Kevin could see her opening the glove compartment and pulling out something black and rectangular. He saw her adjust a knob and push a lever and then she aimed it at him.

He waited. For a second he pictured his head exploding right off his shoulder. Who is this woman that he should trust her? Then, he felt a small pop. Almost like a gas bubble bursting. It must be done, he thought, his heart beating rapidly.

Ashleigh got out of the car and walked toward him. "It's done," she said. "Go home to your parents. They've suffered enough. But remember, Kevin. If you are called, you better be prepared."

Quickly, and without warning, Kevin leaned forward and kissed her on her cheek. He was crying again. "Thanks . . ."

Twenty-six

David tossed the newspaper that the guard brought to him, on the cot. He wasn't in the mood to sit and read as if he were relaxing in his own living room. He was feeling much too anxious.

The guard was doing paper work. He could see this through the small window on the outer door, and other than that, no other activity existed.

Except one. There was a scratching sound. A thin sounding noise coming from under the cot. David couldn't see anything, but the sound was real.

Bending over, he peered beneath the cot, looking for whatever was making the noise. He could see nothing. Then, reflecting from the little bit of light that was coming in from the small window, David could see eyes staring right back at him.

A mouse, he thought. A dumb little mouse.

Picking the newspaper up from his cot, he twisted it into a spiral and jabbed at the little creature hovering in the corner. Just as he brought the paper out to wind it tighter, the headlines caught his eyes.

August Webster Regression Center was broken into . . .

"Christ," he whispered. God almighty, he thought. There was someone else after Webster too. He finished reading and flung the paper to the floor.

"Open this door!" David commanded. "You can't lock me up when there are others out there sharing my feelings about Webster."

A faint tinkling sound was heard just outside the door and he knew. It was the keys. Someone was going to let him out.

"Please. Let me have my day in court. Let me prove what I say. We have to DO something," he wailed. He was sobbing with terror now. His eyes darting back and forth from the cell to the door.

Vick, the guard, came in with a mug full of coffee. "Relax now, Dr. Wilder. This isn't going to do you any good. Here." He pushed the mug through the bars. "Have a hot cup of coffee. They'll be here to bring you to court in a few minutes. You can have your say then."

David stood staring at Vick. "Look," he said pointing to the paper. "Didn't you read the headlines today? It's all there. Everything I've been trying to tell Detective Antonelli is right there in the paper."

It was now late morning and he had gotten absolutely nowhere. Like all ill-informed people, Vick and Detective Antonelli were ready to take the power side. Not some no nothing scientist's side from the west side of New York.

His mind was clearer, and he suddenly realized that he had done enough for now. He would wait for his arraignment and then, he would calmly, but emphatically lay down all the information and documentation that he could in a very professional manner. No court in the land could ignore a sane man.

But, how sane was he when he lunged across the desk at Antonelli? How credible would he sound in front of the judge when he tried to explain such lunacy? And, he thought further; one case has nothing to do with the other. At the arraignment, they're going to be judging me on MY actions, not Webster's.

It seemed to David that Vick had some sympathy for him. That was good. He needed some leverage. But, time was running short. He needed to use that leverage now. He needed to get out of here.

***

The sun was blinding when he was taken from City Hall. His hands were cuffed behind him so there was no way to shield the piercing glare.

He could feel the stares of the people around him, although the city was very careful to remove its prisoners from the back entrance and avoid scenes. However, there were a number of people in the back, therefore David felt naked among them.

Once inside the patrol car, he rested his head against the seat. His eyes were tearing from the sun's strain and his heart was hammering from anticipation and a little bit of fear.

He had heard Antonelli tell Vick that there would be other charges. It was all he could do to beat this one. Did he even stand a chance of being freed on bail?

David watched as the sun filtered through the trees and cast shadows on the vast lawns of the state buildings. There were dogwood trees in full bloom that were absolutely gorgeous. And as they drove, he wondered if he'd see these trees and enjoy their beauty again. He wondered, and the thought made his stomach queasy, if he would ever see Ashleigh again and tell her he loved her once more, or would he be sent away to do time for something that wasn't as great a crime compared to what Webster was engaged in.

David started to tremble inside. His bowels tightened and his stomach cramped. What was going to happen to David Wilder in the next sixty minutes?

Twenty-seven

"You choose to defend yourself, Dr. Wilder?" the judge asked wiping his wire-rimmed glasses. He looked like a sweet old man to David. Not at all like a judge, but more like a grandfather. However, David knew that this was one of the foremost judges in the judicial system, and unlike a grandfather, had very little patience.

"Yes, sir," David said. "I couldn't contact my own attorney in time, although I did have my partners try repeatedly."

The judge raised his eyebrows in surprise. "Very well. Proceed."

This was not like a normal court case. In cases like this, the accused related his side of the story to the judge. No jury. And then, solely upon his own decision, he passed judgment.

You were lucky to get a judge whose vibes jelled with your own, because in many instances, the case was lost before the first word was spoken.

"Believe me your honor," David began his defense. "I have done nothing but act out of frustration. As you can see by my records, I have had no problem with the law in the past. Quite the contrary, I work for law and order.

That's why, when I found out about the August Webster Regression Center, I felt I had to investigate further and try to put a stop to it."

"I understand that," the judge replied curtly. "But, will you please justify your actions in our Detective Antonelli's office."

Our. David's heart sunk. The judge used the word, our. He let out an audible sigh. He would never win. They were all in this together. All of them were one. *Our court system. Our judge. Our detective Antonelli.*

David shook his head and pictured his small cell at the City Hall. He couldn't end up back there. His heart beat rapidly as he opened his mouth and took his final chance at freedom.

"Your honor. New York City is a big place. If you would just do me the courtesy of letting me finish what I have to say, I'm sure you will see sense to my crime."

"Proceed," the judge said indifferently.

"In that large city, there are nine million people, some regressed . . . some not yet eighteen. Out of those regressed, the suicide rate is horrendous, the mental illness and crime are virtually unstoppable and only a handful are coping with everyday life. Some, your honor, don't even live six months." David looked around waiting for someone to stop him. No one did.

"August Webster takes a soul and allows him to keep his memory . . ." David told his story. The story he told Patrick, Ashleigh and Detective Antonelli numerous times. The story he believed was outrageous, yet when someone didn't agree with it, he found that hard to believe also.

When he was through, the judge looked at him in confusion. "So you're saying, Dr. Wilder, that this Webster fellow is destroying our people in order to preserve our planet?"

"Yes sir." David was encouraged. "He's not playing by the government rules."

The judge nodded and rubbed the stubble on his chin. "I see."

"And so when Detective Antonelli read my files and told me I had no proof of what I was saying, I lost my temper. This has been so hard on us."

"Us?"

"Us. Myself, Patrick Tuchman and Ashleigh Bennett," David explained.

"Bennett." Once again the judge rubbed at his chin in thought.

"Yes sir. She's the counselor in most of the cases, sir. You'll find her name mentioned quite a few times in the files." David paused so that the judge would absorb his words. "Also, your honor, we've come up with a decoder. We've been decoding the microchip so that the memories Webster dredges up are permanently erased. No more nightmares. No more thoughts of suicides."

"And where are these decoders?"

"In our lab. We haven't decoded too many people, only two or three. But with these files, we know where to go. It can't hurt the center, because Webster already knows who's who in their past. He's gotten the necessary information so there's no reason to keep drilling his subjects."

"I see." The judge read, rubbed his chin, and said, "I see."

"Also," David pointed to file *D*. "If you take a look in the D file, you will notice that almost every new soul that Webster has regressed, is dead within a six month period of time." He paused for effect. "I'm talking new souls here. One's that have never lived before."

David stopped talking then. He tried to remain calm and business like. He tried to show the judge just what was happening.

"Have you read these files, your honor?" David finally asked.

"No. No I haven't. And in all fairness to you, young man, I'm going to read them before I pass any judgment."

"But, your honor. What about bail?"

The judge shook his head. "No bail will be set. Not until I've examined the records. And you were really brought in on an assault charge; completely irrelevant to these files." He looked over his glasses at David. "I'm being nice here, Dr. Wilder. I'm tying the two situations together to see what might have caused you to get so upset that you would go for someone's throat.

Anyway, you must remain in town, Dr. Wilder. Might as well save you money on a room."

"But, your honor. I've work to do. I . . ."

The judge banged his gavel on the podium. "Court adjourned until ten tomorrow morning . . ."

Twenty-eight

Patrick Murphy

Detective Richard Stokes

Case Number 565

"Son of a bitch," Detective Richard Stokes said, tiredly closing a file and leaning back in his chair. He'd run against these types of guys before. Metal fascinated em'. Put a gun in their hands and it'd be cocked in seconds and flashed at anyone who came within eyesight.

And Stokes knew *this* kid. He had a fascination with guns. Stokes didn't know quite why, but one of those icy cold, metal contraptions just intrigued the boy.

He'd read about Timothy Murphy. A neighborhood good boy gone bad. Brought up in a good Irish Catholic home and then suddenly, he's sitting in handcuffs in the back of a paddy wagon.

"Who can figure?" he said wiping his upper lip of sweat.

Richard turned around at the mention of his name. "Someone want me?" he yelled over the din of voice in the office.

"Got em back!" Someone yelled over to him.

Murphy kept tight control of himself as he was walked into the station. He didn't fidget; he didn't protest; he didn't use foul language. The detectives were doing what they had to do to get him processed. Not that he was officially under arrest, judging from their attitudes. They just had him for questioning. He guessed he was what one considered a suspect.

He supposed he could have left, but every time he even thought of it, they kept coming back to him with questions that they needed answered to help them put together a picture.

Murphy wasn't quite sure what he was suspect to. Probably a robbery or something. In any event, he had nothing to hide. He did what he had to do. He did what he had to in order to maintain peace in the neighborhood. Always had. Always would. He thought about Alexandra then. The urge to see her was almost overwhelming and that was the one urge he had to resist. Not being with her gnawed at him making him feel as though a part of him was missing. He felt disconnected when he wasn't with her. She didn't know it, but he needed her so much more than she could ever need him. He needed to feel the freshness of her person and he needed to see the honesty in her eyes.

And so, everything he did, he did for Alexandra. Everything. If something was going wrong in the neighborhood, he made it right. If some punks came through the neighborhood and started any kind of trouble, he got rid of them. Didn't matter how. He did what he had to do to protect those he loved and cared for.

"Wanna tell me about it?" Detective Stokes asked abruptly.

"I don't know what you're talking about," Murphy replied, dragging his thoughts away from Alexandra. "No one told me what I was picked up for. I assume I'm here for questioning."

They looked at each other, each one trying to read the other's thoughts.

"Johnny Acquino was shot last night," Stokes said.

"So?"

"So, you were seen in the area."

Murphy shifted in his seat. "I'm always in the area, Detective." He put a toothpick in his mouth and chewed on it for a few seconds. "Are there areas in town that we should be or shouldn't be in now?" he asked.

"When there's a shooting, Mr. Murphy, then we need to know just who was in the area and who was not. We'd like to find out if anyone saw anything. Get my drift?"

Murphy nodded. "Yep."

Stokes walked around the back of Murphy, feeling as though he was acting in a Humphrey Bogart movie. "So, I'll ask you again. Did you see anything while you were in the area?"

Murphy leaned forward, put his elbows on the table and brought his hands to his mouth, playing with the toothpick. "I didn't see nothing."

Stokes was getting short tempered. "Listen, Murphy. I don't know where your infatuation with guns came from, but you've got a reputation, you know?"

"Didn't know that."

"So naturally the first person to come into mind when someone in the neighborhood gets shot, is you."

Murphy's mouth lifted in a slight curve. "I'm flattered."

Stokes called Detective Gavin earlier and had the entire investigator's report faxed to him from upstairs. He picked it up from the table. "It says here that you were arrested last week for armed robbery. Two weeks before that, you were arrested for disorderly conduct when you attempted to castrate that Mexican kid that moved into town. Now, you're suspect in a shooting behind Hargrave's Deli." Stokes threw the file on the table. "Do you ever give up?" He asked. "Are you always innocent? What? Trouble just follows you around, Murphy?"

Murphy now leaned back in his chair, one long leg stretched out before him. No matter what an asshole this Stokes was, he always liked him for some reason. "Listen, Detective," he said, smiling. "You might as well put me away now and throw away the keys. I don't know what makes me so infatuated with guns. I don't know why I'm always for the underdog and the first one in on the scene when there's trouble. I can't figure it out either. But, seriously, it's like I'm drawn to it all like a magnet. You know?" He stood up. "I'm not so sure that I'm not going to do something that grave someday." He shook his head. "I'm really not so sure, Detective."

"Great!" Stokes said, slapping at his forehead. "I've got a lunatic on my hands."

But Murphy looked straight into Stokes' eyes. "I'm serious, Detective Stokes. I'm really serious. I love guns. I love guns. I'm worried about it myself," he sat back down. "So what do I do?"

"Ya lay low, kid, and you stop thinking about it. That's what you do. And you can't keep runnin your mouth off like this either. I know you. I know your folks. But someone, someday isn't going to know you and guess what? They're gonna lock you up when you talk like that. They're gonna fuckin lock you up. Now if you haven't anything else to say and you really didn't see anything last night, please go on home, Murphy." He picked up the file and opened the door. "Go on home and don't go out for a month, ya hear?"

The smile on Murphy's face spooked him.

***

It was late. Murphy was waiting for Alexandra. She should have been there by now. He looked at his watch and then he looked out the window onto the streets below. You never know who's out there anymore. You can't trust anyone. Everyone is out for his or her own skin and no one would help you for love or money. That's why he had so many guns. He had to protect himself. He had to protect those he loved.

There was a knock on the door, but he knew it wasn't Alexandra. She never knocked. She just let herself in with her own key.

"Who is it?" he yelled through the door. He was meaning to put in a peephole. This was dangerous, he thought. If that damn Johnny Grande didn't go berserk on him last year, he'd have a door for Christ sakes.

"Detective Stokes." The voice sounded strained, but Murphy had no doubt that it was Stokes.

"Comin'," he yelled, working the locks from the top to the bottom.

Like a tornado bursting through the door, Stokes was in before Murphy could invite him. "Here's the love of your life, Murphy," he yelled waving a gun in his face. "Isn't this what you love? The gun? Look at the gun all shiny and new. It's full of death. It delivers the same. Lookee here, Murphy. I've got her cold in my hand."

Murphy immediately saw what was happening. He had seen it three times just this year. Stokes' chip activated. Stokes was trippin as if he was on a bad blast of crack. He came to Murphy's because Murphy was the last thing on his mind before he activated. Therefore, he had to play out the part.

Murphy knew that Stokes didn't even have to have a past to go on back to. Just the activation of the chip alone could cause a temporary insanity. And sometimes, not so temporary.

He had to convince Stokes that he wasn't well and in the morning he would regret using that gun to kill him. He had to try, although at this point, Stokes' mind was reeling all on its own. He would be hard pressed to hear anything Murphy had to say to him.

"Detective Stokes, it's me, Tim Murphy." He walked towards him with his hands in the air showing that he was free of any weapons. "We're friends, Detective. Don't you remember? Today you told me that you knew my mother and father, remember? So why would you be comin' in here like this?" Jesus, sweet Jesus, he thought fearfully. "Put the gun down, Stokes," he pleaded. "Put it down."

Murphy knew he had been shot. He thought he heard the blast of the gun and he thought he felt a stab of ice shoot through him. But, maybe he was wrong. Maybe he was dreaming. And maybe, just maybe he wasn't dead.

Twenty-nine

By early afternoon, Kevin Black's whole outlook on life had changed. The fears he had were now pushed out of his mind and he felt lighter, happier. This feeling existed without the use of cocaine and although he was considered an addict, there was no urgency to take a blast. Kevin felt that Ashleigh Bennett was an angel from heaven who came down to save his life.

But that didn't stop him from carrying on his earlier plans. Plans that he made before Ashleigh came into his life. At four o'clock, he looked at his watch, which was an hour from now, the school would prepare for a protest. He had already informed the press of this, and the staff at TJJ Television. Some of the students were gathered in the cafeteria and the rest were on the football field in the back of the school.

His bowels tightened to think that these students paid heed to what he said and his suggestion of a protest turned into a reality. No one had ever listened to him before. He knew that it was a direct reflection of his changed personality. And soon, he was sure that all the students would feel the liberty he was feeling now. He made plans with Ashleigh to return and help them all out of their fears with the decoder.

Kevin would make sure everyone was warned of what this August Webster was capable of and then, after the protest . . .

after he felt that he did what he could to save all the Nathanial Black's out there . . . then he would go home to his parents.

Kevin took the small bag of white powder out of his shirt pocket and opened it. He scattered the substance about the school grounds and with his foot, mixed it in with the dirt. There would be no more highs. If he felt the urgency, he would fight it. He was finally a man.

From the corner of his eye he caught the glimpse of a van with large letters on it. The television crew was already here. This was it, he thought.

It didn't take long before all the students were rallying in the front of the school, each with a sign. DOWN WITH WEBSTER . . . NO MEMORY NO DEATH . . . LET US LIVE . . . THOUGHTS ARE PERSONAL . . .

Along with the students, the press and the cameras, were the police. They were calmly standing in front of their squad cars with Billy clubs in one hand and the other on their pistols.

Kevin beamed with pride. He couldn't believe that he was the sole one responsible for this turn out. He hadn't realized how many of his classmates hated Webster and harbored the same fears. He wished that Ashleigh could do the same for them as she had for him.

At that moment, as if to prove the truth in Kevin's words, Ashleigh appeared at the west end of the building, her back erect, her hair blowing loosely about her shoulders and the decoder in her hands.

Kevin grinned mischievously. This had been a good day.

Ashleigh's hands clasped the decoder in front of her. This would be a great accomplishment, she thought wearily, wishing David could be here to see this. But, if anything would help get him out of the mess he was in, this kind of publicity would.

She had discussed this with Patrick and he was as excited about it as she was. More so because he had intended the decoder to work only on people who had already been regressed. But, Ashleigh had detonated the boy's chip even before his eighteenth birthday. That meant that she was going against government regulation and could be severely punished for it.

But, he knew what was in the back of her head. She was out to save the young ones. He could tell how her mind was working. What were a few hundred souls next to the eight million people in the city? She could do them good this way. It would be a way to save their lives.

***

Ashleigh knew that the chance she was taking was extreme. She picked up a megaphone and began to speak. "Will you all please enter the school and meet me in the cafeteria. I have an important message for you. . . ."

Without a word, which was unusual for a crowd of teenagers this size, seemingly knowing the importance of what she intended to say, they made their way, in an orderly fashion, into the building.

It didn't take but a few minutes for her to have them seated and quiet.

"My name is Ashleigh Bennett, and I'm here to help you all," she began. "I have to put my trust in you because I don't believe you would be here if we weren't on the same side. You should all be here in protest of Webster's tactics and regressions."

The crowd cheered briefly and then quieted to hear more.

"The chance I'm taking in being here is grave. It is punishable by law. I hope you will spare me such a terrible ordeal and stand behind me. As you leave this room to protest, your chip will be detonated, much like a bomb is. You will never have to suffer the pain that some of your family and friends are suffering. Unfortunately, I can't help them all."

Kevin stood up and walked to Ashleigh's side. "Miss Bennett is the counselor for the August Webster Center." The crowd began to jeer. Kevin lifted his hands and opened them. "Wait," he yelled. "Wait . . ."

Once again, they quieted down. "Miss Bennett and August Webster have never met. She was just assigned his Center to do the counseling for the city. That's how she got the goods on the man, guys. She's on our side." Kevin sat at the edge of one of the long lunchroom tables.

"You all know who I am. I'm Kevin Black. I'm the guy you laughed at and stayed away from, unless you're a junkie. Now I'm your best friend." He paused for a few moments. "You all knew my brother, Nat, and you've all heard that he killed himself. Webster was the reason." He looked around and tried to make eye-to-eye contact with each one of them. It was important that they feel his pain. That they believe in him. "I know I've never proven anything to you other than I'm a junkie and a drop out. Believe me, I'm not anymore. As of today, my chip has been detonated. I'm totally independent of it." His eyes grew wet so that the room began to blur and he had to squeeze them shut in order to focus again. "So independent, in fact, that I'm coming back to school and I'm going somewhere in life," he looked at Ashleigh. "Thanks to this woman."

Ashleigh, her eyes down, was glad that she had made this decision. It was her turn to give them instructions and hope that they would stand by her. "You all must be regressed when you're eighteen. Some of you are very close to that point in time." She swallowed hard. "When you're time comes, you will not be able to automatically go back to your other lives, if any, so you'll have to fake it." She looked at Kevin and smiled. "The only thing I ask of you, for your own protection, is that you never say you're a new soul. Make up some former life by reading about someone in history. Study his or her habits and dialect and know what you're talking about before you make your appointment."

Ashleigh's voice began to quiver as she noticed Patrick standing in the door of the lunchroom. It was time to begin, she thought. Our hour is near.

"That's all I have to say to you, kids. Please leave in the same orderly fashion that you arrived in. And thank you." She looked at Kevin and took his hand. "Thank you for your support, Kevin."

As the students left the room, Ashleigh and Patrick and even

Kevin, with David's decoder, began to detonate their chips. They felt good. The young people had a second chance.

"They're going to march, you know," Kevin said, as the three of them walked out of the building.

Ashleigh looked surprised. "March? I thought they were going to protest right here at the school."

Kevin laughed. "No. We're going to march right down to the Webster Center and protest right in front of it."

"You'll cause a riot, Kevin. It won't be just a march."

Patrick looked at Kevin and frowned. "Do you think this is wise, son. We want the media here, of course. We need the publicity. But to cause a riot would be ludicrous. People could get hurt." He stopped walking and looked directly at Kevin. "I wish you'd think about this and reconsider."

Kevin laughed. "No chance, man."

Thirty

Webster couldn't take his eyes off the shadowy forms that were moving toward him. Don't let fear take you, he said to himself. Don't let them see you with your guard down.

He wasn't particularly found of the chain of events that had occurred during week. First the robbery; then the report of the robbery in the paper; and now this. Had he been a weaker man, this would have taken its toll.

He stood at the window of his office and watched as they marched their way down East 56th Street. He had an instinct, even though it could have been any one of a number of reasons why they were coming this way, he knew that they were coming for him.

The faces were getting larger as the bodies got closer. Teenagers. They were just young people, he noticed. They had long hair, even the boys, and odd apparel. What did they want with him?

He quickly put on his suit jacket, straightened his tie and went from his office to the front foyer. Opening the doors, he stepped out on the top stair and faced his enemy.

"Stop right there!" he yelled. But there was no authority in his voice, just stark fear. He looked around him. They were coming from everywhere. His heart was hammering, as was his head. He pictured a vice gripping at his temples squeezing until the top of his head exploded in relief. At this moment he would have wished for that vice. He would have wished for anything that would relieve him of the impending danger and pain that he felt coming on.

He ducked back into the building. His files. They were after his files. *That Patrick Tuchman will pay for this, whoever he is.* And, whoever he was, Webster felt that he was exceedingly close. He could almost feel the man's breath against his face.

"This is a mistake, Ash," Patrick said. "The kids shouldn't be here protesting. It could land them in jail."

"Which one of us is going to tell them that, Pat?" she replied. "Look at their faces. They're determined young people. They've found a secret, I'm afraid."

"What secret?"

"That there's strength in numbers, Pat," she answered. "The secret to life."

Patrick looked at her in disbelief. "Do you have any idea what their intentions are?"

"No more than you do. But, you can be sure that they're not going to stop until they've said their piece."

Finally, the students did stop walking and held up their signs. One voice in particular sang out in chant. The others followed. "PLEASE HEAR US . . . PLEASE HEAR US . . . PLEASE HEAR US . . ."

The news team began to question the students one at a time. They seemed to be orderly. They seemed to be unionized, until August Webster showed his face again.

"What do you want with me?" he screamed from the door. "Get out of here. I've called the police."

"You can't do anything, Webster," a young female voice yelled back. "We're within our legal rights."

"You're disturbing my practice!" he yelled.

"Good," another voice yelled, a young male this time.

Webster shook his fist at the crowd of students. He implored the older man in the front of the line to talk to them and have them break this up before someone got hurt. He had no idea that he was pleading with Patrick Tuchman.

Patrick began to speak. There was no forethought on his actions. It seemed as if the words just seem to fall out of his mouth. "Dr. Webster, it is you who is at fault. You have not been following government law. You punish your people. You torture your people and ultimately lead them to suicide, if you don't kill them yourself first."

Webster was astounded. How could they know? Where could they have gotten this information? His mind went fleetingly to his missing files, but he dismissed that thought. "You have to prove what you're saying, young man."

"We can. We have solid proof. Why don't you just give yourself up and tell the authorities all of it. They will help you. There are people out there to help you."

Webster's eyes squinted in rage. "I don't need help! I help people!"

Suddenly, a gust of wind blew in from the Hudson, and the sky opened up to unexpected torrential rains.

"Leave now!" Webster yelled, grateful for this act of God, not that he ever believed in a supreme being. "Leave now and I will not press charges against you all."

***

Once again the students chanted. "NEW SOULS MUST LIVE . . . OLD SOULS MUST NOT REMEMBER . . . NEW SOULS MUST LIVE . . . OLD SOULS MUST NOT REMEMBER . . ."

The noise of the chanting brought with it a more severe headache. Webster squeezed his eyes closed and tried to control the sickness that was threatening to rise in his throat. He once more went back into his building, raced back to his office and locked the door behind him.

He could see his prescription bottle on the sink of the bathroom and he quickly went for it, knowing that within minutes after taking his pills, he would be able to think again.

His hands shook badly as he tried to pry the cap off. "Damn

safety caps," he muttered as he wrenched it free from the bottle. Downing two pills, he rested against the sink and breathed in deeply. And then he cried. He cried for a good long time, as wracking sobs forced him to hold onto the sink. And as quickly as the tears came, they went, and he composed himself, as if nothing had happened at all.

Webster knew that it would take a few minutes for the pills to work, but subconsciously, knowing he had taken them was enough for him to begin feeling better. He gathered his personal files, stuffed them in his briefcase and locked his doors. There was nothing more he could do here.

He looked out the back window for signs of students. They were all in the front. If he could get out the back door, move quickly behind the buildings, he could possibly make it to the corner and grab a cab home. He needed rest. He didn't want to know the outcome of this protest anyway.

The rain felt good against his face and head as he weaved his way between the buildings behind his own. Some of the structures jutted out further in the back than the others, which meant that he had to walk around buildings instead of in a straight line. Once at the corner, he hailed a taxi. As he got in the cab, he ignored the look of pain on his face through the window, and the tears that mingled in with the rain. And as he passed his building and watched the looks of hate on the student's faces, he knew he had to make some plans. He had to make some excuses. He had to make some sense to the government. For surely he would be investigated. Surely this protest had kindled their appetites a little.

It was insane. A few blocks away people were gathering in unison holding up signs and yelling some unintelligible garble. They didn't know what they were doing. They didn't know how serious this game was that they were playing. He had all the control. Not them. He was the one who called the shots. Not them. This new world was nothing like the old world. People were afraid then. Children never spoke up. Cities never fought back the way they do today.

August Webster realized then that he was a product of the

new world. He realized then that he belonged in the past where he was the happiest.

Thirty-one

> A protest march in front of the August Webster Regression Center yesterday afternoon, in New York City, sparked an investigation from the state. Dr. Webster was unavailable for comment. Here are scenes from that protest walk now...

Tony Antonelli slammed his fists on the top of his television set as he watched the six a.m. news. He watched as the students rallied with signs and chants.

Obviously, there was someone else in the city concerned with Webster's tactics besides David Wilder.

Antonelli paced back and forth in his small Washington apartment. He was alone. His wife was an airline stewardess and away for a few days, but Antonelli didn't mind being alone. In fact, he enjoyed it.

He was in deep thought as he sipped at his coffee. Maybe there was something to this New York center after all. Maybe he shouldn't have doubted Wilder so vehemently.

But, there was something about that man that really pissed

him off. He made an appointment, showed up precisely on time and then, like some hot shot lawyer, came up with all that shit about the center.

Antonelli had to admit that at the end, he was beginning to feel sorry for the sap. But Antonelli never goes back on his word. He wouldn't drop the charges.

Now, things may be different. He may have no choice but to drop . . .

"Antonelli, are you in there?" It was Ed Marcetti, an investigator on the night shift.

Antonelli opened the door to a dark haired man in a rain jacket and hat. "Marcetti, what are *you* doing here. I thought you were on nights."

Marcetti pushed his way into the apartment. "Yea. Yea, I usually am, but this Wilder case is bugging me."

Antonelli didn't know what it was about the man that reminded him of *Columbo*, an old detective series that shows even now sometimes, late at night. The man was much smarter than he acted and once or twice you got fooled by his innocent way. "How did you get involved, Ed?"

"I have a niece in the city of Manhattan. She's going through a bad time of it." He shook his head and puffed on an unlit cigar. "You know, Antonelli, the trouble she's having came about right after her session with Webster." Another puff. "And I know it's true because she's my favorite. And to be a favorite niece, Antonelli, she had to be special. She had to love to laugh and she had to have some kind of love for life. But, that all ended in regression."

Antonelli didn't answer. Instead, he followed Marcetti into the living room and sat down.

"It's my sister's kid, Antonelli. You understand how it is. You want to protect them. Father's a loser. You'll find him in the bowery somewhere slummin'." He looked out the window at the passing cars. "Now, it looks as if she's gonna lose her kid, too."

Antonelli rested his head on the back of the couch and looked up at the ceiling. "How long you been suspecting Webster, Ed?"

he asked.

"Couple months."

"Why haven't you said something?"

Marcetti shrugged. "I never say nothin' until I've got proof." He put his hands in his pocket and turned to face Antonelli. "I'd say now, it's time to talk."

Antonelli covered his face with his hands and rubbed at his tired red eyes. "You know that I'm directly involved with this case, don't you Ed?" he asked.

Marcetti nodded. "Word gets out, Tony."

Antonelli exhaled loudly. "Well then you know that I'm directly responsible for putting that young David Wilder in the can."

Again, Marcetti nodded. "What are you going to do about that Tony?"

Antonelli shook his head. "I don't know. Wilder comes into my office the other day and starts charging this center with all kinds of things. Things that I should have been on top of. I read the files he had prepared and as soon as I read the first page, I didn't bother reading any more. I couldn't let him show me up. It was my job that was on the line."

Marcetti smiled. "So, it's your ego that keeps young Wilder in the can, huh?"

"My ego and my pride."

"Drop the charges, Tony. Don't be a foolish old man."

"I'll look like a fool if I do, Ed."

"You look more like a fool if you don't. Come on," he urged. "Be a hero to the kid."

Antonelli reached his hand out and picked up the phone.

***

David Wilder lay on his cot in the county jail. He thought about Ashleigh and how he wanted to hold her. He thought about Patrick and decided that he had no better friend. And then, he made the promises all humans make when frightened or cornered. He promised to show them how he felt. He promised to never take their friendship for granted.

Vick had told him the news about the protest march in front of Webster's center. "Now, they should at least investigate further about what you have come here to tell 'em," Vick said.

But, after a while, it looked as if they had just forgotten about him. Not one more word was said.

A little past three o'clock that afternoon, David could hear keys jingle in his dreams. He woke up to hear a door opening and Vick telling him he was free to go.

"You can go now, Dr. Wilder. You're free." Vick said, shaking him. "You're a free man."

Suddenly, as if shocked by an electrical current, David jumped up from his cot to face Vick. It wasn't a dream. He was being released.

"The judge must have read the files. He must have believed what I had to say," he told Vick.

Vick shook his head. "No, my man. It wasn't the judge that freed you, it was Mr. Antonelli. He dropped all charges against you."

David was leery. "Why?" he asked. "What's in it for him?"

Vick looked at him and grew serious all of a sudden. Then, without a moment's hesitation, he spoke as if he knew the man better than anyone else. "His conscience, Dr. Wilder. His conscience finally gave out."

***

"I'm sorry sir, but the next plane to Kennedy doesn't leave for another hour. There's been a delay."

It had taken David one hour, after he was released, to get to the hotel, pack and head for the airport. Now, there was a delay in his schedule. How perfectly fantastic, he thought.

He turned from the ticket counter, glanced at his watch and sighed. He looked around. Lockers to the right, vending machines to the left, baggage claim areas down the escalators, and small cafes and gift shops surrounding everything. The thought of spending another hour in Washington was revolting.

He had far too much to do.

Thirty-two

Patrick Tuchman had a premonition. He wasn't clairvoyant, and maybe this was just a gut feeling, but it was going to happen. He knew it. He tried to pinpoint just what it was that was going to happen to him tonight, but he couldn't. He only knew that it wasn't going to be good. Even his apartment gave way to an eerie feeling, unlike the warm, informality it usually held.

He was good on premonition. Always had been. And that's what scared him the most. Sometimes he would try to push it out of his mind and immediately replace it with other thoughts. But, it never once worked. When he felt something was on the verge of happening, no matter where he took the feeling, and no matter how he replaced it with other thoughts, it happened. It hovered close to him until he had no choice but to notice. And now, that feeling was back.

When he was a kid, he remembered having the feelings that someone was walking behind him when he was on his way home in the darkness. He was just a kid, maybe twelve or thirteen. This was the age when a man felt like a man, but couldn't hide the many emotions in him that were still a little boy . . . like fear.

Fear. The number one feeling that pushes a man back to the womb where he is protected and safe.

Where most kids do make it home and find there is absolutely no one behind them, Patrick was different. There was always someone behind him when he had these feelings . . . some gang member who was teasing him or some old drunk that tried to scare him into giving up his money. Whatever the situation, the premonitions were always accurate. Not almost always, Patrick was sure to remind himself, but *always* accurate.

It wasn't just a feeling that something, anything, was going to happen. It was a feeling of impending death to Patrick himself. This time, the feeling was so pungent he couldn't escape it. And it was close. It was close enough to bite him.

The phone rang. He hesitated to answer it. But the repeated ringing of the person who wouldn't give up, urged him to pick up the receiver.

"Patrick?" It was Ashleigh.

"Oh, Ashleigh. Thank God it's you."

"Is something wrong?" she asked. His relief was so visible to her that her heart started hammering in her chest. Had he heard something about David in just the short time that she had spoken to him?

"Nothing I can't handle," he lied.

"Well, I just wanted you to know that I called Washington a little while ago to ask how David was and they said he was released a couple hours ago. Have you heard anything since?"

Patrick voice perked up. "No. This is the first news I've gotten. Good God, Ash, that's great! And, if you know David, he's on his way home already."

Ashleigh laughed. "I hope so." Things were quiet for a few moments, then . . . "Patrick, why don't you tell me what's on your mind."

"Why don't you come over for a cup of coffee, Ash? It's nothing important. Just a premonition. A feeling that something's going to happen, and yet, I can't put my finger on."

Ashleigh closed her eyes. She hated premonitions, especially bad ones. "I'll be right over, Pat. Sit tight."

"Thanks." They hung up, but Patrick didn't feel any better.

In fact, considering how he felt, he wondered if it was smart asking Ashleigh to come over. Was he putting her in any danger?

Patrick went to the door and locked it securely. He then went to his desk to secure the duplicate files that David had taken with him.

"Patrick?"

He jumped, spilling the contents of two of the files on the floor. Turning around to where the voice came from, he saw nothing. There was no one there.

"This is the craziest . . ." Patrick's heart began to hammer within the walls of his chest. There was someone in the apartment with him. Someone calling out his name.

Patrick checked out the only other room in the house. The bathroom. He didn't have a bedroom. The apartment was an efficiency. There was no one there. He picked up his straight razor and went slowly back into the living room, keeping his ears pealed for the slightest noise.

"Hello, Patrick." The tall man standing in his living room smiled widely, exposing a great deal of teeth, most of them black with rot. "Webster sends his regards."

All the paranoid feelings that had been going on in Patrick's mind had suddenly surfaced. He had been right all along. All his feelings had been accurate. For now, standing in front of him was a man he had never seen before.

Patrick tried in vain to speak, but the words were locked in his throat. He watched as the tall man walked toward him. Instinctively, he knew that the man was concealing a gun.

"Please excuse the intrusion," the man said as though he had potatoes in his mouth. "But Webster hired me for this evening." He grinned again, this time, more in a sneer that gratefully didn't show so many teeth. "Otherwise, I would have been out to dinner with my girl."

"What do you want?" Patrick finally managed.

"Me?" the stranger said, pointing to himself. "I don't want a thing, friend. It's my boss. He wants you, and if I'm ever going to get to dinner, I'd better get you for him."

"But why? I don't even know August Webster."

"For someone who doesn't know anyone, you leave your pens in awful strange places."

That stopped Patrick in his place. "My pen . . ." he whispered.

"Yeah, you're pen. Hellava spot to leave it, eh? Brought you some trouble with the old man, I guess." He put his hands in his pockets and stood with most of his weight on one leg. "You see, the man don't like anyone in his office." He grinned. "It's a personal thing, you know?"

Patrick's mind reeled. This was impossible. What was happening to him? The stranger then grabbed at Patrick's hands and squeezed the razor from them, cutting deeply into Patrick's palms. Patrick was almost frozen in horror. But something in him told him to fight back.

Patrick grabbed at the stranger's face, tearing the flesh with his fingernails and leaving deep grooves along the cheeks. His first thoughts were that he was fighting like a woman, that the stranger was too strong.

Feeling a cool object against his head, Patrick felt his guard go done, almost as if he had given up. It was a gun, and it was pointed to the right temple. *Oh, God no*, he thought as he heard the crack of the stranger's knuckle when he applied pressure to the trigger. *Oh, God no . . .*

***

The door was opened about three inches when Ashleigh arrived. "Patrick?" she called from the hall, knocking softly. "Are you in there?"

The silence from the apartment was deafening. Ashleigh pushed the door with the tips of her fingers until it opened all the way. There on the floor was Patrick. His eyes were opened and a last look of horror was still on his face.

Stiffling a cry, Ashleigh walked around him. "Patrick? This isn't funny," she said in a quivering voice. "Get up. Please!" The tears came. "Please get up." She moved around to his desk and picked up the receiver of the phone, dialing 911. "My friend has committed suicide," she said calmly. "Please send someone." Then, she numbly sat down and waited.

Once or twice she glanced at Patrick. But there was too much blood. "Poor Pat," she whispered.

She didn't look for a suicide note. She stopped crying. Simply because none of those things would matter anyway.

Thirty-three

George and Ginny Gere

Case number 45

George Gere promised his wife Ginny a trip to Rome, and a trip to Rome was what he gave her. It was something that both of them would not soon forget. And now, with just three more days left of their vacation, George and Ginny promised themselves they would rent a car and tour Florence and Naples on their own. No more public tours.

On the morning of their road trip, George became concerned because he didn't understand most of the road signs that were on the highway. There were many, and they were so different from those in the States that he wasn't sure he would be able to properly drive the three to four hours from Rome to Naples without causing some confusion to himself and chaos to the others on the road that day. Besides, there was something compelling him to do otherwise. "I'm going to see if we can take some scenic routes," he told Ginny. "That way, it won't be boring and we'll be able to see some of the countryside, the way they really live here."

Ginny made him promise that he would get back on the highway if he had more trouble going through the towns than he had on the highway.

The sky was a perfect gray. It made the countryside seem even more historic and quaint. They marveled at the way people were still living, even in these days of modern convenience. There was farmland as far as the eye could see. Olive trees with nets swimming under them to catch the ripe, freshly fallen olives. There were grapevines, and sheep and goats covering the pastures, devouring the land's green grass and vegetation.

George felt as though he belonged here, especially in this particular little town of Pito' which bordered on two sides of other towns with similar surroundings.

Suddenly, the clouds grew thicker and George knew they were approaching a storm. The gray and bluish clouds were moving fast and the wind whipped up around them, causing debris to scatter along the streets and onto the car and windshield.

Looking over to warn Ginny to keep her window closed, he noticed that she was sleeping through all this beauty and now, she would sleep through what promised to be a torrential thunderstorm. Lucky Ginny, he thought. He wasn't too thrilled to be driving through it.

George felt cold. Although the weather was climbing to the eighties by mid morning, he was becoming chilled to the bone. And it grew worse. By the time he had gone another two miles, he knew that he was going to be forced to stop and throw the rough old horsehair blanket that someone had left in the back seat of the car, around his shoulders. He couldn't stop shivering as he reached back to retrieve the nasty thing.

The chill was like having a fever climb to 104 degrees, except, without the body aches that usually accompanied it. He tried to call to his wife, but somehow couldn't open his mouth, and he knew full well there was something seriously wrong with him. Yet, he kept going. Somehow he couldn't stop driving, and it seemed that whatever had gotten a hold of him at this particular moment, didn't even allow him to consider stopping the car. George could hear crying. Pathetic sobs that hit him square in the heart. He tried to look from side to side to see who it was that was in such great mental pain, for he was sure it could not be physical. The torment was ripping from the very soul of the victim. But, he couldn't move his head. He just kept driving.

Suddenly, he felt heat on his face and light that actually hurt his eyes. He heard a voice in the distance calling his name.

"George?" Someone was banging on him and screaming his name.

"George! What's wrong? George!"

They were now leaving Pito' and the car swerved to the side of the road and came to a dead stop.

It was Ginny's hand shaking his arm that woke him. He fought his way back to consciousness and yet, he still couldn't speak. He could see the dashboard and the little amber light that made him raise his eyebrows. He had been driving for twenty-five minutes and didn't even realize it.

"George, you were crying so hard I didn't know what was wrong with you. Are you okay?"

Finally finding his voice, George also found his face wet with tears. And then he remembered. He remembered things he didn't understand outside of the town. He had to go back.

"I died here, Ginny."

"What?"

"It was in the sixteen hundreds, Ginny. My name was Rocco Federico. I had a wife and three children who all died from Diphtheria. I ended my own life when my last little boy died." He pointed back to the town. "That's where I will find my grave and I'm going back to find it."

Ginny couldn't speak for a moment. "What are you talking about, honey?" she asked softly, suddenly afraid that she would find out they were abducted and on another planet.

"I died here. I saw it all. I don't know how, but I just know it." He slammed his hand on the wheel. "I just know it, Gin."

Turning the car around, Ginny slunked down in the seat and didn't say a word. He would play this out no matter what she said, so she said nothing.

"I need to ask someone about Rocco Federico, Gin. Someone has to know about him."

Patronizing him, she said, "But you don't know how long ago he lived."

"He lived," he stated blatantly. "That's all I need to know." He put his foot to the pedal as though he were in a tremendous hurry. "Someone has to know who he was. There are libraries, news articles, legend, everything and anything will do right now."

The scenery was new to him since he hadn't seen it the first time he came through. It was right out of the history books. There were even some outhouses and definitely plaque houses. Every plaque house had a 'plaque' on the outside with the date it was built. There were many, many of these homes built in the sixteen hundreds. More than three hundred years ago. Surely there was information on these houses. There would be a history to all of them and he was meaning to find out.

George couldn't believe what he was saying. Maybe in the morning he would feel absolutely foolish about what he was doing. And he suddenly wished that Ginny were not with him at all. That way, he could keep the whole incident from her, if this were to be a fruitless search. But now she was here, and she was just as sucked into this as he was. The only thing he could do was follow the instinct through.

There was an old man. A very old man smoking a cigar just outside a grocery store. George looked at Ginny.

"Surely you don't think that this man would remember Rocco, George. He's old, but come on!"

George closed his eyes briefly. "You can't be serious yourself, Gin. You really don't believe that I'm even entertaining that notion, do you?"

Ginny shrugged. "I really don't know what to believe anymore, George."

Pulling over to the side of the road, they sat there for a few minutes. It was obvious that he was trying to collect his thoughts and figure out a way to ask about Rocco without looking absolutely ridiculous.

The old man eyed him suspiciously. Neither George or Ginny could speak a word of Italian, but they were hoping to meet someone who could at least communicate with them and possibly translate.

"Hello," George said, extending his hand to the old man. "My name is George." He pointed to himself, then to Ginny and said, "And this is my wife, Ginny. We are looking for the Federico family."

The old man's eyes brightened. "Ah, Federico. Si, si. Federico."

George and Ginny exchanged glances. "I'm looking for Federico. Rocco Federico who lived in the 1600's."

Just then, a young woman came up from behind the old man. "Papa?"

The old man spoke just enough Italian for his daughter to understand and just enough for the Gere's not to.

"Pardon my father," the young woman said with barely a trace of an accent. "He is very much part of the old school. It isn't often that we have such glamorous visitors from America in our piazza." She smiled. "You must forgive his rudeness." She extended her hand. "My name is Mary Matola. This is my papa, Vincent Matola," she said, looking at the both of them alternately. "And you?"

George shook her hand. "George and Ginny Gere," he said with relief. "We are looking for any information on an old family named Federico. Particularly a Rocco Federico. He was born in the 1600's, and if you have any history books or libraries, we would be interested in searching for this family's background."

The young woman shook her head. "I'm afraid not, Mr. Gere. We have no schools in this piazza, nor do we have libraries. We are mainly comprised of elderly people. I'm only here checking up on my father."

"Sort of like exiling them to an island," Ginny mumbled.

Mary smiled softly. "That's probably just what it looks like, and it probably has a lot of truth to it. But we find them much happier this way. They play cards and bocci ball." She nodded. "It's better for them this way."

"So where would I look?" he asked.

"Probably a couple of piazzas over. Maybe thirty miles or so." She turned and pulled her father's jacket closed. "On second thought," she said. "There's a very old cemetery way in back of the church property. You may find what you're looking for in there, or at least some familia. I can't promise you, but it's worth a try, no?"

Ginny thanked her. "Yes. Yes it's worth a try." She pulled on George's arm. "Come on dear," she said. "Let's go check out the cemetery."

***

It wasn't hard to find. Right on Caruso Drive and left on Meglio Courtyard. There was a church. A church that neither one of them had ever seen the likes of before. It was old. There was no question about that. But, it was absolutely magnificent.

The grass around the church was damp and soft and a little difficult to maneuver through. But they made their way through to the historical cemetery.

Ginny took one side of the small square plot of land and George walked around the other side. Neither knew which one of them was feeling more foolish. But they would have always wondered what brought on such a dramatic exit out of the little city.

Ginny glanced over at George, just to check on him. *Where is he?* Her heart began pounding in her chest, threatening to cut off any air that was left from her sudden fear. "George?" She then heard the cries. Oh no, she thought. He found his own grave. How difficult this must be for him. How could she doubt it? They had never been to Italy before. They had never even heard the name Rocco Federico. How then, could this be a figment of his imagination?

She tripped twice, trying to get to him. But when she did, she herself couldn't believe what was before her.

George was kneeling in front of a grave that someone had etched with a primitive object:

> Here lies Rocco Federico
> Who took his own life.
> He now joins his family,
> Three children and a wife.
> Born 1636 - Died 1665

Right next to that grave were four smaller ones. Rocco's wife, Emelia rested in one, and the three in front of it belonged to their three children, all succumbed to Diphtheria.

"I'm so sorry, George," Ginny said touching his shoulder.

"Why?" he replied sadly. "In a way, this is so incredible. How it all came to me and how I was lead to this site. Now I wonder how many times I lived before. I wonder why it is that I didn't feel the transition in these lives, or if I did, why it is that I was not allowed to remember it." He pushed himself up from the ground. "I'm not sad, Gin." George looked at her. "What are you doing?" he asked.

Ginny was aiming a camera at the grave. "I'm going to take a picture for you to remember this."

"I'll remember it Ginny. I don't want a picture, and I don't want to speak of this again. This belongs only to us. No one else." He laughed as he put his arms around her shoulders and guided her back to the car. "Besides, who in the world would believe us?"

Thirty-four

David had never been to the city morgue. It just wasn't a place he desired to be. Especially having to identify his best friend's body.

He pushed through the scratched and dull metal doors that led to the storage room . . . the refrigeration area. There he saw empty gurneys. Some with blood on them, and some with bodies on them. He assumed that Patrick was one of the bodies ready to go into the refrigerated box that was built into the wall.

The atmosphere was as repulsive as his mind had told him it would be on the drive over here. The smell of antiseptic and body fluid made it difficult for David to breathe.

For a few minutes, he stood in the holding room reflecting on the unanticipated quickness of Patrick's death. Thoughts about what his friend was thinking at the moment of his demise filtered through his mind. Those thoughts bothered him infinitely.

In a shabby office sat the morgue worker.

"I came to identify a body," David said to the fat, hairy man. His white jacket was full of blood and he was still wearing his plastic hat and gloves. But, what upset David more was the fact that the man was chewing on a salami sandwich.

"What's his name?" he asked with a mouth full of food.

"Patrick Tuchman," David replied bitterly. Somehow it reduced Patrick to just a slab of meat by the disrespect this man showed to the dead.

David pointed to the half-eaten sandwich that lay on the desk. "How can you do that?" he asked, shaking his head.

"Do what?"

"Eat with your gloves on. Didn't you just finish up on a body?"

The man looked at him with slanted eyes and a curled upper lip. "So? I washed them. What's it to you?"

David's anger was building. "My best friend is in there," he said pointing to the body room. "I'd like for there to be a little respect for him."

The man put his hands on the desk and leaned toward David. "So there'll be respect for him at the funeral parlor. You ain't got no rights comin' in here and shootin' off your big mouth."

For the second time in a week, David was about to lunge at someone, but thought twice about it. The last time he reacted that way, he ended up in the can.

"Look," David said, finally. "I don't want any trouble. I'm just upset. I just want to identify my friend's body and get out of here."

The man grunted, belched, and waddled toward the door. "Follow me," he said.

David followed him through the double swinging door into the holding room. The gurney that he had assumed was the one Patrick occupied was the one that he walked to. He could see the stamp that was placed on the bottom of his feet identifying him. At one time, they used to tag the toes. Now, the body went to his grave with a stamp. David smiled to himself. Almost like Patrick was being mailed to his final reward.

Patrick was a dusky bluish gray by now. His eyes were closed, thankfully. There was a large piece of gauze covering one whole side of his face and head.

"That's where the bullet entered," the man said. He looked at David with the first show of sympathy on his face. "What made the poor sucker do this, anyway?" he asked.

David shrugged. "I can't tell you, pal. I guess one never knows what goes on in the mind of another. Not even your best friend."

The man nodded. "You know him?"

David knew that he had to ask that question. He was here to identify. "Yes," he whispered, his eyes welling up with tears. "He's Patrick Tuchman . . . And he didn't even wait for me to say good-bye."

***

You could have cut the tension in the air with a knife that evening.

Ashleigh and David sat in the lounge chair on the terrace in her apartment. It was a cool evening and the smell of jasmine floated up to their nostrils as they reclined in each other's arms.

"This is one of the worst times in my life," David said. "Even more so than when my mom and brother died. I couldn't have done anything to prevent that. I felt sad, not guilty."

Ashleigh was resting against his chest, her hair fanned out around her. "You couldn't have done anything to prevent this, David. It was what he wanted and what he intended to do." She looked up into the stars. "God only knows how long he had been planning it."

He leaned over and kissed the bridge of her nose, and as she arched toward him, the scent of her perfumed body beckoned to him.

She was wearing a white, short sleeve angora sweater with a low front. He slipped his fingers down beneath her breasts and felt them welcome him. His entire body shivered with passion. His voice was a hoarse whisper as he told her he loved her. This time, meaning to show her.

Swooping her up, he carried her to her bedroom. Pulling the sweater over her head, he caressed her breasts with his lips. Her body felt like satin beneath his own, and quickly and intently, they rode the waves of pleasure together.

***

David made preparations at the Thornton Funeral Parlor for Patrick's burial. For some reason, the little that was left of his family encouraged him to do so.

That afternoon, the funeral director was to send his men to the hospital morgue and pick his body up for embalming. They would hold a service in the morning and bury him in the Washington Cemetery in Brooklyn where he was born.

As David left the funeral parlor, Ashleigh paged him. He stopped at a nearby phone booth and called her. "What's up, honey?" he asked.

"David. Just got a call from the hospital. They want you to stop by there as soon as you can."

David was confused. "Why? Did they tell you why, Ash?"

"Uh uh. They just asked that you be there."

He could hear ice jingle in a glass and he pictured her sipping her usual ice tea. "Want to meet me there? I'll head over there now."

Ashleigh gulped down a mouthful. "Sure. I'll meet you there in half an hour."

When he hung the phone up, his eagerness got the best of him, and he jumped in the car and raced to the hospital. Irrationally, the thought crossed his mind that Patrick wasn't really dead. That it had all been a terrible mistake. But, knowing that wasn't the case, he tried to reason other things out. Like what had he to do with anything the hospital might have found out? Or why call him instead of his family with any other news?

He fought traffic all the way, weaving in and out of cars and speeding up at yellow lights. The reflection on the glass of the streetlights appeared as diamonds along the roads. He couldn't even imagine what it was like when the bulbs hung on a tall pole. It certainly couldn't have provided the cars with much lighting. Now they were encased flush with the road, and lined the streets brilliantly.

He made a right hand turn into the hospital parking lot and

found a space at the end of the third row near the emergency room. The morgue was one flight down from emergency.

Ashleigh was already there when he arrived. She must have been already out the door after they spoke. "Hi!" she whispered. "They'll be right out. But," she looked toward the double metal doors of the body room. "I don't think they want me around for this. They keep asking for only you."

David nodded, somehow feeling flattered by this. "Don't worry. I'll take care of that, Ash. We're partners. They want to talk to me? Then they talk to you too."

Ashleigh nodded and smiled.

The same fat man with the plastic gloves and cap came heavily through the doors. He gestured to David to take a seat against the wall, and he eyed Ashleigh suspiciously.

"This is my associate," David quickly said, reading his expression. "She stays."

"Very well," the fat man grumbled. He cleared his throat. "I have some information that might be valuable to you," he said gruffly, but not much above a whisper. "I understand you were working on the August Webster investigation."

David and Ashleigh exchanged glances. "We weren't aware there *was* an investigation."

"Well, since the protest, he's been under some heavy scrutiny." Then, he waved his hand as if to dismiss that part of the conversation and get onto the other, more interesting stuff. "Anyway, your friend didn't commit suicide," he said matter of factly, as if it was a common everyday part of life.

David grabbed at Ashleigh's hand. "I knew it," he murmured.

The fat man continued despite the display of emotion he witnessed. "The man was shot in the right temple. Now, as far as I figure, Dr. Tuchman was left-handed. Am I correct?"

Ashleigh looked at David and winced as if trying to remember. "Yes! Yes!" she said, excitedly. "He was left handed!"

"We always pushed him out of the way when we ate because his elbow would be in our way," David added.

"S'far as I can see, the man would have to be a contortionist to get his hand whipped around to shoot himself in the right side of the head," the fat man said. "And judging from the angle and everything else I find, I'd stake my life on this case being a homicide."

David stood up and ran his fingers through his hair. "I hope you're sure, Mr . . ." Funny thing. He'd never got the fat man's name.

"Sullivan. Johnny Sullivan," the man said extending his hand.

David looked at the plastic wrapped hand and bile rose to his throat. Swallowing hard, he felt obligated to grasp it. "Thank you Dr. Sullivan. Again, I hope what you say is true. I . . ."

"Young man," the fat man bellowed turning from them and walking back into the body room. "Johnny Sullivan never lies and never stakes his life on anything. I'll be in touch," he said, raising one finger to them. "I'm going to call the authorities now."

Johnny Sullivan disappeared behind the metal swinging door. They could hear him whistle as he walked.

David looked at Ashleigh, closed his eyes slowly, and whispered. "Thank God for Johnny Sullivan."

"You know you don't have to continue treating his patients, don't you?" David said to Ashleigh.

"I know I don't. But look at Patrick. Look at what happened to our good friend. It would be senseless to quit the Center now. I could still get a lot of valuable information." She looked back at the hospital morgue doors. "For Patrick."

"I understand, Ash. But remember, things are getting hotter. Webster is going to be fishing like crazy to find out who is trying to take him down. We know he had Patrick killed. Next, he will try to find us, and perhaps he will try the very same thing."

"Patrick was unaware of it. We are not. I'm sure we will be watching each other's backs, as well as our own from now on."

"Patrick was unaware, all right. That breaks my heart. I can't imagine what he must have gone through at the end. We don't really know if he was warned or not. We don't know if he was followed and didn't want to bother us with it. You know Patrick, Ash."

"I don't mean to sound cold, David. But now Patrick is gone. He'll always be in our hearts, but he is gone. There are many more out there who are suffering. Many chips are activating. Many lives are going on with horrendous memories that they can't erase. When you deal with a barbarian, you fight like a barbarian. Isn't that what you always told me when we were younger?" She touched his arm. "We have to continue on and take the man down. We have to try and detonate as many chips as we can and help those whose chips have been activated before they take care of it themselves."

David sighed. "I hate to admit it, but you're right."

"Okay. We got the files. We know where these people live. What we don't know is how many of them are still alive and how many of them are still within their own sane minds."

David raised his eyebrows. "Seems to me we should start with your first file. Get them separated into location so that we don't have to drive all over the city to do this. How many do you suppose we have?"

"Hundreds," Ashleigh replied. "Thousands, if you count those who haven't reached their birthdays yet."

"Let's not forget the newborns. We've got to get to them as well. But we can do them in one fell swoop."

"We can wait on them, cant we?" Ashleigh asked.

David shook his head. "It'd be harder, Ash. They leave the hospital the day after they're born now, so we have to visit the hospital once a day. Otherwise, how would we know where they've gone? In eighteen years, we'll have the same problem."

Ashleigh was listening with no expression, restlessly tapping her notebook. Clicking her pen, she said. "I agree. Okay. Tonight, we can work on location and hospitals, how many there are, diameter of nurseries for decoding?" She suddenly stopped walking and turned to him. "What happens to a baby if he is still there on the next night. The night after we've detonated his chip and are back there to do the others? Can we hurt him?"

David shook his head. "No. Once they're detonated, they're detonated. There's no affect on the child if it's done again, or repeatedly for that matter."

A teenager with a Mohawk and numerous body piercings came from behind them weeping like a baby. He looked so unlike the sensitive type. But, it was obvious by the way he was carrying on that he'd just identified someone very close to him.

"Pain is everywhere," Ashleigh whispered, wanting to put her arm around the young man.

Outside, it was cool. A numbing rain beat down on them, and the line of cabs around the station didn't end. They walked hand in hand, determined, no matter what their future had in store for them.

Thirty-five

Louise Fletcher

Case number 98989

Madness. She had seen it before, and now it was all around her. "Who is this?" she asked, thinking that she shouldn't have answered the phone after all.

"The Duke of Windsor," came the ridiculous answer. And then, all in a single blink of time she heard him say. "I am Horace, the God of the Dead."

And then there was no thought. Only an overwhelming fear that gripped her somewhere below her stomach and worked its way to her throat. This had to stop. Every single night this person called her. Always at the same time. Always using the same words.

Louise Fletcher found herself standing at the window, staring out into the night. She had to figure out who it was that was calling her. But there were other things. Like the burning. There seemed to be several areas of distinct burning that seemed to be coming from around the back of her house. This scared her. Scared her because she lived miles from the nearest neighbor and no one would be there soon enough to help her.

Scared because she wasn't sure what was burning and how close it was to her house.

Louise lived alone. Her husband, Earl, had passed away from the virus some five years before. They had control over the virus by then, but with Earl, it had lived dormant within him for several years before it decided to wake up and kill him.

And, as if all this was not enough, there was some lunatic calling her at night, scaring the living shit out of her.

Louise was having a problem trying to figure out if her chip had accidentally activated. She had heard about others that had activated from the newspaper articles; they were absolutely devastating, from suicides to sheer craziness. And that's what she felt was happening to her. Sheer craziness.

And then, there was this clicking sound and sleepless nights, night sweats, and nightmares. She was sure that her chip had activated untimely. All of this was so sudden.

The phone rang again. At first, she wasn't going to answer it. Then she decided that she would face her demon and forge ahead of her fear.

"Please don't call me again," she shouted into the receiver.

There was no one.

"If there is something I should know, please, by all means, speak. I'm listening. Otherwise, don't call here again." Louise hung up feeling very good about her bravery. And tomorrow evening, she would have her sister, who was coming to visit, pick up the phone instead of herself. She had to prove to herself that she wasn't crazy like she was beginning to think. And this would prove that the chip had not activated.

She thought of her sister then. Catherine had no idea what was happening and would be very upset. She would worry about what mental condition Louise was in and if it came from a terrible physical condition that had been overlooked. Catherine was the surrogate doctor in the family. No degree, mind you, but she knew all there was to know about medicine, or so she said.

***

After an intolerable night of bad dreams, shaking, and an unquenchable thirst, Louise, exhausted and on the verge of a nervous breakdown, prepared for the arrival of Catherine.

She was anxious to see her sister. Although Catherine was very difficult to have around for an extended length of time, they really hadn't been together for a month of Sundays. And although her reasons for having her over were more of a selfish nature than the want to see her, it promised to be a good visit. She was glad that Catherine had accepted.

Looking in the full-length mirror, Louise was shocked to see how much weight she had lost in the last month. Her eyes were hollow and her skin sallow. Catherine was sure to notice.

***

At five thirty, Catherine showed up. But it was Louise who was shocked. Catherine had gained at least fifty pounds since she had seen her last.

"My, my, sister Louise," Catherine sang. "It is so good to see you. What's left of you that is . . ."

"Well, dear sister, it's obvious that whatever weight I may have lost, you seemed to have found."

They both laughed at that, and it seemed as if they truly would have a delightful time together.

"How long can you stay, Catherine?"

"Long enough for you to get sick of me and kick me out."

Louise laughed and looked at the clock. It was six o'clock. One more hour and that phone would ring. She just needed to know that her chip hadn't activated, and that was why she made sure that Catherine was sitting right next to the phone so that she would answer when it rang.

The time dragged by. Louise was so anxious to have her sister experience what she had been going through these past few weeks that the wait was intolerable.

The phone rang three times since Louise planted her sister by it, and all three times Catherine picked it up on the first ring.

"Hello," she would sing. "This is Louise's sister Catherine." She certainly wasn't shy.

By five minutes to seven, Louise was getting jumpy. Her nerves were wiry, and the anticipation was almost too much to bear. *What if he didn't call,* she thought. *What if this one night, he chose not to call?*

And then it rang. It rang like an explosion hitting the room.

Louise looked at Catherine who was sipping tea. *Why isn't she answering it? She's answered every call on the first ring.*

The ringing seemed to get louder, and Louise watched Catherine with perplexity. She acted as if nothing happened.

Getting up, Louise decided to leave the room so that Catherine would not wait for her to pick up the receiver. She would do it herself. But Louise could hear the ringing from the kitchen.

"Catherine, would you please get that?" she shouted from the kitchen.

"Get what, dear?"

"The phone. Will you please see who it is?"

Catherine got up and walked to the kitchen door. "My Lord, child, I think you're hearing things. That phone hasn't rung once."

And Louise heard the clicking.

Thirty-six

He should have known. He should have known just by the chain of events that the day would end as it had begun.

August Webster's life as he wanted it, as he knew it, looked like it was coming to an end. His dreams of the longed for utopia were fast fading. He didn't know how many were involved in seeing his world's demise, but he knew it was more than *one* Patrick Tuchman.

Rubbing his temples, Webster made himself a drink and sat on the veranda. He had to think. He had to pump his own ideas into his own head because there was no one to get different views from. Who could he trust? This was a one-man show. He couldn't afford to share his plans with anyone, simply because he knew about true leadership. You turn around and someone's ready to stab you in the back.

One simply had to look at some of the past presidents of the country. There were those assassinated and there were those who had lived through attempted assassinations. Who did they trust?

Conversely, there were madmen out there who had no interest in the politics of the world. They hated the leader. Nothing more than that. Boom! That leader was gone.

So, Webster felt, and rightly so, that he could trust no one then or now. He would deal with this on his own. He would come to the right decision and conclusion, alone.

He felt as though he was being kicked in the throat. He felt he could only depend on the goons that had taken care of Tuchman. At least, until someone came along and offered them something better offer.

Picking up the phone, he called Jimbo. "We've got to move fast on the others. I don't know how many there are, but we need to find out and get to work on them. You need to go over to the other side of the Hudson and open my warehouse. I've got to start moving records over there as soon as possible. I have a small boat at the pier. Look for it. It's called Aryan. Also, I saw a woman with Tuchman the day of the protest march. I'm assuming she's in on this."

"I thought you didn't know Tuchman before this, boss."

"I didn't. But when I saw his picture in the paper, his obituary notice, I recognized him as one of the leader's of the protest. She was standing right next to him. Whispering to him. Leading the others. So, Jimbo, that leads me to believe she is a prime suspect. Meet me at the pier."

Webster pulled on his trench coat and quickly left through the back door. Everyone was suspicious to him now. He looked behind him when he walked. He picked up the phone and listened before he said hello. He looked at every cab driver as if they could be terrorists. He was becoming neurotic and not in touch with reality.

This, of course, was Webster's annoyance. He needed to be in control always. Always.

So now, he would send Jimbo across the river to open the warehouse, and he would begin protecting himself and his clients.

Waiting for him on the dock was Jimbo wearing bright orange and blue coveralls.

"Dr. Webster?" He was deathly afraid of the man.

"Yes. What the hell are you dressed for? Halloween? Why didn't you just wear a flare in your hat?"

"Sorry sir. These are my boating clothes."

Webster handed him a bag. "We'll start with these files."

The gap between the pier and the boat yawned and narrowed as the surge pushed the boat against the pier. Grabbing the rail, he boarded, followed by Jimbo.

"You're going to need to put these on just in case of an accident. Leave the files on the floor just in case you go in." He handed him arm floats. "And if you do go in, don't take them over with you. Obviously, you're not a great boat man."

"But, boss. Am I driving?"

"Of course."

"I can't drive a boat."

"Jimbo . . . that's just the chance you have to take. I know it's not a pretty sight, but you going in could happen. The water's maybe in the fifties. Do you get seasick?"

"I don't get seasick, boss, but I do get claustrophobic."

"You'll be okay. Stay on the deck." He handed him keys. "Here are the keys to the warehouse."

He climbed back onto the pier and yelled, "Wind's blowing out of the northwest at fifteen knots. You'll be okay."

Jimbo veered the boat a little two much to the right when he pulled out and the back hit the pier. Webster waited until he was well underway before he headed back to the house.

The cab ride back was tense. He kept thinking the driver was looking at him through the rearview mirror. Every time the cab stopped, he scanned the doors making sure no one would jump in.

"Hard day?" said his driver, a portly black man. "Must have argued all day, huh?"

Webster opened his calendar book hoping the man would recognize that he was not listening.

"I remember one me and the wife had. It was in a Burger King of all places. Tells me I'm too fat to be eatin' French fries. Can you believe it? Well, I'll tell you we had it out. Yup. She walked on out the door and told me I could eat it all for that matter and then drop on the ground dead for all she cared. She took the car. Me? I walked five miles to the nearest saloon." He began to chuckle then, his whole body rippling and rolling.

***

When Webster finally returned home, his headache was so intense that it burned at his eyes. His joints ached and he longed for sleep.

Dragging himself to his bedroom, he began undressing as he walked. Usually a very neat man, Webster tossed his tie on the banister, his shirt dragged behind him, and his jacket was on the floor in the doorway. He unbuckled his pants and they fell to his ankles. With one foot, he pushed the shoe off the other and left his socks on.

Webster sat down on the unmade bed and let out a small guttural sigh. "Dear me," he said, rubbing at his temples, which lifted the corners of his lips up into a cynical smile. "Jimbo better be doing his job. Moron probably capsized the damn boat." But he was much too tired to even worry about that. Besides, maybe once he was asleep his headache would fade away.

***

The morning sun came in through the slated blinds and made lines of light on Webster's face and pillow. If he moved just slightly, it would hit his eyes. If he stayed just the way he was, he could possibly get in another ten or fifteen minutes of sleep.

Still with his eyes closed, Webster tuned in on his headache, searching for it. With a sigh of relief, he noticed no pain. Turning onto his side and shielding his eyes from the brightness of the sun, he lifted himself off the bed and went into the bathroom. The sun usually started another migraine for him. He tried to avoid it as much as he could, never looking directly into it.

The phone was ringing in the living room. He could hear it from the bathroom. Who would be calling him at this time of the morning? He wondered. *Jimbo! It must be Jimbo.*

Running into the living room, Webster stubbed his toe on

the sofa and tripped over the cat. Swearing under his breath, he finally answered the phone on its last ring.

"Jimbo?" There was no one there.

"Jimbo?" he repeated.

Then, a dial tone.

Webster placed the phone on the receiver and closed his eyes. "Big mistake, Webster you stupid bastard," he said to himself. He was yelling Jimbo's name into the phone not knowing if it was even Jimbo on the other end of the line. He just gave away the name of someone he was associated with. And whoever it was, if they ever looked up this Jimbo character, they would know that he was a known killer for the underworld, which astonishingly was beginning to rise again. "Stupid bastard," he said aloud again. He despised himself at that moment.

Webster stood at the window in his living room and looked out over the New York skyline, the little that he could see. The sun was passing behind a cloud and it appeared to be the only cloud in the perfect blue. He wondered why things either progressed smoothly or failed rapidly. There didn't seem to be much else. He had started this center striving to be the greatest. At first it looked like things were certainly going smoothly. He had all the faith in the world that he would be the one to bring the government all of the people that they were looking for. Had it been Einstein, they would have cheered him. Had it been any one of a number of others that were so gallant in the past, then he would have been a hero. A savior.

But now, he felt as though he was always running from something or someone. He constantly felt as though he was being watched or monitored. And maybe it was his paranoia kicking in. Maybe it was that he wasn't playing exactly to the rules of the government and he didn't want to bring attention to it because he couldn't afford for them to stop him. This was the only way the earth's people were going to survive. By bringing them back over and over, and equipping them with enough knowledge to keep fixing the things that were broken in the past.

Webster made a call to his office. "Did you call me, Rita?"

"I did, Dr. Webster."

Webster sounded relieved. "Is something wrong?"

"No sir. But I can't seem to find the files you had in your office yesterday of the clients that you saw."

"What do you need them for?" he asked.

"Our counselor is looking for them."

"What do you mean the counselor is looking for them? I only saw those clients yesterday. Why?"

"Dr. Webster, the government says that we need to send our clients to the counselor who has been assigned to the center. That's what I was about to do when I couldn't find them anywhere."

Webster sounded exasperated, yet scared. "Rita . . . Rita. I've told you before that it isn't exactly a rule by the government. They suggested that we have a counselor visit with each client. But that doesn't mean we are compelled to do so."

"Well sir, since she asked I thought I'd . . ."

"What does she look like, Rita?" he interrupted.

Rita described her.

Right away he knew who she was. Rita was talking about the woman who was walking with Tuchman that day of the protest. It was she, all right. He was positive. Rita was actually talking about a female Charlie Bronson. *She's a walking death wish. A reprised vigilante who is trying to rid the world of the past murderers and rapists.*

Once again he sighed. "I have the files here with me, Rita. Our counselor will just have to wait until I get there." Webster raised his eyebrows. "Do you think she has the time to wait for me? I shall be leaving my house shortly."

"I'll ask her and see, sir," Rita answered and hung up.

Webster smiled, his hand still on the phone. "Patrick Tuchman, dress up pretty. You're getting company . . ."

***

On his way to the office, August Webster was sure he was

going insane. It was the only answer, because insanity would be enough to explain the nightmare that was beginning for him.

The day had started with a truck and car impact on a small two-lane street. This accident backed traffic up for more than forty-five minutes. The truck was carrying small cans of motor oil that burst upon impact, spilling slimy, slippery oil over a major portion of the road. Most of the time was spent waiting for a truck of sand to come and absorb the oil. There were irritated people in lines of cars, bumper to bumper, but none more frustrated then Webster. His mind was clogged with problems that he hadn't yet figured out, and the solution depended on his own strategy. His own keen wit.

As the day continued, things got worse. Between the hours of twelve and one, an ordinary lunch hour to most people, his office turned into a fiasco. He had received numerous phone calls with relation to the suicide of Patrick Tuchman. One particularly from a NYPD detective, questioning him on Tuchman, and requesting some of his records to follow a certain chain of events proceeding his death.

Webster had no files, as of yet, on Tuchman. But that wasn't to say he couldn't arrange to have at least one by the end of the day.

By four o'clock, things had grown progressively worse. Tony Antonelli, an investigator from Washington, had called to make an appointment with him for early morning.

Webster had no idea what he wanted, but the way things were going, he assumed it would fall in line with his day.

At six o'clock, Webster left the office to come home, and once alone, he locked himself in his den and began his own regression once again. Webster regressed at least once a week by recorder. He would ask the pertinent questions on the recorder and give himself ample time to answer them. He needed to constantly know what his next strategic approach was going to be. Only his knowledge from his last life could help him now.

After securing the tapes in his safe, he quickly outlined his plans for the next few days. Webster had a light dinner of poached salmon and a tossed salad. His housekeeper had prepared it for him before she left for the day. While he ate, he spread his papers on the dining room table and studied his defense . . . because he knew he would need one.

Webster had to take control of the situation before it got out of hand. Then it would be too late to do anything. It was a fact that when things went wrong, they snowballed into disaster.

The files that Tuchman had removed from his office held valuable information on new souls. Tuchman knew that these souls were exterminated within a certain period of time. The timing should have been staggered better. It appeared to be much too orderly.

Webster sat back in the chair and ran his fingers through his hair. Then he rubbed them over his face as if to erase all the problems with his hands. His heart pounded with fear every time he thought about what would eventually happen if this got away from him. If he lost control.

He thought back to the earlier days when his wife, Esta, was around. She had helped him through those first years. She had supported him financially and mentally while he worked the kinks out of his life. Then, with his obsession for the younger woman, his mistake was made. He took the girl to his home at the wrong time. Esta walked in, then walked out, and never returned again.

He had never really stopped loving her. But he knew it was fruitless. She hadn't spoken a word to him since, and that was over twelve years ago. Even now that he was wealthy, she had no use for him. That was the one heavy pain in August Webster's heart. For the first time in his entire life, he had no control over something.

The night turned into day. Webster spent the remaining hours till morning on his terrace, rocking back and forth on his redwood rocker. He reminded himself of his grandfather, a man who spent countless hours rocking when he had a problem, as if that chair would give him some deep seated solution. It never did. It only gave him a sense of serenity.

And when the sun showed its face on the horizon, peeking

between the buildings and casting a romantic glow about the city, Webster was still sitting there. If he could only do things differently, he thought. If only he wasn't who he was in his last life, his present life wouldn't be turning out this way. But there was no stopping fate. This was how it was meant to be. This was how it would be.

Getting up from his rocker, he stretched and pulled at his tired muscles. He longed to get into bed and sleep for a few hours, but his day wouldn't be put off. As he closed the terrace doors behind him, he wondered what problems would be added to his life by five o'clock this evening.

***

Tony Antonelli tossed some Chicklets into his mouth as he waited for Marcetti to come out of the men's room. He tried ignoring his reflection in the terminal window, but it seemed to be yelling out at him, fat . . . fat . . . fat . . .

He had put on more weight since he'd come back from vacation a month ago. Funny, he thought. While he was off work, he had hardly eaten a thing. He'd been too busy fishing, sailing, and doing all the little things that he never had the time for throughout the year. But, as soon as he got behind that desk, his appetite exploded like an atom bomb.

In the evenings, during every commercial break, his habit was to get up from the couch and put a hit on the refrigerator. It must be a subconscious act, because many times he would find himself with the door open, staring at the food, yet could not remember getting there.

He raised his eyebrows and shrugged. Maybe he was destined to be fat, although it was just in his stomach. He touched the round bulge, shook his head and sighed. A few pounds ought to do it, he thought, looking at his reflection again, twisting from side to side to get an all around view. After all, he smiled smugly, while downing an egg crème, the rest of his body was perfect.

"Where'd you get that?" Marcetti said, strolling toward him, still wiping his hands.

"Little concession next to the gate. Want one?"

Marcetti extended his palms to him. "No. Run right through me like a river." He pointed to the men's room. "I'd be back there by the time I swallowed my first sip. You know," he said walking with his hands clasped in the back of him. "My wife has the same problem. Can't touch anything with creme in it. Ba ba boom . . . right through her too."

Antonelli looked at his watch, not wanting to hear any more of the bathroom problems in the Marcetti household. "Twenty minutes to take off pal. We'd better get a move on."

"Does Webster know I'm tagging along," Marcetti asked.

"No," Antonelli said. "Actually, I didn't want to scare him into any kind of preparation. Right now, this is just a friendly little tete` a tete`." Antonelli put a dollar in the newspaper vending machine and retrieved the New York Times.

"Good," Marcetti replied. "From what I've got here," he patted his breast pocket, "it looks like your guy Wilder really had this Webster pegged to a tee." He shook his head. "Too bad you didn't give the guy a little more leg room. Could've taught us a lot more about this August Webster character. Could've helped us a lot."

Antonelli stopped in his tracks and looked at Marcetti. "Give me a break, Ed. I was wrong and I admitted it. I'm full of enough guilt and shit to last me a lifetime. I don't want to hear your views on it too. I don't know how the hell to make it up to the man."

"Have you seen him since he's been released?"

"Nah . . . He took off so damn fast, I don't know what's happened to him." He continued walking again. "Look, we were only set back the couple of days that Wilder was in the can."

"From what I can see, Tony, we couldn't afford to give this Webster guy a couple of *hours*. He's that dangerous."

"What kind of investigation did you do?"

"We went through all his client files that were entered into the system. The man should have staggered his method affecting the new souls. It was too consistent between the timing of the regressions to the time of the deaths. They were all within a period of six months, Tony. None of them went beyond that amount of time." He snickered. "If he had just allowed some to go on a year or more, it would have been hard to figure out."

Antonelli sighed. "Well, hopefully, he's slipped up a few more times."

Marcetti seemed to deliberate for a few seconds, apparently weighing the situation that they were going to be facing in a couple of hours.

"I'd wager that he's slipped up a bundle," he said softly, as if to himself. "But let's not underestimate him. He's a very intelligent man. So intelligent, that I believe he misses the little things."

As they raced toward the gate, Antonelli had to admire the spunk that Marcetti had. He understood from one of the other detectives that for the last thirty years, Ed had dedicatedly worked the night shift. Sometimes two shifts, but the force was careful about allowing that. He had a great sense of humor, and for some reason, he seemed to be hiding something. His brown eyes could tell a story and it seemed to Antonelli that there was a perpetual grin playing around his lips, making people unaware of what he was actually thinking.

About thirty minutes into the flight, Antonelli decided that he trusted this man seated next to him. "Ed. Did you know that the states are having a meeting this afternoon on the Regression Act of 2035?"

Marcetti looked up at him in surprise. "Where'd you hear that?"

"It was announced in the bulletin this morning."

Marcetti shook his head and skimmed over the front of his teeth with his tongue. "Didn't get to the office this morning. Shit! What's happening?"

"Looks like they're going to be reviewing the necessity of the act. What they've come across is not sufficient to keep it going. The budget committee insists that the rewards are too little in comparison to the costs of keeping it going.

"Don't forget, Ed, the government is funding all these centers. Added to that, you have the August Webster's of the world." He shook his head. "God only knows how many games are being played. God only knows how this turned out to be a power struggle. Whoever finds the most prominent soul wins the brass ring."

Marcetti rested his head against the back of his seat and closed his eyes. "It was a stupid idea in the first place, Tony. A stupid, stupid dream."

Antonelli looked at him in surprise. "Stupid?" He laughed. "Funny you should say that, Ed. My birthday's coming up in a few weeks. That means it's my turn up at bat. I can't sleep." He was going to say he couldn't eat, but thought better of it. "I'm scared shitless, and if I were someone else, I'd enjoy a nice nervous breakdown over it."

Marcetti smiled, eyes closed. "I know. I've been thinking about my own regression. It's in two months. Hope they do away with the Goddamn program before then."

"Do you think there's a chance of that?" Antonelli asked.

"Who the hell knows? But if we don't have the smarts to further this planet on our own, like our forefathers did, then we deserve this shit."

Marcetti slept the rest of the way in discontent.

Thirty-seven

Ashleigh Bennett was looking in the mirror. She wasn't bad looking, yet, she wasn't what she would have designed for herself. And she wasn't being modest. She had some girlfriends that were perfectly content with what they saw in the mirror. Not Ashleigh.

She turned to the side and examined her figure. Slim. That was it. It was not an hourglass figure like she would have wanted. It was just a slim unflattering figure.

"Good morning, beautiful," David said slipping his arms around her waist. "What are we looking at?"

Ashleigh smiled. Her thoughts were her own. "Just wondering how I got so lucky."

David rubbed his hands up and down her smooth body and turned her toward him. "I'm glad you stayed the night, Ash. It's going to be a tough day. What time do we have to be at the funeral parlor?"

"The service starts at nine," she answered picking up a towel and shampoo. "I'll be out in a few minutes." Suddenly she stopped and turned to look at him. "David, what are we going to do about the fact that murder is suspected in Patrick's death?"

David shrugged. "I've thought about that ever since Dr. Sullivan told us, but like he said, the murder was so clean, only the police would know what to look for. I wouldn't." He plopped back down on the bed. "I didn't even remember that he was left handed, Ash."

Ashleigh folded the towel in her lap and sat on the little stool near the bed. "I didn't either, David. At least not until I was reminded of it. But, I don't think I'll rest if I can't at least keep on top of the case," she said lowering her head. "I miss not having him to call. We grew close very fast, you know."

David smiled. He was worried about that at one time. But for some reason, Patrick was a real bookworm, in the true sense. He wasn't really interested in having a romantic side to his life. Computers, books, and research were his romance. "I miss him too," he replied.

"Well, it's been reported to the authorities," Ashleigh said. "So now, instead of suicide ruled on his death certificate, it says deferred. Homicide investigation is pending, and Patrick will soon rest in peace."

Her stomach growled graciously. Tiny little quivers of rumbling permeated through her intestines. Why was it that food seemed to rule her life lately?

"You hungry?" David asked.

"Ummm." She stood up and looked out the window at the fluffy white cumulus clouds and immediately thought of biscuits. Her mouth watered. The geraniums bordering his terrace reminded her of wet, juicy strawberries. "Starved," she added.

David slipped his arms around her body again. "Do you promise that if we ever become a permanent fixture, that you'll bring your own food?"

Ashleigh turned around. "Why? Do you think I eat too much?"

"Nah. It's just that you eat more than me." He laughed and pinched the cheeks on her behind.

"I don't know what it is, David. I'm always hungry. I've always been reminded of food in everything I see."

"God knows what's going to happen to you when you become pregnant."

"Are you proposing, David?" she asked, snuggling to his chest.

"Could be," he smiled. "Could very well be."

***

Ashleigh showered and David made them a breakfast of French toast, scrambled eggs, and bacon. When finally the food was being lovingly shoveled into her mouth, a smile of satisfaction hit her lips. "Delicious," she cooed.

"Today, Antonelli is suppose to have a meeting with Webster." he stated.

Ashleigh's hand stopped midway between her dish and her mouth. "What?"

David nodded. "Yea. He's here to question him."

"How did you find that out?"

"Rita. I called to make an appointment for my own regression," he said in between large gulps of coffee. "But, she couldn't make the time for me this morning. I asked her why. Was he all booked up? She told me that August Webster had a meeting with someone from Washington and that it would take most of the morning."

"How do you know it's Antonelli?" she asked.

"She said that she believed Detective Antonelli would be in with him most of the morning." He poured them more coffee while he spoke. "I made an appointment for late next week and hung up."

Ashleigh whistled. "Whew! That's incredible. How can we find out what the meeting's about?"

"I'm going to be there," he said smugly. "I'm going to be right in the room."

Ashleigh looked at David as though he'd lost the last of his marbles. "You've got to be kidding. It's beyond me why you would want to get yourself killed. Why you would want to get yourself put back in jail."

"Ash, don't worry about it."

"Don't worry?" Ashleigh's voice rose. "You know how they

all feel about you. I don't understand you. I don't understand how you can even get close to that man."

"Who? Antonelli?"

"No," she stated. "Webster. But now that you mentioned Antonelli, he's the one that put you in jail while you were so sick. He had no sympathy for you. What makes you think he wouldn't do it again?"

David smiled. "I think Mr. Antonelli knows what's going on now, Ash. I think he knows that we are on the same side."

"You are in enough hot water as it is. You don't need to give them any more ammunition."

"I'm not," he said gulping down his coffee. "Believe me, I'm not. You're just paranoid."

Ashleigh looked shocked. "I am not paranoid; Dr. Wilder. Tony Antonelli, and August Webster are the paranoid ones. They've made it a cardinal rule that paranoia should follow people around day and night until someone breaks. Someone even wrote a book about it."

"You seem to think that my visiting with the old gang is some sort of punishment to you. Maybe you should think about it more positively. Look at it as a way to evaluate things. Evaluate the situation. Webster is the only bad guy, Ash," he said slowly. "Do you agree so far?"

She nodded.

"Okay. Antonelli and this Marcetti are the detectives working on capturing him. That's if Marcetti shows up with Antonelli." He gathered some papers and threw them into his briefcase. "Now. If both those men are out to get Webster . . . And I'm out to get Webster…Then, who's the only one on the opposite side of the fence?"

Ashleigh wouldn't answer him.

David smiled. "Ah. I knew you'd come up with the right answer, love." He grabbed his briefcase and sunglasses and kissed her on the top of the head.

Just as he drove away, Ashleigh closed the door and whispered, "Stay safe David, I'm pregnant."

Thirty-eight

August Webster cleared his desk of paperwork. The Washington man would be here soon and he didn't want him snooping around. Probably just a few questions about Patrick Tuchman's death. Yet, why did he have such a baneful feeling lately? It hung over him like death.

Sometimes, Webster felt as if he wanted to chuck everything he worked for away and live in peace. He thought about growing old in Miami, like everyone else did, and dying at a ripe old age in some condo on the beach. Then, his body would be shipped back here by Concord and buried in his family cemetery only to be reborn again to take another shot at happiness.

But he could no more give up this life than he could even think about beginning another. He had too many blessings. If there were a God, as some people believed there was, he surely would have many thanks. But knowing there wasn't, only made him more imperious to his own power.

Sometimes Webster wished there was a God. It would be so easy to have someone to blame things on instead of admonishing himself for all that went wrong. It would be so easy to pray for things and expect them to manifest immediately, instead of working until they patterned themselves out. The only thing that would be hard to take would be thanking him for some fine accomplishment. For that truly belonged to Webster.

Walking over to his personal file cabinet, he lightly touched it. Within those metal walls were files of forgotten souls. Souls that were already trying to make it back. Souls that may be already back on this earth again. What a favor he had done these people.

Now, if his resourceful mind served him well, it was beginning to look like the end for him. There wasn't anything that he could do about it. He was careless.

Webster returned to his chair and sat down. He swiveled it around to face the window and meditated. There was only one thing that he could do at the moment. When the Washington man arrived, Webster would play it cool. He wouldn't let on that he was a blubbering mass of nerves. He would let the man believe exactly what he wanted to believe, except for the detrimental suggestion. That, Webster could cunningly redirect in the proper direction.

Then, if it didn't resolve itself the way he desired, he would give in. He'd do what his heart told him he would never do. Retire.

***

"Dr. Webster," Rita said, sticking her head in the door. "There are two gentlemen here to see you."

"Two?" Webster asked, shocked. "I thought we were only expecting one man." He cleared his throat and looked on his appointment pad. "A Mr. Tony Antonelli, I believe."

Rita stepped into the room and quietly shut the door behind her. "Dr. Webster. I'm afraid we were both mistaken because there are two men outside that door. Could I show them in?"

"Uh . . . uh, yes. Yes, by all means show them in," he stammered and quickly tried to recover himself.

Within seconds, two men walked into Webster's office. Let the games begin, he thought shakily.

After brief salutations, they got to the point directly.

"Dr. Webster," Antonelli began. "I understand that you have made the acquaintance of Patrick Tuchman?"

Webster shifted in his seat. An answer that he could easily answer. "Yes. Not too well, I'm afraid. But I did sit with him a few times."

"And tell me, sir. What was it that you noticed most that could account for the young man to take his own life?"

"Depression," Webster said. "Severe depression."

"Had he met with his own regression yet, Dr. Webster?" Ed Marcetti asked.

Something about this man irritated Webster. Maybe because he was an unexpected and uninvited guest. "No. He wasn't due for a few months."

Right away, Antonelli knew that he had caught the man. Tuchman's birthday was this month and he was to have his appointment here at the clinic in a couple of weeks. "I see," Marcetti said, pulling out a long cigar.

Webster looked at the cigar in disgust and Marcetti caught the look. "Don't worry, Dr. Webster. I never light a cigar indoors." *Not unless I could get away with it.*

Antonelli cut in quickly, excited that they may have pinned the man to the wall. "Sir, if I may be so bold. What happens to the new souls in your agency? Where do you send them?"

Webster started squirming in his seat. This was it, he thought. He'd better come up with the right answers or he would create suspicion. "Well, after the regression session, if I find out that there was no previous life, I make no further appointments with them. They are free to go and do as they please."

Somehow, Antonelli wasn't buying. Webster could feel it.

"Seems to me," Antonelli said, opening his notes, "that almost every one of your new souls have perished within a six month period of their first meeting with you."

Marcetti cut in immediately. "Can you explain that, Dr. Webster?"

"I can. But I won't. I have rights. Perhaps you'd like to tell me what you're doing in my house. Presumably you have a warrant?" His eyes flickered back and forth. "You . . . You have to Mirandize me." He paused and swallowed.

"You're not under arrest yet, Dr. Webster," Marcetti said, watching him closely. "Now, sit down."

Webster did what he was told, sweat rolling down the sides of his face. Very frightened now, he said, "You won't get away with this, you know. You can't prove anything. This is an illegal search and seizure."

The room was still for a few moments. Then, Webster, who looked as if he were going to cry, said, "I just wanted to form an Aryan society. In order to have a more perfect union, you must do away with the substandard. The unacceptable."

Antonelli and Marcetti looked at one another and nodded. This was it.

"What about Patrick Tuchman, Dr. Webster?" Antonelli asked.

Webster looked at the two men blankly. "Tuchman?" he asked. "Tuchman was a trouble maker. A snoop. Found his pen in my office. Had him followed. No one needs troublemakers. Do you agree gentlemen?" He began to speak in short phrases. "Took my files. Nobody touches my files."

Antonelli stood up, followed by Marcetti. "We quite agree, Dr. Webster," Antonelli said. "Listen, if you don't mind, Marcetti here is going to stay with you and go over a few things. I'm going to get with Rita for a few minutes and then, we'll be on our way." He went to the door and gestured for Marcetti to follow.

Webster stood staring blankly into space.

"He's sick," Marcetti said. "He's a very sick man." He glanced over at Webster. "Looks like he was trying to prepare for us, but it was just too overwhelming for him." He shook his head. "I feel for the guy."

"He's a bastard, Ed," Antonelli said. "A bastard who finally snapped. I'll be damned if he doesn't remind me of . . ."

"Dr. Webster?" Rita pushed against the door to get in. "Is Dr. Webster all right?" she asked fearfully.

Antonelli gently escorted her out of the room. "Rita. Dr.

Webster is ill. I'd like to get the medics from Bellevue here immediately."

Rita was in shock. She nodded and picked up the phone, but Antonelli sensed that she knew this would eventually happen.

Inside Webster's office, Ed Marcetti spoke gently to the man. "Have you had your own regression yet, Dr. Webster?"

Webster suddenly appeared to gather his wits about him for a brief moment. "Of course, young man. Of course. I was a very very important man. I was what I am today. I formed an Aryan society then and I'll form one again." He then looked up at Marcetti, looking very much like a little child and asked. "Won't I?"

Thirty-nine

Tony Antonelli had no intention of bringing August Webster to his knees this morning. It was obvious that he was already at the breaking point.

"It's the easiest case we've had yet, as far as bringing someone in," Marcetti said, as they watched Webster mumbling to himself. "I figured an investigation would take months, and I really didn't figure this man to budge at all. If he weren't at his limit, I think we would have been in for a struggle."

Antonelli nodded. "I agree. We'll have him analyzed, but don't kid yourself. Without Webster around for answers, we've a long road to haul when figuring out what really happened here." He leaned back in his chair and watched August Webster's eyes roll, and hands clench and unclench a number of times. "If he doesn't snap back soon, I doubt he ever will."

"Good morning, Antonelli!" David Wilder stood at the door. "Hear you've got a star witness."

Antonelli jumped up from his chair. "Wilder," he said softly. "How'd you know I'd be here?"

David smiled. "Purely accidental. But since you are, perhaps you could fill me in on the details."

Antonelli turned his back to David and walked slowly back to his chair. "First I want to apologize for my arrogant ego at your expense."

Marcetti looked at Antonelli and then at Wilder. This was an incredible scene. Antonelli apologizing to someone.

"It's an extraordinary case, Wilder," Antonelli continued. "For the first time in my career, I'm unnerved." He got up and introduced David to Marcetti. "This is my partner, Ed Marcetti. He's collaborating with me on this case."

David nodded his acknowledgments and continued on with his speculation. "It seems he's snapped, Antonelli. What good is he going to be this way?"

"None. But, if he can hold onto his sanity a little longer, or if he could at least come up with brief moments of sanity, he could very well be helpful. What have you found out?"

David shrugged and moved into the room more. "Tuchman was murdered."

Antonelli nodded. "We know. The coroner reported it to NYPD this morning. We got word of it before we got on the plane."

"Who did it?"

Antonelli inhaled deeply. "Well, that's going to take some time, Wilder. We know that Webster here was directly involved, although he wouldn't soil himself by pulling a trigger. To find out who actually did, will presumably take some investigating." For the first time, he looked directly into Wilder's eyes. "For now, Webster will be kept in a safe place for questioning."

"You mean an institution, don't you?"

Antonelli shrugged. "I don't think we've any choice, Wilder. Look at him."

David looked past Antonelli to Webster. He was sitting in his chair, his suit suddenly rumpled and his hair disheveled. His eyes sagged and watered, and confusion was making its home there. If one didn't know it was August Webster, they would have surely been observing a very, very tired old man who would be at peace to just give up.

"I almost feel sorry for him, you know?" David said.

Marcetti stood up and patted David on the shoulder. "Listen

son. People get themselves into situations like this. He knew he wasn't following the right course. Granted, he may have thought his course of action was much better. We all know it wasn't. But, when things began to go wrong, Webster began to snap. This was long in coming, believe me.

"And another thing I'd bet my job on, men . . . August Webster's actions in this life have a whole hell of a lot to do with one of his past lives."

Within minutes, they could hear the siren coming down the street. "Webster will more than likely be admitted to the psychiatric ward for observation and questioning," Antonelli said to no one in particular. "Then, we'll probably be getting the news on the meeting in Washington later this afternoon."

David looked at Marcetti and then at Antonelli. "What meeting?"

Marcetti shrugged and tightened his lips. "They're thinking about doing away with the Regression Act."

David's heart began to pound. "But what about the rest of the people? It's all well and good that they would want to stop putting that ridiculous chip in a baby's head. But what about the chips already activated, old and new? What about them?"

Antonelli faced the window. Everything out there looked pretty normal, but God only knew what nightmares they had to clean up. "They haven't made that decision yet, I suppose. But it will happen. I know it will happen." He turned to David. "Tuchman left a legacy, Wilder. We're going to put his decoders to work."

David choked back tears of relief.

***

Webster's phone rang, and then it stopped.

Obviously, Rita was taking care of matters from the reception area. Within a few seconds, her voice came over the intercom loud and clear. "Mr. Marcetti, it's for you."

Marcetti looked at the others. "Me? Who the hell knows I'm here? I left this number with only one . . . oh, oh." He picked up the phone and faced the wall. "Yeah. Yeah," he kept saying. "When? I see." He swallowed hard and his voice cracked. "I'll be there as soon as I can. Yes . . ."

Antonelli quickly went to Marcetti. "Ed. What's wrong? What's happened?"

Marcetti looked at Antonelli and broke into tears. "My niece," he cried. "My niece."

Antonelli knew instantly. "When, Ed?"

"'Bout an hour ago." Marcetti turned around with the most immense pain in his eyes that Antonelli and David had ever seen. So intense that they could feel it way deep in their souls. "And all because of that rotten bastard!" he screamed leaping across the desk at Webster. "All because of you," he grabbed at Webster's collar and began choking and shaking. "You! You!" He cried and choked out the words of hate that he had saved up in his throat. "She was a good girl, you son-of-a-bitch. She didn't do anything to you."

Antonelli and David began pulling him off Webster. They sat him down and Rita brought in some water. "Please," David said soothingly. "We know how hard this is. But," he pointed to Webster. "Look at him. He's a vegetable now. He doesn't even know what's going on."

Marcetti looked at the pathetic August Webster. He sat there as if he were enjoying full retirement. He had a smile on his face and a blank stare in his eyes. He knew nothing of what was going on. But, occasionally, he did speak.

"When we exterminate those souls, we go on to the next assemblage. Life is good . . ."

Forty

"What are we doing here, David?" Ashleigh asked as she laid her head against his chest.

They were sitting on her sofa looking out the window into the black sky and out onto the sparkling black Hudson. "Where did we all go wrong?"

"We're waiting to see what's going to happen next, Ash," David said softly into her hair. "Just waiting. And we didn't go wrong. What we did, was go wrong, trying so damn hard to go right."

There was nothing left for them to do now. They only had each other. Webster was put away. Patrick was dead. Antonelli was now a good friend and asked that they visit when they were in Washington. It seemed that the only logical thing for them to do would be to get back to their normal lives.

"I'm not saying that things didn't turn out good, David. I mean we lost Patrick and all. But, the horror stories might stop now, and the world may be able to continue on by our own intelligence and volition." Ashleigh shook her head and snuggled closer. "What's out there for us, David?" she asked. "What's the only logical thing for us to do?"

David pushed her away from him and looked into her big beautiful eyes. "Well, we could get married. That would give us something new to work on."

Ashleigh's face brightened. "We could . . . but that's a very long job, David."

David smiled and nodded. "I'm well aware of that, Ash. Anyway . . ."

The words coming in from the other room stopped them immediately. A Special Report was coming in from Washington on the conference with the other nations concerning the Regression Act.

"Shhh . . ." David said putting his finger to his lips. "Listen."

"THE REGRESSION ACT HAS BEEN REVIEWED AND REPEALED AS OF MONDAY, JUNE 26, 2040. ONCE AGAIN, THE ACT HAS BEEN REPEALED. ALL THOSE WITH CHIPS, KINDLY MAKE AN APPOINTMENT AT THE CENTER CLOSEST TO YOU. AT THAT TIME, YOU WILL TAKE AN MCD TEST, FOLLOWED BY IMMEDIATE DETONATION OF YOUR CHIP.

I REPEAT . . . ALL THOSE SUCCESSFULLY OR UNSUCCESSFULLY REGRESSED, KINDLY COME IN. WE'D LIKE TO HELP IN ERASING YOUR PAIN. FOR THIS WE APOLOGIZE."

The commentator's voice cracked. *"LOOK'S LIKE WE'RE ON OUR OWN AGAIN, FOLKS. THANK THE LORD."*

Ashleigh and David wept freely at these words. They'd fought hard. They'd lost a friend in doing so, but the planet was on the mend once again. Thank the Lord.

"Hey," Ashleigh turned her face up towards him. "How would you like a little Patrick in your life?"

Epilogue

A full month had gone by since the Regression Act was repealed. People felt safer, and life began to go on more naturally and without the constant fear of their chip activating on them.

There was still the pain of the loved ones lost so unnecessarily, but there was now a future. Somehow, the people of the earth took the deaths of their loved ones as a learning experience. They never again would have someone take over their lives so easily. The destruction was right there in front of them. Friends and relatives were snatched from their lives in a moment of blinding horror and suicide, all because of the selfish intentions of one man.

They placed no blame on the government. The earth was in such a state that decisions made out of desperation were not always accurate. And, although it was a very good idea, this Regression Act, it had put some people in power that never should have been in power. Hence, August Webster.

August Webster had the desire to not only run the city of New York and its surrounding areas, but the entire world. He was the one who had to find the greats of the past. He was the one who decided who lived and who died in the present. And he was also the one who decided that his clients would retain the memories of their past with them throughout this entire lifetime. He was the one who made that decision and, although it was one city in the world that came across this kind of misfortune, the governments could not and would not take a chance of it happening again. No matter how thorough the screening was of the center's leaders, no one could know what was inside that person's mind, so they had no idea if they were putting in the leader of today, or someone from the past, good or evil.

***

David and Ashleigh Wilder walked into the Bellevue Hospital Mental Ward. Detective Antonelli followed behind.

"It's been quite a while," Ashleigh stated. "Has he shown any improvement?"

Antonelli shook his head. "No. He's the same way. He regressed back into his own past life quite spontaneously that day in his office, and it took us some time to finally realize who he really was. I'm afraid that Dr. Webster has locked himself into that life and will probably remain that way for the rest of his present life. He's quite happy now, living in his little dream world. In his sick mind, he has won."

They entered the large, doleful building and took the elevator to the thirteenth floor. Antonelli now led the procession.

They walked down to a set of double doors with a gate in front of them. Antonelli pushed a buzzer and, after an extended period of time, someone came and unlocked the door and the gate. He turned to David and Ashleigh and put a finger to his lips. "Make as little noise as you can," he told them. "I'd like to warn you about what you are about to witness, but I think I want to see the shock in your eyes." He patted Ashleigh's bulging stomach. "I hope the shock won't be too much for little Patrick in there," he said smiling.

The three of them then proceeded down another hall to room 47B.

They hesitated for a brief moment outside the room, unsure

of what they would find. Then, Antonelli slowly pushed open the door.

Sitting on a stool in front of a large caged window, was August Webster. He seemed to be giving a speech to his people . . . waving and nodding . . . smiling and nodding again. "In a thousand years, people will still remember my name."

He didn't hear them come in.

Antonelli stepped forward, with Ashleigh and David directly behind him. To make his presence known, he clicked his heels together and saluted.

"Good Morning Mein Fuehrer Hitler . . ."

A Spectral Visions Imprint

Riverwatch by Joseph Nassise

When his construction team finds the tunnel hidden beneath the cellar floor in the old Blake family mansion in Harrington Falls, Jake Caruso is excited by the possibility of what he might find hidden there. Exploring its depths, he discovers an even greater mystery: a sealed stone chamber at the end of that tunnel.

When the seal on that long forgotten chamber is broken, a reign of terror and death comes unbidden to the residents of the small mountain community. Something is stalking its citizens; something that comes in the dark of night on silent wings and strikes without warning, leaving a trail of blood in its wake. Something that should never have been released from the prison the Guardian had fashioned for it years before.

Now Jake, with the help of his friends Sam Travers and Katelynn Riley, will be forced to confront this ancient evil in an effort to stop the creature's rampage. The Nightshade, however, has other plans.

NOW AVAILABLE

* * *

A Spectral Visions Imprint

Night Terrors by Drew Williams

He came to them in summer, while everyone slept . . .

For Detective Steve Wyckoff, the summer brought four suicides and a grisly murder to his hometown. Deaths that would haunt his dreams and lead him to the brink of madness.

For David Cavanaugh, the summer brought back long forgotten dreams of childhood. Dreams that became nightmares for which there would be no escape.

For Nathan Espy, the summer brought freedom from a life of abuse. Freedom purchased at the cost of his own soul.

From an abyss of darkness, he came to their dreams and whispered his name.

"Dust"

NOW AVAILABLE

Published By Barclay Books, LLC
http://www.barclaybooks.com

A Spectral Visions Imprint

Island Life by William Meikle

On a small, sparsely populated island in the Scottish Outer Hebrides, a group of archeology students are opening what seems to be an early Neolithic burial mound. Marine biologist Duncan McKenzie is also working on the island, staying with the lighthouse caretakers, Dick and Tom, while he completes his studies of the local water supply.

One afternoon the three men are disturbed in their work by the appearance of a dazed female student from the excavation, who is badly traumatized. She tells of the slaughter of the rest of her party by something released from the mound.

Soon everyone Duncan knows is either missing or dead and there are things moving in the fog.

Large, hulking, unholy things.

Things with a taste for human flesh.

NOW AVAILABLE

* * *

A Spectral Visions Imprint

Dark Resurrection by John Karr

When Victor Galloway, a prominent surgeon and family man, suffers a heart attack while home alone, he claws his way to the phone and manages to dial 911. The paramedics arrive, smile down at him, and, to his horror, give him a lethal injection.

As Victor's life is ending, his nightmare begins. Rushed to the Holy Evangelical Lady of the Lake Medical Center, he is met in the emergency room by Randolph Tobias, CEO of H.E. L.L. "I need your skills as a surgeon to harvest the living and feed my people," says Tobias. "Join us and you may remain with your family. Join us and you will never die again."

Despite his refusal of Tobias' offer, Victor is pressed into the ranks of the undead. Like Tobias and his people, Victor begins to crave human flesh. His humanity, however, refuses to be vanquished. Risking the lives of his wife and son, Victor wages a battle against Tobias in an attempt to stop him and his people from preying further upon the living.

NOW AVAILABLE

Published By Barclay Books, LLC
http://www.barclaybooks.com

A Spectral Visions Imprint
The Apostate by Paul Lonardo

An invasive evil is spreading through Caldera, a burgeoning desert metropolis that has been heralded as the gateway of the new millennium. However, as the malevolent shadow spreads across the land, the prospects for the 21st century begin to look bleak.

Then three seemingly ordinary people are brought together:

Julian, an environmentalist, is sent to Caldera to investigate bizarre ecological occurrences.

Saney, a relocated psychiatrist, is trying to understand why the city's inhabitants are experiencing an unusually high frequency of mental disorders.

Finally, Chris, a runaway teenage boy, happens along and the three of them quickly discover that they are the only people who can defeat the true source of the region's evil, which may or may not be the Devil himself.

When a man claiming to work for a mysterious global organization informs the trio that Satan has, in fact, chosen Caldera as the site of the final battle between good and evil, only one question remains . . . Is it too late for humanity?

NOW AVAILABLE

* * *

A Spectral Visions Imprint
Phantom Feast by Diana Barron

A haunted antique circus wagon . . .

A murderous dwarf . . .

A disappearing town under siege . . .

The citizens of sleepy little Hester, New York are plunged into unimaginable terror when their town is transformed into snowy old-growth forests, lush, steamy jungles, and grassy, golden savannas by a powerful, supernatural force determined to live . . . again.

Danger and death stalk two handsome young cops, a retired couple and their dog, the town 'bad girl', her younger sister's boyfriend, and three members of the local motorcycle gang.

They find themselves battling the elements, restless spirits, and each other on a perilous journey into the unknown, where nothing is familiar, and people are not what they at first appear to be. Who, or what, are the real monsters?

NOW AVAILABLE
Published By Barclay Books, LLC
http://www.barclaybooks.com

A Spectral Visions Imprint
Spirit Of Independence by Keith Rommel

Travis Winter, the Spirit of Independence, was viciously murdered in World War II. Soon after his untimely death, he discovers he is a chosen celestial knight—a new breed of Angel destined to fight the age-old war between Heaven and Hell. Yet, confusion reigns for Travis when he is pulled into Hell and is confronted by the Devil himself, somewhat disguised as a saddened creature who begs only to be heard.

Freed by a band of Angels sent to rescue him, Travis rejects the Devil's plea and begins a fifty-year-long odyssey to uncover the true reasons why Heaven and Hell war.

Now, in this, the present day, Travis comes to you, the reader, to share recent and extraordinary revelations that will no doubt change the way you view the Kingdom of Heaven and Hell. And what is revealed will change your own afterlife in ways you could never imagine!

NOW AVAILABLE

* * *

A Spectral Visions Imprint
Psyclone by Roger Sharp

Dr. David Brooks is a front-runner in the cloning realm and a renowned Geneticist. He is a highly successful scientist who seems to stumble into one discovery after another. However, Dr. Brooks cannot find anyone close to him that shares his views on the cloning of humans.

Therefore he works in secrecy on a cloning project and has hidden his most recent discovery, the ability to clone beyond infancy. It is a clone of himself that this successful and secret experiment has rendered. The goal he has in mind is to recreate, in this clone, his twin brother, who had been abducted over twenty years ago.

Though the clone grows rapidly and is identical to David in appearance, a major question remains: Can anyone really clone a soul? Or is the clone an open vessel to an opportunistic spirit . . . a demon? The answer comes to Dr. Brooks soon, and at a cost . . . that of material destruction and the slaughter of innocent lives.

NOW AVAILABLE
Published By Barclay Books, LLC
http://www.barclaybooks.com

A Spectral Visions Imprint

Third Ring by Phillip Tomasso III

Private Investigator, Nicholas Tartaglia, is back . . .

Two men burglarize the home of the city's most prominent CEO, searching for a mystical book. They are discovered in the midst of the crime by a family member and in the chaos, one of the burglars winds up dead. So does the CEO's only son.

When Tartaglia receives a call defense attorney Lynn Scannella, an old friend, he learns that she has just been assigned to represent the man accused of the burglary and murder. With time being of the essence, Scannella needs Tartaglia's help investigating the circumstances in order to establish a defense for her client.

In a desperate search for answers, Tartaglia finds himself submerged in a raging river of deception and witchcraft. It quickly becomes apparent that getting a man out of jail might be the least of Tartaglia's concerns as he uncovers an underworld consumed by the use of black magic . . . and a plot that scares the hell out of him.

NOW AVAILABLE

* * *

Suspense

The Institut by John Warmus

LaRochelle, France: 1938: "Gently," Inspector Edmund Defont ordered the body to be cut down. Those who did not know him would suspect he feared he might hurt the dead girl—or wake her. The two policemen who worked silently under his command knew his sole intent was to preserve the crime scene. Thus, begins Edmond Defont's police investigation into the nightmares of David Proust, a young, affable priest who dreams and women die. When Defont's prime suspect and best friend both disappear in the middle of the night, his search takes him to the *Institut d'Infantiles*: an ancient Roman fortress in the middle of the Carpathian Mountains in the wilds of Poland: a place that conceals the mysteries of centuries.

NOW AVAILABLE

Published By Barclay Books, LLC
http://www.barclaybooks.com

Mystery\Suspense

Soft Case by John Misak

New York City homicide detective John Keegan wants nothing more than a dose of excitement. After nine years on the job and countless cases, his life has fallen into a series of routines. He no longer sees purpose in his job or his life, and with each day that passes, he tries to think of another way to break the monotony. It would take a miracle case to restore his faith and enthusiasm. A miracle case he wants, a disastrous one he receives. Excitement he gets in droves.

When software giant Ronald Mullins is apparently murdered, the case falls on his desk, thanks to his eager partner. At first reluctant to take on the high profile murder, Keegan dives in head first, only to find that there is a lot more to it than any one could have imagined. Along the way he will not only have to examine the clouded facts of the case, but the facts of his own life as well. To investigate the case of his life, he'll have to fend off the media, handle his over-zealous partner, and confront conspiracy and corruption which go to the top of the city government.

When the entire police organization turns against him, Keegan is forced to handle the case alone. Armed with a sardonic wit and a distrust of everyone around him, Keegan must risk his job, his friendships, and even his life to solve the biggest case the city has seen in decades.

NOW AVAILABLE

* * *

Mystery\Fantasy

The House On The Bluff by Elena Dorothy Bowman

A deserted house in New England contains a secret reaching back to the Crusades.

In a White Stone Abbey, situated in a dense English forest, a scroll, which held the secret to the present day Pierce House on the opposite side of the Atlantic, lay hidden in a chamber behind an alter, protected down thru the ages by brown robed monks until the 18th Century. On the quill scripted parchment were words that foretold the future of a dwelling, its surrounding properties, and, through the generations, to its final location in consecrated grounds to a distant land across the seas. It also foretold of the horrendous trials set before it, and who the true owner would ultimately be.

To the day she entered her ancestral home, with its promise of terror or fulfillment, The House On The Bluff maintained its enchantment and its ageless elegance, standing as a silent sentinel waiting for the one long destined to enter with her Consort, to claim ownership.

NOW AVAILABLE

Published By Barclay Books, LLC
http://www.barclaybooks.com

Mystery

Death On The Hill by James R. Snedden

As a favor to an old friend, a vacationing Chicago investigative reporter is pressed into action to cover the story. Due to the nature of the killing, it soon becomes obvious that standard police investigative procedures won't be enough to solve the crime.

After the murdered woman's identity is established, it becomes apparent that things aren't what they appear to be. During a visit to the dead woman's office, the reporter notices a picture of the woman and two Chinese men. He recognizes one as the key figure in the Democratic National Committee fundraising scandal, and the other turns out to be a Triad leader wanted in Hong Kong.

Calling on his contacts in Washington, he is put in touch with three local Asian sources in the Los Angeles area to help him dig out information. Enlisting the help of influential members of the local Chinese community and two tenacious detectives from Hong Kong, the mystery is solved . . . but in the most bizarre way imaginable!

NOW AVAILABLE

* * *

Nonfiction Health\Fitness

The Workout Notebook by Karen Madrid

Karen has always had an interest in staying in shape. After the latest fad diet on the market left her with acne and exhaustion, she decided to develop her own plan and devise easy methods that work for weight control. She decided that she didn't want any more suffering from diet plans that were concocted by people who were just plain CRAZY! Her goal is to have *The Workout Notebook* all medical doctors as a natural way to help their patients manage weight control and good health; it is already being used by many with positive results.

NOW AVAILABLE

Published By Barclay Books, LLC
http://www.barclaybooks.com

Action\Adventure
Vultures In The Sky by Shields McTavish

Lieutenant-Colonel Douglas Mark White, a fighter squadron commander stationed on Vancouver Island, analyzes evidence surrounding the crash of an Arcturus maritime patrol plane: he concludes that the aircraft was shot down by a hostile fighter. Aggressively, Doug pushes for authorities to investigate the incident. Subsequently, large-scale air activity in Canadian air space is detected involving unregistered jet transports and fighters. The armed aircraft are marked with the insignia of the United States Air Force.

Doug attempts to solve the mystery despite the resistance of the Wing Commander, the seeming disinterest of authorities at higher HQ, and a lack of resources. Accidental damage to his eyes, which places his position as a flyer and squadron commander in jeopardy, complicates his quest. Ultimately, he discovers that there is a large-scale drug-smuggling operation flying from Mexico and Columbia to a fake USAF air base in British Columbia.

Doug, despite eyesight difficulties and self-doubt related to the death of a squadron pilot, struggles to defeat the smugglers. His fight to destroy the 'Vultures' culminates in an air battle and personal clash for survival with their detestable leader.

COMING JANUARY 2002

* * *

Action\Adventure\Suspense
Appointment In Samara by Clive Warner

A part time job with the CIA is fun. That's what Martin Conley thinks until one day a dying KGB agent gives him information that changes his life. Conley sets off for the Wadi Hadhramout to retrieve the codes to a biological weapon that can wipe out America. A beautiful Lebanese girl, Alia, acts as his guide. A storm wrecks their boat on the Yemen shore, leaving them to struggle on, and Alia is abducted by tribesmen. Realizing he has fallen in love with her, Conley rescues Alia, and is drawn into a civil war between North and South Yemen.

Conley delivers the codes to his masters but new evidence makes him wonder if the weapon will neutralized —or used against China?

There is only one thing to be done: destroy the weapon himself. Defying his CIA masters, Conley and Alia set off on a mission to find and destroy it—but time has run out.

COMING JANUARY 2002

Published By Barclay Books, LLC
http://www.barclaybooks.com

Drama

Do No Harm by James R. Snedden

Three young men with totally different aspirations meet in medical school where they form a lasting friendship. The author follows their lives, cleverly weaving their stories of intrigue and sex, probing the events influencing their lives, ambitions, and career:

Charles, poor boy from up state New York, whose goal is wealth and social status. He sets up practice in the City of New York; however, when legitimate means don't produce financial rewards quickly enough, he resorts to criminal activity, consorting with members of the underworld and making himself vulnerable to blackmail.

Abner, a farm boy from rural Illinois, inspired by the doctor who cared for his family. His altruistic motives turn to disappointment when reality replaces dreams. Returning to his hometown, he is met with resentment and hostility and must decide to leave or stay and fight.

David, the rich boy from San Francisco. The only son of a wealthy businessman, he chooses medical school to escape his parents and their plans for him to carry on the family business. An adventurer and ladies man, tragedy strikes just as he finds purpose in his life.

COMING JANUARY 2002

* * *

Dark Drama

Silent Screams by Annette Gisby

Jessica is a troubled young girl whose life is full of secrets, dark secrets that she can't tell. She believes she would be better off dead than living in the hell in which she finds herself. She slashes her wrists.

Someone is calling her, calling her back from the darkness, the emptiness. The voice is faint but getting stronger. She struggles to open her eyes, but they rebel against the bright lights. Is this heaven?

He is stalking her. He says she has been a naughty girl; naughty girls have to be punished.

Footsteps. Footsteps on the stairs. She hears the last stair creaking. Any minute now. She jumps from the bed and dives underneath. It's useless to hide; she knows he will find her. As her bedroom door opens, she holds her breath and peeks out. First she sees the shiny black shoes and the bottoms of black trousers.

She has always wondered about the black. She has always assumed that the devil wears red. She tries to scream, but no sound escapes from her locked throat. Her screams, as always, are silent.

COMING JANUARY 2002
Published By Barclay Books, LLC
http://www.barclaybooks.com

A Spectral Visions Imprint
Monstrosity by Paul Lonardo

A prominent New England university is slowly falling under the influence of an alien cult that promises to deliver an elixir of immortality to its followers. Jack McRae is the only person in town who suspects that the cult may not be delivering exactly what it has promised. But he is a young outcast whose only connection to Bister University is his girlfriend, Katie. However, after a string of disappearances, Katie falls prey to the Second Chance Cult and its charismatic leader, and it is now up to Jack to rescue her from its greedy clutches. His suspicions lead him on a perilous journey into the inner sanctum of one of the Nation's oldest private institutions. As Jack closes in on the truth behind the alien mystery, he witnesses cult members undergoing bizarre transformations, discovers grotesque insect/rodent creatures hiding in the walls and floors all around the university, and then uncovers the possible plotting of a mass suicide ritual. All the evidence leads Jack to affirm his belief that an alien intelligence may not exist. But Jack soon finds out that what's really going on involves something even more sinister, though very much terrestrial.

COMING JANUARY 2002

* * *

A Spectral Visions Imprint
The Burning Of Her Sin by Patty Henderson

Meet Brenda Strange. Wealthy. Dead Ringer for Princess Diana. Once a junior Partner in a thriving and prestigious New Jersey law firm, she had everything going for her. But something went wrong. When a disgruntled client goes on a killing spree in the offices, Brenda is counted among the dead. Except she came back.

After learning to cope with her near death experience and newfound psychic abilities, Brenda and her lover decide to move to Tampa, Florida and the house of their dreams. Malfour House is a very old Victorian located in The Tides of Palmetto, an exclusive community for the rich.

But after she and Tina move in, Brenda finds the dingy walls and empty rooms screaming their secrets in her mind. Brenda begins tracing a path filled with murder, betrayal, ghosts, and the deadly curses of Santeria, a dark and exotic religion. Realizing that Malfour House will not let her leave until she unravels the clues to the horrifying murders long buried in it's past, Brenda renews her career as a private investigator.

And if that isn't enough of a puzzle to solve, she must confront the mysterious intruder trying to chase her and Tina away.

COMING JANUARY 2002
Published By Barclay Books, LLC
http://www.barclaybooks.com

A Spectral Visions Imprint
Watchers Of The Wall by William Meikle

Since the time of the Bruce, dark shadows have ruled Scotland, and lusted after the rich pickings of the nation to the south. The Old Protector staked one King before the Tower of London, thus ending the previous bid for the throne. But now, in 1745, the ruler by blood, the Boy-King, is massing his vampire army and heading south. Only the ancient wall stands in their way, and the watchers who protect it. This is the story of two of them.

COMING Winter 2002

*** * ***

A Spectral Visions Imprint
Spirit Of Independence Repentance\Iniquity by Keith Rommel

Travis Winter, the Spirit of Independence, has battled the Devil since his redemption. Travis seeks, by direct intervention, to change the evil men do. But every turn, at every intervention, he finds his efforts thwarted by the Devil. For it is the Devil's wish to prevent Travis from earning his way back into the Kingdom of Heaven.

Desperate to save his charges—and himself—from the unseen forces of temptation, Travis follows the Devil into his sadistic world of corruption. What he discovers along the way will either break his faith or bring him to salvation. That is, until an elder Spirit named Wallace comes to Travis and reveals hidden messages in the Bible that show Earth engulfed in fire and destruction. Without immediate change, the world is fated to this foretold ruination.

Now Travis must find a way to keep mankind from such a future. No matter what the Devil and the recently discovered hidden messages of the Bible have to say about it!

COMING Winter 2002

Published By Barclay Books, LLC
http://www.barclaybooks.com

Mystery\Suspense\Sci-Fi

Time Stand Still by John Misak

When private investigator Darren Camponi is hired to find an old classmate, he considers it a routine job with the opportunity to see a friend from the past. After locating him, Camponi learns that his classmate is working on a top-secret project: time travel. Torn between earning his pay and helping his classmate out, Camponi gets caught in the middle of a conspiracy and cover-up that appears to go to the top of the federal government, and down to his own family. With no other choices, Camponi enlists to help his classmate, and even volunteers to help finish the research, if only to get to the bottom of the trouble.

Along the way, Camponi follows a string of coincidental events, leading from the death of a fellow PI to a conspicuous medical malpractice suit brought against his father. When trouble comes to his family, Camponi will stop at nothing to end the problems, and clear his classmates' name. He volunteers to test the time machine, only to find out his past was better the first time around.

COMING Winter 2002

* * *

Drama

Angel With A Broken Wing by Leslie Bremner

Mariah's world is torn apart with an announcement by her husband, Michael, that he is leaving to join a cult. Despite his having become increasingly distant during the past year, never in her wildest dreams would she have imagined this. Apparently love was not enough.

Oak Forest, a sleepy mountain community, beckons Mariah to return to the cabin where she was raised. Abandoned, she must now provide the financial and emotional support for herself and her eight-year-old daughter. Torn apart by Michaels desertion, the future now rests on her shoulders alone.

COMING Winter 2002
Published By Barclay Books, LLC
http://www.barclaybooks.com

Mystery\Fantasy\Sci-Fi
Time In A Rift by
Elena Dorothy Bowman

A young, beautiful, lonely girl, searching for ancient treasures off the shores of Hawaii, is caught in an undersea earthquake. This opens a "doorway" between the present and the past, and she quickly finds herself immersed in the political events of the islands. These circumstances lead to love, mystery, cataclysmic explosions, and an end to a way of life. She uses special technology to triumph and find her way back home. Most of all, she finds a new beginning when past becomes present as foretold by the legends.

COMING Winter 2002

* * *

Psychological Suspense
Off Pace by Brittan Barclay

Meagan, a Registered Nurse with a Pre-Med degree, has always wanted to be a doctor. Yet, financial and personal issues have prevented her from going to medical school. So, when a major national pacemaker company offers her a job with promises of community prestige and significant financial rewards, she decides to accept this new career.

Although Meagan builds her assigned territory to a peak, she discovers that success comes with many prices and personal sacrifices.

As the sole female representative among male colleagues, not only does Meagan learn of the unethical and corrupt methods in which business is obtained by others, she begins to suspect that the apparently accidental deaths of certain people with ties to the pacemaker industry are not really accidents. No one takes her suspicions seriously, however. Not until she becomes the killer's obvious target.

COMING Winter 2002

Published By Barclay Books, LLC
http://www.barclaybooks.com